No Proper Lady

No Proper Lady

ISABEL COOPER

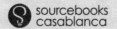

sourcebooks
casablanca

Published by Sourcebooks Casablanca, an imprint of Sourcebooks, Inc.
P.O. Box 4410, Naperville, Illinois 60567-4410
(630) 961-3900
Fax: (630) 961-2168
www.sourcebooks.com

Printed and bound in Canada.
WC 10 9 8 7 6 5 4 3 2 1

To my parents, Dan and Kathy, for love, support, and never finding the small library I hid under my bed.

Prologue

JOAN CAN'T HEAR MUCH SCREAMING.

The tunnels are long, and a lot of doors line each side. The doors are heavy, metal ones, the kind you have to shut by turning a wheel. They do a fairly good job of containing the sounds of the screams within. Of course, screaming wastes breath and time, and there's nobody to hear or help.

Some of the Dark Ones don't let you scream anyhow.

Joan's right hand twitches. Here in this windowless white-walled room, the priests are working on the circle, making sure everything's right and performing the last few rites they hadn't been able to complete in advance. Joan has never done any real magic. She can't fight either, not this time—if she got killed now, it'd be the end of everything—and she's convinced herself of this enough to hold most of her body still. It's just her hand that doesn't listen.

So Joan wraps it around the hilt of her sword. She'd rather have a gun, but the priests have said that would be a spectacularly bad idea in here. The sword's hilt is wood, smooth from long use and solid. More solid than she feels right now.

Behind her, the circle has started glowing blue. She knows this because the hair at the back of her neck stands on end. She doesn't look. She doesn't want to see the circle before she has to, and she definitely doesn't want to meet anyone's eyes.

Nobody speaks. The priests chant incantations, all fifty-seven Secret Names and the tongue-warping syllables of summoning, but nobody talks to each other. All the plans were final months ago. There's nothing to say. Joan doesn't want thanks or pity, and she's not really sure she wants hope.

So she stays silent, and she's the first one to hear the noises: metal clanging and gunfire and wet sounds she knows too well. And now some screaming. Sometimes you can't help it.

Joan wants to tell herself she doesn't know any of the voices, but she can't believe that, and it doesn't matter. Everyone outside knows their duty. When the first set of claws shears through the metal door, she knows whose bodies lie in the hallway beyond.

She jerks the sword out of its sheath and slashes at a hand almost the size of her body—too big for the tunnels, but when have the Dark Ones ever concerned themselves with normal sizes and shapes? There's a screech and the hand jerks back. Only for a moment, though. Smaller creatures pour through the hole. But they're not that much smaller.

The situation is familiar now, even with the surging power behind her, the increasingly panicked voices of the priests, and the names she's trying not to think. Fighting settles around Joan's shoulders like a warm blanket. She stabs at things with too many eyes and dodges lashing tentacles and claws and bursts of greenish-black fire. There are others at her sides, the inner guards. She knows their presence like she knows her own hands.

One of the guards falls, smearing red against the wall. Another ducks, catches a glistening whip behind the heel, and is dragged forward struggling. Joan lunges forward, slashing—but someone from behind jerks her back. She starts to fight but then remembers where she is and sees human eyes glaring down at her.

"Go now," says Elizabeth, her face bloodless. "*Now*." She doesn't wait for a response and shoves Joan forward into the circle.

Light rises around her almost at once: blue at first and then shimmering in a million different shades. Outside the barrier of light, the room spins and fades, and the floor falls away beneath Joan's feet.

The last thing she sees is her sword hitting the floor.

Chapter 1

THE FOREST NEAR ENGLEFIELD HALL WAS LUSH AND green with early summer but the view out his study window might have been invisible as far as Simon Grenville was concerned. All he could see was his aunt's letter, the careful penmanship hiding polite rage:

> I find it quite impossible to understand what you mean by departing so suddenly and without giving notice to any of our acquaintance save through me. Your actions seem calculated to provoke gossip, if not to give offense outright.

> You, of course, have long demonstrated that you care little for the good opinion of society. Such hasty conduct, however, cannot but reflect on Eleanor's place in society—to say nothing of her own mind and temper.

He'd stopped reading then and dressed for a ride. With considerable effort, he'd kept himself from tossing the letter into the fire on his way out.

The devil of it was that Aunt Sarah was right. Leaving London on short notice by himself might have caused rumors. But taking his schoolgirl sister away with him, so soon after a mysterious incident at a gentleman's house, would have the gossips talking for weeks. It hadn't been a prudent course of action. It had simply been the only one he could take.

When his horse shied, Simon realized that he'd clenched his fists.

Easy, he told himself. *The beast's twitchy as it is. No call to spook him.*

The path wasn't much more than a game trail, and the underbrush was thick at each side. Nearby, trees seemed to grow through one another or leaned to the side like old cripples. It was the sort of place where one almost expected to meet a druid. There had been standing stones once. Simon remembered Father joking about them when he was small. Back then, the idea had been funny. When Simon had become older, the memory had made him curious—but he'd never had time to investigate.

Now it just reminded him of things he'd prefer not to think about. The way Eleanor had been keeping to her rooms since they'd arrived, for instance. Or the obituary in the morning's paper: "Lieutenant Frederick Carter, a credit to his regiment and beloved by all who knew him."

All except one.

Simon shivered. At first, he attributed that to nerves. Then he realized that the light had faded and looked up to see dark clouds covering the sun.

Stifling a sigh, he turned Aladdin around, making for the place where he remembered the path splitting from the main trail—but the trail wasn't there. A three-way fork faced Simon instead, each path as thick as the next. He could see no clear sign of which way he'd come because the grass was too thick for hoofprints.

He stared at the junction, confusion and frustration rising as one. He'd turned *once—*

So you thought, said a damnable little voice in the back of his head. *You were hardly paying attention, you know*.

Simon drew a breath through his teeth and then took the right-hand path. One was as good as another just now, and he suddenly felt that he should be moving. It wasn't just the darkening sky; the very air seemed thicker than it should be.

When he first saw movement to his left, Simon told himself that it was a bird or perhaps a squirrel. There were enough of them in the forest. Then, as he caught a glimpse of something gray and low to the ground, he tried to make himself think of badgers or perhaps a stray dog. No matter that his fingers were already moving in the beginnings of a warding spell. That was just nerves. This was his family's land. There was nothing dangerous on it.

Then Aladdin bolted.

Simon flattened himself against the horse's neck just as a tree branch snapped and fell through the air above him, scraping his back and sending down a shower of leaves and small twigs. He swore and yanked hard on the reins, but Aladdin ran on. Simon saw no trace of gray in the undergrowth now, no movement other than theirs, but the bloody horse seemed not to care.

Simon darted a glance behind himself just to be sure. The forest there looked empty too, but when he snapped his head back to the front, he saw a fallen tree looming ahead. He closed his eyes and hung on.

The landing was hard enough to bruise, but Simon sent up a quick prayer of thanksgiving just for being alive and still on the gelding's back. When he opened his eyes again, he saw a clearing ahead—and a ring of stones inside it. Time and neglect had covered most of the stones with vines and grass, but their shapes were unmistakable. They were square-cut dark stones, each only a little shorter than a man.

The ground at the center of the ring was glowing.

At first, the light was a blue dot, only about the size of his fist, but then it blazed like a newly lit gas lamp. Rings of the same glowing blue energy spread out from it, rippling across the mossy ground and out to the stones.

Some kind of energy was building here. Simon wasn't sure he wanted to be present when it peaked, and he knew he didn't want to be on the back of a panicking horse. He kicked free of his stirrups, tightened his fists in Aladdin's mane, and yanked backward with all his strength.

He was expecting to be thrown, which let him tuck his head and take most of the impact on his shoulder, but it still hurt spectacularly when he landed. Aladdin, damn his hide, bolted onward across the clearing and into the forest beyond.

The ground hummed with power. As Simon got to his knees, he saw the stones out of the corner of his eye—dark rock outlined in blue-white fire. His hair lifted, standing on end.

Instinctively, he turned away from the circle, closing his eyes and throwing one arm up to shield his face. A second later, the earth shook and a light flashed blindingly bright, even through Simon's closed eyelids. He had the momentary sense of some Power passing over him, of something great enough to terrify any mortal man.

Then the light was gone, leaving only a faint blue afterimage and the rapid hammering of Simon's heart. He opened his eyes.

There was a girl in the circle.

She was almost Simon's height and slat-thin, with lightly tanned skin and darkish hair that hung down her back in a lank braid. The leather trousers and vest she wore did little in the service of modesty, but moral outrage was not the first thing that came to mind upon seeing her. Caution was.

The woman had a knife strapped to each wrist, another at her waist, and an angular silver pistol holstered beside the knife. She might have had more weapons yet in the large pack on her back. Simon wouldn't have been at all surprised.

As he began getting to his feet, she heard and snapped her head around. Her eyes were narrow, her body tense. She reminded Simon of a wild animal poised to run or fight.

She'd clearly been doing the latter already. Looking more closely at her in that moment of stillness, Simon saw that the upper part of her right boot and the leg of her trousers above it hung in shreds. He glimpsed red beneath the tatters and more on her vest near her collarbone.

"You're bleeding," he said.

She relaxed, at the shock in his voice more than anything else, and felt at her face before looking down the length of her body. "Not mine," she finally said. Her accent was strange—not quite American but close to it—and her voice was low. "Not mostly. Some scratches on the leg."

"You should have them seen to," Simon said. "I'd—"

He stopped himself for a second, wondering if he really meant to take this half-wild creature back to the house. But she was a woman alone, however well armed, and wounded, with both night and rain coming on.

Simon sighed. "I'm Simon Grenville. And I'd be glad to show you back to the house."

If I can find it.

The woman stepped forward and offered a hand. Simon took it, unsure for a moment what she expected, but she evidently had no such doubts. She shook hands like a man. "Joan," she said. "Daughter of Arthur and Leia."

Simon wouldn't have been surprised to hear Sultana or Yen Xing—or Titania, for that matter, as unlikely a fairy as "Joan" would have made—but he'd expected nothing so ordinary. "A pleasure. I'm—"

"*Down*," Joan barked. Then she swept Simon's legs out from under him.

She followed him to the ground with more control, one hand darting to her belt. Her weight hit Simon's chest, and her hair fell into his face, blocking his vision.

Oh, good. She's mad. I'm going to die here.

There were three short, high-pitched noises. Three bursts of silvery light flew overhead. Then there were screams.

They weren't human screams. No human throat could make those noises. They had a shrillness and a buzzing quality around the edges that put Simon in mind of angry bees, only many times larger.

"Fuck," Joan snarled, and fired again.

Another scream stopped midway through, cut off by a quieter, much wetter noise. Then silence.

Joan was lying atop him, most of her body pressed firmly against his. Simon had imagined the general situation in his youth; it was not nearly as pleasurable in fact.

For one thing, he was getting quite tired of being knocked to the ground, especially now that he had a large rock pressing into his back. For another, Joan was all angles, and one of her elbows was practically stabbing him in the ribs. Up close, she also smelled: not dirty, but rather acrid and sharp, as if she'd washed her hair with lye. Her hair wasn't really dark at all, he realized then. It was simply covered with something viscous.

She got off him quickly. It wasn't a moment too soon.

Away from her, the smell was different and worse, rank-sweet like burnt honey. Two...creatures...lay in the grass near the stones.

Both were more than half Simon's size and doglike but with six legs each and horns. Hairless. Gray. Simon understood the wet noise now. One of the creatures no longer had a head, only a mass of bone and red meat. That was still less horrible than the twisted, eyeless flesh of the other and its gaping, razor-lined mouth.

Simon turned away toward Joan, and that was almost worse. She was looking thoughtfully at the bodies, the silver gun in one hand. Clear tubes ran out of the gun and into her arm just below her elbow, pulsing slowly. Simon could see her blood moving through them.

No oath could have expressed his shock, and none came close to encompassing his disgust. He made an inarticulate sound in his throat.

Joan looked up and absently tapped the top of the gun with her free hand. The tubes detached from her arm and began recoiling. Their ends were covered with tiny teeth. Simon watched them, hypnotized by his revulsion.

"You're in a hell of a lot of trouble here, Simon Grenville," Joan said.

Chapter 2

SIMON TOOK IT WELL. NO RUNNING, YELLING, OR PASSING out. He just stepped back and kept his eyes on her. Smart.

"I'm not your problem," Joan said, keeping her eyes on him but not letting them rest entirely on his face. With a lot of men, you saw lies in the hands first: little tics and shaking, those nervous habits that said, "I'm a bastard. Please put a bullet in my head now." Nothing yet. She gestured to one of the cerberi. "You ever seen these before?"

"Lord, no."

For a moment, she'd thought that they'd screwed up at home, that they hadn't sent her back early enough. The clear horror on Simon's face—not just "Oh, I'm screwed," but "This can't be happening"—put solid ground under Joan's feet again.

Besides, this place was too green and the air too clear to be anything but the Old World. Simon was evidence too. She'd felt solid muscle under her for that moment when the cerberi attacked. Simon was probably even lean for this time and place, but he wasn't *just* muscle and bone. His cheekbones were high but not sharp enough to cut rock, and his black hair was thick, even faintly curly. Also, his clothes—tan pants, dark green jacket, and extremely white shirt under a black vest— were whole. None of them looked armored, and only his shiny boots were leather.

This was a man with plenty to eat and plenty to wear. Probably a man who'd always had those things.

Joan's skin prickled. *You're not back home*, she told herself, and tucked her hands behind her back so she wouldn't put one of them on her knife hilt. She imagined she already looked threatening enough. The spot inside her elbow where the flashgun had attached itself to her vein still burned a little. Reattaching would be easy for the next minute or two, and the knowledge comforted her even though it shouldn't have. She didn't want to have to use the gun again so quickly.

It helped that Simon wasn't armed. Another difference, one she almost couldn't process just then.

She walked over to one of the cerberi. "They were summoned," she told him. "People can do that."

"I know."

Joan blinked. "Most people don't know, though. Right?"

Simon laughed humorlessly. "Most people would think the idea mad. I've some experience with magic."

"Huh," said Joan.

She knelt by the cerberus and opened its neck with one flick of her knife. Steam rose up. Joan held her breath against the smell. Using the knife blade, she pushed the dark-purple muscle back until she could see the bone. It was marked with a dark sigil at the base of the skull. "Like I thought. It's somebody's pet."

"I hope you don't mean that literally," he said, clearly trying not to breathe too much.

"Probably not. Not here and now. Mostly, they're hunters."

"Hunting…me." He didn't sound as shocked as Joan had thought he would. Surprised, sure. Dismayed, definitely. But it was as if once he knew about the cerberi, learning he was the target was just confirming something he'd dreaded all along.

"Probably."

"Do you have enemies here?"

"If anyone sent these things after me," she said, trying to keep her voice level, "they've got more and weirder power than I've ever heard of. And we're totally screwed."

He was silent for a second. Then he asked, "We?"

"The world."

Joan wiped her hands on the grass. She hated to do it because the grass was so damn green, at least where the cerberi and their bits hadn't landed, but it was better than on her pants. She was trying to get the last of the gunk off when Simon stepped forward.

"Here." He held out a square of cloth. White cloth. Totally unstained.

Joan shook her head. "That's—linen?" It was hard to be sure. She'd seen linen at dedications, but it had been yellow with age. "You can't get this stuff out."

"It's a handkerchief." *You crazy woman*, his tone of voice added. "I've dozens more at home. Possibly hundreds."

"Oh."

"If you don't take it," Simon said, "I'll drop it out of a carriage window. I'll wait for a particularly muddy day too."

Joan laughed dizzily and took the square of cloth. "Thanks." Wincing again, she began to wipe off her fingers. "So. Somebody summoned these on purpose. We're not on anyone's territory, are we?"

"No. It's my family's land. And magical claims tend

to be more static." Simon took a deep breath. "Someone sent them after me, didn't they?"

Joan nodded. "Cerberi—"

"As in Cerberus?"

"Yeah. Plural. They need something to trace. Blood's best and then other fluids, but hair or nails work too. Even something you use."

Simon was staring at her. His eyes were blue and very bright. That probably didn't mean much here. At home, he'd have been trained as a precog or maybe a clairvoyant. "My God, anyone could—it's not as if I keep watch over my hair or my nails, and everyone loses gloves. A servant could have dropped something. Anyone could have—

"Well," she said, "who'd want to?"

She knew the look on his face from times when the leg would have to come off or the men were beyond rescue. Pain. Resignation. And more than a hint of anger.

"Reynell."

Simon didn't speak loudly. It was a breath of a word, a suggestion. It damn near knocked Joan on her ass.

"Reynell?" she repeated, and the sound of her voice speaking that word was loud and terrible. She flinched from it.

"Alexander Reynell. We were—" Simon stopped and looked at Joan.

She was aware again of how luxurious his clothing was and how well he filled it out, and again she had to stop her hand from falling to her knife.

His voice turned cold and careful. "What do you know about him?"

"What makes you think I know anything?"

"I'm not blind."

Reynell had sent the cerberi, she thought. Simon clearly hated him, she thought, but she had no proof and no way to get proof. "It's not personal," she said. "I have…things I have to do. I don't know that I can—"

"—trust me? I assure you, the feeling is mutual."

For a moment, they stood in silence. Joan heard the noise from the treetops for the first time: birds, of course, but more than she'd ever heard in one place before. *It's so* alive *here!*

She almost looked up. In that second, Simon's face softened again.

"It's…bad, isn't it?" he asked. "Wherever it is you're from?"

"You can't imagine."

"Alex Reynell and I learned magic together, for the most part," Simon said. "Until perhaps a year ago, we were the best of friends. Then he developed habits that I couldn't overlook. When I confronted him, he apologized and promised to reform. I chose to believe him—until a few weeks ago."

"What happened then?"

"He made my younger sister the host for a demon." Simon's voice was flat.

Ah, hell. Joan remembered the Red Room: the darkness and the priests' steady, hopeless chanting. "Is she—"

"One of her friends warned me in time. I managed an exorcism." He laughed curtly. "Perhaps the shoddiest that's ever been done, but it worked. Mostly. She's… taking some time to recover."

"If she's sane after that, you're both lucky," Joan said. "Not many people come back from possession."

In her time, you got two weeks in the Red Room, tied up well so you couldn't gouge your flesh. Two weeks and then someone with a knife. It was the kindest way, and it didn't waste ammunition.

"And then he sent demons after you."

Simon nodded. "I suppose he wanted revenge. I probably wounded his pride when I spoke to him at first, and I wounded more than that when I found him and Eleanor." He rubbed his mouth with the back of his hand. "Two days ago, Eleanor's friend died. In his sleep, they say."

"Young man?"

"Not yet five and twenty. The room was locked."

"Wouldn't make much difference to a grue or a succubus."

The wind picked up, gusting around them. In the distance Joan heard thunder. Simon blinked, shaken out of his thoughts, and sighed. "We'd better start back toward the house," he said, "though we're likely to get soaked in any case."

"Are there people there?" Joan asked.

"Yes, of course. Servants, mostly, but—oh." Simon looked at her clothes.

Joan chuckled. "Don't worry. I did come prepared." She shrugged off her battered leather knapsack, opened it, and drew out the dress.

It had taken forever to find—her height didn't help—and the people back home had packaged it as carefully as they could in layers of plastic wrap that Joan peeled off carefully as Simon stared. When she finally held it up for inspection, he stared even harder and made a choked noise deep in his throat. It could have been laughter. Or horror.

"Not what girls wear here, huh?" They'd known so little. When one of the teams had found the dress in a shop, everyone had felt amazingly lucky.

True, it had faded a bit. The black dots weren't as dark as they'd probably been, and the fabric around them had once been a much brighter turquoise. But beggars couldn't be choosers. The dress was long and had bows, one on the waist and one at each shoulder, and that was what everyone said women had worn back then. Plus, it was satin.

"If I put my coat around you and we move very fast, it might do. For now."

"Great." Joan started undoing her vest. Simon hastily turned around.

Right. Nudity, taboo. She shucked her clothes and belt quickly, and then reluctantly stripped the knives from her wrists and dumped everything into her backpack.

The dress fell over Joan with a light grace she'd never felt before, and she couldn't resist one barefoot spin to see the skirt swirl out around her. *Hot damn. Did they wear this all the time back then? Not really practical, but then it wouldn't have had to be, would it?*

She shoved her boots back on and turned to face Simon. "So?"

"The less said the better." He held out his coat. Joan slipped it on. It was thick and warm, and she winced when her sticky hair hit the fabric. So did Simon.

"Sorry," Joan said. "Thanks."

"Quite all right."

Neither of them spoke again until they'd been walking for a while, Simon probably because he was looking for the path and Joan because she kept getting distracted.

There was so much here that there hadn't been at home: the sharp smell of pine, the lush green of the trees around them, and the sudden small movements and sounds of animals. It was nothing like her world.

When they stepped onto a broader path, Simon relaxed and then looked over at her. "Now," he said, "I'm afraid I must insist on knowing more—your connection with Reynell, and where you're from, and why you're here."

"What year is it?" Joan asked.

"Eighteen hundred and eighty-eight," he said slowly. "What year was it when you left?"

"Hard to tell," Joan said, not really surprised that he'd caught on. "About two hundred years from now, we think. A hundred years after Alex Reynell breaks the world."

Chapter 3

SIMON FELT AS IF THE LIGHTNING FLICKERING IN THE distance had struck next to him.

"He lives that long?" He was almost stunned to hear his own voice.

That wasn't one of the questions that really mattered. He'd wanted to ask how birdsong and grass had ended up so rare, as well as how she could shrug off demons and look at linen as if it were gold. He'd wanted to ask what Reynell had done.

Mostly, he'd wanted to ask if Joan was sure.

He couldn't manage any of those questions. There was too much to get his mind around. He'd nibbled off a corner and was glad he'd managed that much.

"Not so far as we know," Joan said. "But there's a lot we don't know—a lot that got lost. We know about the book, though."

"The book?" Simon made himself start walking again.

"The one that Reynell writes, everything you never needed to know about..." She glanced around uneasily. "There are places outside the world, and there are Things that live there. You know what I mean?"

"I have some idea." He'd read rumors in books and seen glimpses of places when he was scrying. *All hope abandon, ye who enter here.*

"He wrote it. Probably with...help. Then someone used it."

"Used it?" Simon asked, though he knew what she meant. "Who would—"

"Nobody knows. Some people say it started in Tokyo. There's a song—code, we think—that talks about America. Maybe it was the military. Maybe it was a cult. Maybe it was just some guy whose girlfriend dumped him." Joan shrugged. "It doesn't matter. Things happen. It was a hundred years ago."

A hundred years in the future, then. Like almost every man of his acquaintance, Simon had speculated about what might happen in that time, what wonderful new advances mankind would make. Now he knew.

"The spells in the book opened a doorway," Joan said, "and the Dark Ones came through. Not just the little ones, the cerberi and their friends, but the big boys."

"The Lords of the Places Beyond," said Simon, remembering the title of a book he hadn't wanted to read.

"Yeah," said Joan. "Them."

The thunder sounded very loud. "But people survived," Simon said. "People must have survived."

It was raining now. The water ran over Joan's face, coursing down her cheeks like tears, but her eyes were calm and her voice was steady. "Sure. The old governments built tunnels for war. That's where I grew up. That's where everyone lives—everyone except the Dark Ones' pets. Or livestock."

"And you came back? I take it this is more than a sightseeing trip."

Joan was silent for several minutes. In the dim light, she looked insubstantial, ghostlike. "We were losing," she said. "We fought for four generations. We did a good job. We put some marks on the sons of bitches. But there were fewer of us every year and more of them."

Looking away from her face, Simon could see a long twisting scar on her upper arm. A rope might make a scar like that. Or a very thin knife. Or a tentacle.

"About seven years ago," Joan said, "one of our priests got visions. Very specific ones: a name, a year, and the kind of patterns you need for real power. The kind you need to send someone back and let them change things."

Joan's voice fell when she spoke again, but Simon still heard her clearly. "That's our only chance now."

Close to the house, the path was broader and Simon didn't have nearly as many branches to duck under.

He caught himself looking at the scar on Joan's arm again. It made the whole thing more real somehow and more appalling. Simon was a progressive man, but this was no Athena, no shining leader like her namesake. The war she fought was neither clean nor glorious, only desperate. "What do you expect to do?"

Joan turned to look at him, surprised that he'd ask. "My primary objective is to destroy the book. My secondary objective is to kill Reynell."

He'd thought as much, and he braced himself. She wasn't going to react well, but he had to say it. "It doesn't work that way here."

"What do you mean?"

"You don't just…assassinate a man."

Joan stopped walking and turned to look at him. "I wasn't," she said in an overly patient voice, "just going

to walk up and stab him. That doesn't generally work
very well. And I'm not stupid. Besides, I have to find
the book first. That's what 'primary objective' means."

"That's not what I meant."

"Are you serious?" Joan stared at Simon as if he had
grown a second head. "He's killed once. At least. And
what he did to your sister…we slit men's throats back
home for that, and we give their bodies to the dogs. It's
worse than rape, and you get killed for that."

Eleanor claimed she didn't remember anything of the
physical world between the time she was mesmerized
and when she woke. If there'd been any physical viola-
tion, she hadn't told Simon, nor had her servants. And
he hadn't known how to ask, hadn't been able to put it as
frankly as Joan did. Not even in his own mind.

If the demon hadn't been there, or if Simon's punch
hadn't put Alex out, the night might well have ended
in murder. Simon realized that he'd spent the last week
hiding from that as much as anything else, from the possibilities that he could have killed Alex and that Alex
had become someone who deserved death.

Still, what Joan proposed was different.

"We hang men," he said slowly, "but that's a matter
for the law—"

"The law made by people who wouldn't know a
demon if one bit them in the face? Good luck with that."

Simon pressed his lips together for a second, re-
minding himself that Joan was a stranger to his world
and that her mission was an urgent one, and then went
on. "Of course I don't propose telling the law about
this, but we should apply the same principles. A man
deserves the chance to face his accusers, the chance to

know his crimes and their consequences, and to repent, if he will."

Joan's eyebrows shot upward. "Reynell? After what he did?"

Maybe Alex hadn't intended things to go so far with Eleanor. Maybe Lieutenant Carter had died naturally. Simon remembered Alex as the boy who'd brought him home for the holidays, knowing he'd dreaded spending Christmas with Aunt Sarah or rattling around at Englefield alone. Had that boy gone completely? Was there still some goodness left in Alex? Simon couldn't think it likely. But—

"It doesn't matter what I think," he said. "He still deserves the chance."

"The chance to kill you." Joan snorted. "Or to run away and continue his work elsewhere. To end the world—or don't you believe me?"

It was a struggle not to look away. Her anger was a burning thing, one that might leap from her eyes at any moment like the shots from her strange gun. Simon knew he didn't want to be in its way, and yet, for a moment, it gave her a fey sort of beauty.

"I believe you think so," he said carefully, "but unless you're concealing something from me, neither of us knows the whole truth. It could be enough to destroy his manuscript. It could even have been enough that you've come here."

Joan's face was like stone. "This is why I'm here," she said. "This is what I have to do," she went on. "If it's wrong, if the price is being damned, then I'll pay it. Gladly. You don't have to help me, but I won't let you stand in my way."

Simon thought of Lieutenant Carter's pale and still

boyish face, of Eleanor, thin and silent, of the men who'd left the gaming tables ruined because they'd crossed Alex in some way they might not even have known. He thought of a broken world.

"I'll help you," he said, "as much as I can, on this condition: that if Alex must die, you allow me to do it."

Joan looked up at him, anger still on her face but with that turning rapidly to confusion.

"If I fail…well, I'll likely be dead, and you can do as you please," Simon said. "But he was my friend, whatever he has or will become. I can give him the chance to die like a man, at least. I want your promise that you'll let me do that."

Through the curtain of water, Joan met his eyes. "Is there any promise you'll believe?"

He had told her about Alex in part because she was enough removed from his circle and Eleanor's to be safe. It hadn't all been trust. Still—

"Give me an oath you value," Simon said, "and I'll believe you."

Joan stepped back, reached into a slit he hadn't seen in her skirt, and withdrew a dagger slowly, clearly not wanting to alarm him. Balancing it on one hand, she slid her forefinger lightly across the blade. Before the rain washed it away, Simon saw red there. "By blood and iron," she said, "I swear it. I'll give you the first chance to deal with Reynell."

Something hung in the air briefly as she put the dagger away, a pale echo of the power Simon had felt in the ring of stones. A shiver went up his spine as he started to walk again—and he didn't think a hot bath and a meal would banish the feeling entirely.

Chapter 4

THE HOUSE WAS A LONG REDBRICK SQUARE RISING FROM a lake of green. Four floors of windows watched Joan as she approached, all wondering who this drowned rat was and whether she really meant to come inside.

"Give me your hand," Simon said. "Try to look quiet and frightened. I'll tell them that you were set upon in the woods, that you hit your head and lost your memory."

"Amnesia doesn't work that way." Joan rested her hand on his arm. Beneath her palm, his shirt was soaked and clammy, but the faint warmth of his body felt good.

"Fortunately for us, I doubt any of my servants know that."

Servants. Right. Joan remembered some of her briefing. She was increasingly aware of how scanty it had been.

"How easy is it to become a servant?"

"Here?" He sounded startled.

"At Reynell's."

"Difficult. He hasn't had a vacancy in quite a while, and he's quite thorough about new applicants. Interviews them personally."

"Worried about assassins?"

"Or afraid for the good silver."

She wasn't sure what silver had to do with it, or what the difference was between good and bad, but she didn't have time to ask. Figures were coming out of the house now, hurrying toward her and Simon with black umbrellas over their heads. She shifted her weight a little to lean against Simon and tried to look dizzy and confused.

That wasn't hard. She'd had maybe an hour of sleep, and her last meal had been almost a full day earlier. It had been a good meal—they'd even found beef somewhere—and she'd gone longer than usual without eating, but she was starting to feel the lack. She lowered her voice and looked up at Simon. "Anything else I should do?"

"Don't shoot anyone."

"Sir! Mister Grenville!" It was one of two young men, both sturdy enough to make Joan wary, neither armed, and both in clothes like Simon's. The one talking was short and blond. "It's good to see you, sir. We thought—oh."

He looked from Joan to Simon, silent for a second, until his taller, red-haired companion kicked him on the ankle and took over. "Glad you're all right. We'll have you inside in no time." He handed an umbrella to Simon—it was sort of futile at this point, but the gesture was nice—and then turned, the blond following him, and opened the doors.

Lots of deference, Joan noted. No suspicion of an ambush. Neither of the men had scouted the area or even looked behind her and Simon while they were talking. Back home, even in relative safety, anyone outdoors would have done those things.

Being attacked wasn't just unlikely in this world. It didn't happen. Period.

She would have stopped to think that over, but there was no time. And then they walked through the doors.

Part of Joan went on thinking coolly, too trained to do anything else. *It* marked the exits, the lit fire in the fireplace, and the heavy iron tools by it. The rest of her mind boggled.

The walls and floor were pale, but not the rough, industrial gray-white of the caves. These walls were warmer colored with traces of gold and tan and polished so that they glowed in the firelight. Brighter paintings hung high on the walls, and the dark furniture that sat against the walls was made of black and gold enamel or solid reddish wood carved into whorls and curves, and it had velvet cushions. Inside glass globes, gas flames flickered, brighter and warmer than any fluorescent Joan had seen. Even light was different here.

It was gorgeous. It was terrifying. Again she told herself that luxury here didn't mean what it had meant back home, that this wasn't a trap or a sign that Simon had sold out. Still, she wished she had her gun in her hand.

The servants Simon had mentioned came out, headed by a woman in a long gray dress with a high collar and long sleeves. She was shorter than Simon, though she'd still have been on the tall side back home—Joan was something of a freak there—and plump, with thick brown hair under her white cap. She started talking to the men who'd brought them in, giving them orders. Then she looked over to Simon... and saw Joan.

She was disciplined in her own way, this woman. She didn't gape or cry out. Her large brown eyes got larger for a moment, and she took a deep breath. That was all, but it was enough for Joan to recognize the look as horror and then pity.

Joan bristled at first, but she couldn't blame the woman. She'd read the reports back home about malnutrition, vitamin deficiency, and all the conditions people got when their food mostly came powdered. Nobody back home had been eating right for a long time, but she'd never really thought about that. Now it came home to her. The servants and Simon looked the way people should, and Joan didn't.

"James," said the woman, "go to the village and get Doctor—"

"No," Joan said quickly. She might be able to explain the claw marks on her leg or the scar where the flashgun had latched onto her arm, but she didn't think people in this time had warding tattoos. "Thank you."

"The scoundrels ran away at the first sign of anyone competent, Mrs. Edgar." Simon took a step forward, lowering his voice. "But I can't…Well…I don't think she's in any state for such an examination."

Mrs. Edgar put a hand to her mouth. "Oh, you poor dear—"

"I don't remember anything," Joan said. "My head hurt for a while, but it's stopped now."

Everyone was staring at her. She was aware of everything that Simon's coat concealed: her ludicrous dress, her tattoos, and the long-healed scars from past battles. Joan folded her arms across her chest.

"Food and rest are what's needed, I think," said Simon. "And privacy."

"Very good, sir," said Mrs. Edgar. "If you'll follow me, miss—"

"MacArthur, wasn't it?" Simon offered.

At least it mostly kept her father's name. "Yes—I think so. It sounds familiar."

"Very good. I've had Rose light a fire in one of the guest rooms, and we should be able to make you quite comfortable. This way, miss."

Joan followed, wincing at first when her shoes made squelching noises on the marble. Then she stopped thinking about it because she had too much else to take in. The staircase itself was a marvel with a dark wood railing carved with roses, a thick, tan carpet on the stairs, and small windows made of red and blue glass on each landing. You didn't have windows back home unless you had to. Windows broke.

The upstairs room into which Mrs. Edgar led Joan had blue walls and a large fireplace. The fire was starting to blaze now, and a young blonde woman in a pale dress and white apron was rising from her knees in front of it.

"This is Rose," said Mrs. Edgar. "She'll be in again shortly to draw you a bath and bring some food. If that's all right, miss?"

The question was an afterthought. The woman had clearly put Joan into whatever mental category she used for children and invalids. That meant less trouble for Joan, but it was still vaguely insulting.

"Fine," Joan said. "Thank you."

She looked around. The room was vast. The *bed* was vast. Joan's briefing had covered at least a little about this time's weird morals, or she would have asked where the other two people were. A tall dark cabinet stood in one corner, a chest of drawers with a mirror over it opposite the bed, and a desk by one of the windows. Thick blue drapes covered the windows, and a blue and gold rope hung down by the canopied bed.

Joan watched the other women leave, waited until they'd closed the door, and then dumped Simon's coat onto the floor. She shrugged her knapsack off on top of it, flicked the bag open, and swiftly unpacked its contents into the desk. The flashgun and the knives went into the bottom of one drawer, and she set two wrist sheaths full of poisoned darts over them. Then there were a small metal flask with a sigil on it, in case anything poisoned *her*, and a thin wire garrote coated in silver, because you never knew, plus a first-aid kit, a case of lock picks, and two sticks of camouflage face paint. Finally, there was another metal flask, this one smaller and with a different sigil, containing liquid fire. The priests back home had enchanted it.

On top of everything, including the knapsack itself, she laid the black clothing she'd brought: leather pants, shirt, gloves, and soft-soled shoes. With everything piled right, the drawer appeared to contain nothing but a mass of black cloth. Now only her tattoos and the magic-sensitive patch behind her right ear would show that she wasn't from this time, and the sensor was almost invisible even when she was naked. She closed the drawer and stepped back just as someone tapped on the door.

"Come in," Joan said.

"I've come to run your bath, miss." Rose was carrying towels and a clean white nightgown over her arm. Her eyes widened for a second when she saw Joan's dress, but she didn't say anything. Not waiting for a response from Joan, she opened the door on the far wall, revealing a small bathroom. She knelt by the tin tub and began to run the water.

Joan looked away. They said this was how the Traitor

Lords lived, with people waiting on them hand and foot. When Rose stood and stepped toward her, Joan stumbled backward, revolted in a way that had nothing to do with the marks on her own body or the girl herself. "I can bathe on my own," she said quickly, forcing herself back to pleasant neutrality. "Dress myself too. Thanks."

"Of course, miss," said Rose, surprise changing to sympathy on her face. "I'll set the tray by your bed then, when I bring it up?"

"Thank you," Joan said.

When Rose left, Joan took a deep breath, then closed her eyes and let it out slowly. *This isn't a bad place*, she told herself, *and you're not a bad person for enjoying it. Missions have benefits. If this one's got more than most, there's a reason for that.*

Then she opened her eyes and shucked off the wet dress as fast as she could, peeling it down her torso and kicking it away from her legs. Her boots went too, and she finally curled her bare feet into the carpet. The thick, golden-red patterned stuff was better than even the captains or the administrators had back home.

Talk about hazard pay!

Joan got into the bath slowly with one foot, then the other, gradually sinking down until everything below her neck was submerged. The water was hot enough to make her wince when it hit the cuts on her leg and some scratches on her back she hadn't been aware of, but she wasn't complaining. No way. If she'd closed her eyes, she'd have fallen asleep then and there.

Instead, Joan made good use of the washcloth and some soap that smelled like roses. She scrubbed hard. Seeing dirt peel away from her skin was satisfying, if a bit disturbing. It took three washings before she thought she had gotten all the demon blood out of her hair, and when she got out of the tub, the water was dingy brown.

The nightgown was warm and very soft. Back in the bedroom, she found dinner on her nightstand, sitting under a silver dome and smelling delicious, with a glass of red wine beside it. Joan had mostly been able to ignore her stomach before, but now it woke up and screamed like a spoiled child. She lifted the dome quickly, revealing half a chicken, hot bread with real butter, and soup with beans and carrots floating in it.

If she hadn't been trained, if she hadn't seen men die after gorging themselves on an unexpected feast, Joan would have fallen on the meal like a hungry dog. She made herself eat slowly instead. It was very pleasant torture. Nothing on the plate was gritty or hard, and the meat was so tender she almost didn't have to chew it. And apparently this wasn't anything special here, just a meal for a rainy day.

Joan couldn't eat all of it or even much more than half. When Rose, returning, gave the tray a wide-eyed look, Joan dropped her eyes and looked away. "I hadn't been eating much," she said, speaking only partly to the girl. She could feel the shades of her family and her comrades watching her, their eyes hollow and hungry.

"Yes, miss," Rose said with another one of those sympathetic looks. "Shall I put out the light for you?"

"Yes. Please."

Tired as she was, Joan woke sometime before morning. She didn't know when. At first, she didn't know where she was. She knew that it was dark and that she was alone.

For a long moment, she held still, waiting to hear the

sounds or see the movements that would tell her what to do next. There was nothing at first, then the slow and comfortless return of memory.

She *was* alone—alone in a world she knew even less about than she'd thought.

Earlier, she'd taken pleasure in being well fed and clean and in the softness and warmth of the bed. Later, she might enjoy those things again. Now, in the dark, they only reminded her of what lay ahead.

Nothing came for free. Not even in this world, pleasant as it seemed. Joan already knew the price she'd have to pay.

Chapter 5

WHATEVER THE SERVANTS MIGHT HAVE THOUGHT OF "Miss MacArthur's" curious appearance or of the story Simon had put forward to explain it, they kept very much to themselves. Mathers, Simon's valet, was the only one who knew him well enough to inquire about the matter. "If I may be permitted to ask, sir," he began, as Simon dressed after his bath, "how long do you believe that Miss MacArthur will be with us?"

"I can't say. She doesn't remember any family, and she looks like she'd been in the devil of a situation for some time. Unless you've heard of any missing women"—Simon paused long enough for Mathers to shake his head—"she'll stay here for a while."

"Yes, sir."

Simon nodded, running a hand absently through his hair. By God, it was good to be clean and dry again—and well fed too. He hadn't realized he was so sharp-set, but he'd attacked dinner thoroughly enough to nearly leave the plates gleaming. *Being near death is very good for the appetite, of course. Ask any jailer.*

A quiet cough drew his attention back to Mathers. "Yes?"

"With your permission, sir, I'll have one of the maids engage the village dressmaker tomorrow. And the cobbler as well."

"Ah. Yes. Good idea." One, Simon was embarrassed

to realize, that had never crossed his mind. He knew very little about the essentials of female life.

Realizing that made him think of Eleanor—and wonder.

However aware Ellie had been of the unseen world before her fateful encounter with Alex, she certainly knew about at least a part of it now. Joan would have no need to pretend amnesia with Ellie. Besides, Ellie knew more about women's life than Simon. She could be a guide where his own experience failed him.

If she could stand the experience.

Simon frowned into the mirror. If he could trust Joan to keep quiet about the more alarming parts of her history and about her connection with Alex, the arrangement might benefit everyone. Still, it wasn't a decision to make lightly, and he was glad that he had at least one task to put behind himself before he could speak to Eleanor.

There was some benefit to having a house far too large for its occupants. Simon had taken over the smallest of the bedrooms, in addition to his own suite, and had sent the room's furniture upstairs for the servants' use. The gesture had, as he'd hoped, left most of them unwilling to question the source of their luck too closely. He claimed that he used the room to practice fencing. One of these days, he kept thinking, he should buy a foil.

The room was an airy little place with a good eastern view. The walls were light colored and the floor was bare wood, far from comfortable on a cold and rainy day but most convenient for Simon's purposes. The only object was a large rosewood chest against one wall. The chest's contents would have amazed most people, disturbed others, and told all more about Simon than he particularly wanted any of them to know.

Before Simon took out the key to the chest, he locked the door behind himself and then tried the handle. He'd never seen a spell interrupted, and while quite possibly he would survive unharmed, he preferred not to take chances.

Once he'd made certain that the room was secure, Simon took a small silver censer from the chest and lit it. The room began to fill with the smell of rosewood almost at once. That was a good sign and one that eased his mind considerably. The day and hour, after all, were less than favorable for the sort of magic he intended.

The power came easily, though. Simon began to sense it building before he'd done much more than unfasten his jacket. As usual when he'd gone some time between women, he felt the sensual aspects most strongly. By the time he'd undone his trousers, his cock had risen, thick and hard against his stomach.

He bit his lip and turned his mind sternly to the task ahead of him. Unlike with some of the experiments he'd done in his youth, the laughing half-drunk nights he'd spent with Alex, the purpose of this ritual was in no way to excite the senses. Remembering that, and the consequences should he fail, helped a bit. When he donned his silk tunic, he could at least feel the motion of the fabric against his arousal without losing control.

After the tunic came a shorter red-and-gold robe girdled with a gold sash and a crown of gold and silk. With these, Simon found himself mostly able to ignore his body's urges. Part of it was the ritual—donning the ceremonial garments and putting himself into another state of mind—but much of it was because he knew he looked thoroughly foolish.

Nonetheless, he couldn't completely banish sensual awareness. As the power increased, Simon felt it like a gentle hand tracing up his spine, and when he went to retrieve ink and paper from the chest, he was very aware of the weight between his thighs. He thanked God for his training. The sessions he'd had to hastily abandon in his youth had been numerous. And best not thought of.

Repeating any of the incidents would be damn embarrassing, after all. Even if no history tutor was around to catch him this time.

Instead, Simon focused on the paper as he spread it out on the floor before him and pictured the symbols in his head. This ritual would be one of protection, invoking Mars and Apollo. He took a deep breath, dipped his first quill into the vial of vermilion ink, and began.

Practice let him draw the outer circle in one smooth motion timed with his exhaled breath and the ensuing rush of power. The ink bled onto the parchment, looking startlingly bright. He'd prepared it years ago as part of his initiation, but Mars had been an infrequent influence on his life, and Simon had never felt the need to use the ink until now. It looked remarkably like blood. The civilized man in him wanted to turn away, but the magician relished the sight. Found it exciting.

This was going to be unlike anything he'd done before. He should have had the good sense to be afraid. Had he been outside the room and dressed as an ordinary gentleman, he might have been. Here and now, fear was only heightened anticipation.

Simon began the second, inner circle with golden ink, invoking the sun. This power was more familiar, less preferentially violent but no less capable of destruction. Like that force that had roared out of the stone circle and over Simon's head, it was too large for mercy.

As he drew the innermost shapes in red and gold, he felt his breathing, his movement, even his heartbeat take on a slow, steady rhythm. The power flowed around him, rising and falling with every breath but always increasing a little. The tide was coming in. He felt it in the warmth at his temples and around his hands, below his feet and at his groin.

Calm. Center. Control.

Simon's name came first with the request itself: protection against the Powers of Darkness and all their servants. Then there was his name again and the characters that extended the protection to all of his blood or under his guardianship.

Then the other names. Michael and Gabriel, the warriors of the angelic host. Minerva and Apollo, for wisdom and protection. Bes, a relatively obscure Egyptian god who supposedly fought demons bare-handed, and Sekhmet, before whom evil trembles. Phaleg and Och, Tyr and Freya—a whole circle of names in red and gold with Gevurah, for justice, crowning it.

A space at the bottom provided room for one more entity. With his hand almost shaking with power and dread—even now, there were a few things he feared— Simon drew a final few characters invoking Kali.

The power in the room was almost tangible. Simon could feel its heat as he breathed. It no longer brushed lightly against him but pressed itself close. The power was not as purely sexual as it had been, though his cock was as hard as ever. Rather, it was overwhelming in all ways to all senses, hot and shining and rosewood scented.

Taking the parchment in his hands, Simon knelt and began the invocation:

> *"O Powers who sit at the foundations of the world,*
> *Hear my plea.*
> *I come in an hour of darkness, and I ask for light.*
> *I come in a time of siege, and I ask for aid.*
> *I come a stranger, and I ask for mercy.*
> *Shut not your eyes to my countenance.*
> *Deafen not your ears to my voice.*
> *O Powers, I kneel before you as a supplicant.*
> *O Powers, I ask for aid."*

On the last line, his voice dropped, and he felt the resonance in his chest. He stood in one smooth motion, the graceful ascent of a bowing courtier. The power he'd built rose with him. Simon felt it travel up from the center of his body through his chest and his head and then out, taking wing in one radiant burst of energy. It left him standing breathless in the middle of the room, every muscle in his body tense.

He wanted at once to shout for joy and to snarl defiance, to sing hymns and swear the worst oaths he could think of. He wanted to run like a schoolboy on the first day of summer holidays, to make love to a woman until neither of them could stand, to laugh long and hard and to weep just as intensely.

Life, he thought dimly. *I do think it worked then.*

That made him laugh in a way that he hadn't since perhaps before he'd seen Alex at the gaming tables and the spirit looking over his shoulder. Now laughter rose through his chest like the power had, and it felt astoundingly good.

Everything did. Simon ran a hand down the bulge in his tunic and wrapped his fingers around the swollen shaft beneath the silk. Almost of their own accord, his hips thrust forward, rubbing his cock against the tight grip of his fingers.

If he'd been elsewhere, Simon might have tossed off there and then. He knew it wouldn't have taken long. But this was not the place for any sort of casual release, partnered or not, and there was no time to sneak off to his rooms.

With a considerable effort of will, he opened his hand and turned his mind to old geometry lessons. By the time he finished lacing his boots, Simon was physically presentable, but the euphoria remained. He chose to think of it as a good sign. Calling on the solar powers always had left him somewhat giddy, so it was only logical that such a large working would be even more intoxicating.

Certainly, he thought, he must have been a little drunk to have invoked Kali. Simon hoped that had been wise, but now that he was out of the chamber and back in his normal clothing, he wasn't at all certain. All the other Powers he'd invoked had been relatively minor: servants of something greater, like Michael and Gabriel, or the sort of god who was really just a larger person, like Apollo and even Sekhmet. Kali was a Greater Power herself. And even the most benign of the Great Ones were very dangerous.

She is, however, one very necessary side of a coin.

And she is Chamunda, slayer of demons. Hard to find someone more appropriate.

Abruptly, he thought of Joan.

Perhaps she'd been in his mind all long. Quite possibly, she'd inspired his choice at the end. Certainly neither her presence nor the world from which she came could be absent from Simon's thoughts for very long. They were too unusual, too significant, and too disturbing, Joan herself nearly as much so as her world. Her utter ruthlessness was appalling, her swift determination unsettling, and her whole person so unlike any feminine ideal Simon had ever encountered, even in his progressive circles, as to be utterly alien.

Yet perhaps that disturbing strength and focus was what the situation demanded. The spell Simon had just cast would turn aside demons and curses, but magic wasn't the only threat in the world. Reynell could use men, controlling them by a spell or a fistful of banknotes. The idea had seemed ludicrous earlier—Alex Reynell sending out assassins like some shadowy mastermind in a penny novel—but earlier Simon hadn't had hellhounds trying to rip out his throat.

He hoped he could defend himself. He knew very well that Eleanor could not.

Any men Reynell hired would be men of this world, unused as Simon was to fighting women and likely to underestimate Joan. She could accompany Ellie too in places where Simon couldn't go.

If the gods had sent him a problem, they'd also sent him a tool. He'd be damned indeed if he wouldn't use it.

Eleanor almost crept through the library door, stopping as soon as she was far enough inside for it to close and clasping her hands behind her back. She looked up at Simon uncertainly, the same way she seemed to do everything these days. "You wanted to see me, Simon?"

"I did," he said, and put a hand gently on her shoulder, guiding her to a chair. "Sit down first. I've rung for tea already."

She sat obediently. Never a big girl to begin with, she looked childlike now. Her eyes were huge, bright blue above bruised-looking half circles. The mass of her braided and coiled hair overwhelmed her face, and her pallor was downright ghastly against her black dress. The chair itself seemed to devour her.

Joan was thinner, Simon thought. But nobody would ever mistake her for a child or think her fragile. Even drenched and near starving, she'd had more life about her. *And if she can give Eleanor some of that*, he thought suddenly, *I don't care how if Ellie learns to throw knives and skin deer into the bargain.*

"I heard that there were bandits," Eleanor said, surprising him. She almost never spoke on her own initiative these days. "Are you all right? I'd worried."

"In excellent health. Thank you."

She managed a weak smile.

They'd never really talked, growing up. Simon had gone off to school just as Ellie had started to walk. Now his memories of her were like a gallery of portraits, each one only a moment in time: the laughing child with flyaway curls, the awkward and anxiously mannered twelve-year-old in black school dress and pinafore, the shy young lady with an armful of books. From the time he'd taken over her guardianship, they'd been amiable strangers, but they'd done all right together until April.

Now Simon felt as if he was groping in the dark, breaking fragile heirlooms in a clumsy search for a light that might not even exist.

"You must've heard, then," he said, "that we have a guest."

"Miss MacArthur, they said. She's amnesiac?"

"That's the story I want to give out."

"What do you mean?" Eleanor sat forward a little, an encouraging sign.

"You've heard of other worlds?"

Eleanor blinked. "She's from one?"

Simon nodded. "Human and all that," he added hastily, lest Ellie think of the spirit that Reynell had stuffed into her. "Just foreign, you know. Very foreign."

"How strange." She tilted her head birdlike. The familiar pose gave Simon hope. Ellie had always been a curious girl. Perhaps Joan would be novel enough to draw her out.

"Very," he said, "and she needs our help. Yours most particularly."

"Oh!" Her hand went to her mouth. "I'd be glad to be helpful, of course, but what can I do?"

"You're an accomplished young lady, Ellie. If I needed to learn manners, I'd apply to you. Perhaps I should, in fact." He winked, hoping for a laugh, and contented himself when he got another faint smile.

"Oh. I-I see."

"Would you be willing to help her along? I think she'll learn quickly enough if she has someone to help and to conceal mistakes when she makes them."

"I'll be glad to," Ellie said. And then, in a quick, nervous rush, "It'll be nice to have another girl around."

The word was startling in context. He pictured a girl as a curly-headed tot or a slim young lady in pastels with flowers in her hair, not the bloodstained figure in the stone circle. "She's somewhat older than you," Simon said, "my age or close, and she's quite…rugged."

"I'm sure I'll find her very agreeable," Ellie said politely.

"She will be." He'd make sure of it. Simon cleared his throat. "I'd like you to remain very close to her. Particularly when you leave the house."

He wished he hadn't had to say that. The excitement vanished from Eleanor's face, replaced by the blank, frightened look that was usual these days. She was silent for a moment, and when she did speak, her voice was almost a whisper. "Forgive me, but this isn't just a matter of teaching her, is it?"

If he'd lied to her, she'd have believed him, as she wouldn't have a month ago. So he told the truth. "No. I'm sorry if this upsets you."

"Not at all. I…I mean, thank you." The relief on her face was almost physically painful to see.

That night in April, after she'd come out of her trance, Eleanor had cried on Simon's shoulder for what had seemed like hours, during which he'd patted her hair awkwardly while she shed helpless, hysterical tears. The doctor had come afterward and given her laudanum, which had lasted most of a week. Since then, Simon had seen no strong emotion cross her face. Not until today.

Ah, God, he thought. *I've botched this almost from start to finish. I'd like, for once, to make it right.*

Chapter 6

JOAN SLEPT FOR FOURTEEN HOURS, WAKING EVERY FOUR, as was her habit in strange territory, to check for threats and remember that nobody needed her to take watch. She could have stayed in bed longer, but her stomach started growling and she remembered that the food here was damn good. Still, she didn't head for the kitchen right away, and not only because she didn't know where it was.

This wasn't a vacation. First things first. That meant training: stretching, jumping jacks, forty push-ups balanced on her knuckles, fifty kicks on each leg, and then a regimen of punching techniques. By the time she was done, Joan could have eaten the next thing she saw.

Nobody had knocked on the door, though. Either Simon had told them not to disturb her or they expected her to go and find her own food. She glanced around, didn't see her dress—they'd probably burned it—and decided that the clothes in the desk drawer were a bad idea too. She'd wear the nightgown, then, even though it looked damn silly with her bony wrists and ankles sticking out and with more ruffles than any grown woman should ever wear. With luck, she could grab some bread and coffee without seeing anyone.

Of course she ran into Simon before she reached the end of the hallway.

"Good Lord," he said, shaking his head as he looked at her. "Nobody's told you anything, have they?"

"You sure haven't." Joan drew herself up. "I was looking for breakfast. Your servants probably thought I knew what to do."

"Right," he said. "Pull on the rope by your bed. Rose will bring you a tray."

"I can get it myself. I don't want to be a hassle."

"You're no trouble. Besides, you can't leave your rooms like that."

"I'll be in this for a while, then," Joan said, "unless you keep a bunch of women's clothes around."

"Hardly," Simon said, laughter and shock mixing in his voice. "I've sent for the village dressmaker. She should arrive sometime after you've had breakfast."

Great news in theory: it'd be good if her clothes made her look less freakish. In practice...

"I'll need something to wear while she measures me," Joan said. "There are marks on my back. I can't explain them."

Simon frowned. His eyes went over her body, quick and carefully impersonal. "You'll probably fit in some of Ellie's things for the moment, though they'll be short. I'll ask if she minds."

"Right. I'll pay you back," Joan said abruptly. She didn't know how. She'd figure some way out. "For the room and food too."

Simon's frown didn't go away. Instead, it just got deeper and more surprised. "Do you honestly think I'd ask a lady for payment? Particularly one who saved my life not a day ago? The worst cad in the world would feel some obligation under the circumstances, and I hope I'm not that."

He'd stepped closer to her as he talked. Joan could

feel the heat of his body now and catch a pleasantly spicy smell that was maybe his soap, maybe just him. "That wasn't a favor," she said, snapping her mind back to the conversation. "I wasn't going to stand there and watch you get killed, that's all. And they would've killed me too, afterward."

"Nonetheless, the point stands," said Simon. "Think of it as outfitting the troops, if that's easier for you. We're in this together, after all."

Hearing it that way did help. She wondered how well Simon had known that, and she smiled up at him without thinking about it. "Thanks," she said, not just meaning the clothes.

"Quite welcome," he said, and flashed an unexpected smile of his own. "Now please go back to your room. This isn't the time for me to lurk in hallways with half-dressed women."

Joan had thought that the rope was decoration, but when she pulled it, she did hear a bell somewhere in the wall. Satisfied and a little bored, she wandered over to the drapes and pulled them back.

Outside were blue and green and gold.

Sometime during the night, the rain had stopped and the clouds had rolled back. Now sunlight flooded down onto a mile of green grass. From the window, it looked almost as soft as the carpet. Darker trees bordered the lawn, and off to the west, Joan saw the edge of the forest that she and Simon had come from. To the east were a dozen slate roofs, smoke spiraling up from the chimney on each one. Joan watched the smoke rise into the sky.

After a minute, she thought what she always did, that she was wasting time. She had better things to do. This wasn't a pleasure trip. Good, sound thoughts, these; they'd kept her alive and gotten her here.

For the first time in ten years, Joan rose up against them.

For the first time in ten years, she had time to waste.

After years of preparation, days of ceremony, and those few frenzied hours before the passage, Joan was where she needed to be. Now she had no need to hurry. She'd never been a visionary, but she had the calm knowledge of a warrior and a hunter, and it said *wait*.

This was a beginning. If she watched and waited, this place would give her an opening. If her hands were steady and her feet sure, she would take it. Hurrying wouldn't help.

And there was something else too, something she'd never thought before: *I deserve this*.

Back home, Joan would've squashed the thought. But she wasn't back home. She was miles and years from everything she knew, and she would die in this strange world. The only difference would be whether that death came fast or slow. And even if it was slow, even if she was lucky, the world would probably look less beautiful and be less kind to her before the end. At least now she could enjoy what pleasure there was.

Joan sat on her bed in the morning sunshine, looked out the window, and smiled.

——⁓——

When Rose came in carrying a large tray, she had something white and frothy draped over one arm. It looked like

a dress to Joan but not like either of the dresses she'd seen
Rose or Mrs. Edgar wearing. It was too thin and sleeve-
less. "Your chemise, miss," Rose said, putting it down on
the bed. "Mrs. Simmons will be here in under an hour."

Joan did hurry once Rose left, yanking the nightgown
off and the chemise on, wanting to save time so she
could savor her breakfast. It was worth the effort: two
eggs, sausages, and toast, plus tea that didn't wake her
up as much here as the kind back home did but that also
didn't take the roof off her mouth. She ate as much as
she could and then looked at herself in the mirror. The
chemise hid the tattoos well enough, though there was
nothing she could do about the scar on her upper arm or
the mark from the flashgun. At least the mark was on her
inner arm and less obvious.

Rose returned carrying a brown dress and leading
a slim, dark-haired woman with a large bag. "Mrs.
Simmons, miss."

Did she bow? Shake hands? Joan settled for smiling.
"Good morning."

"Miss MacArthur," said Mrs. Simmons. She took a
quick look around the room and then at Joan. She sniffed
once. *I got here just in time*, that sniff said. "Please move
to the center of the room, miss, and we can get started."

Joan spent the next hour both bored and nervous.
Mrs. Simmons and Rose moved around her, taking
measurements and altering the brown dress. She stared
at the wall and tried not to flinch at having two strangers
in such close proximity. She tried not to think that there
were two of them, that they were healthier than anyone
she knew back home, and that she was unarmed and
wearing only thin cloth.

She did fairly well, Joan thought. Her hands didn't shake at all.

It helped that Rose was silent and that Mrs. Simmons didn't speak except to note measurements and to ask Joan to move. For most of the fitting, the seamstress didn't seem to see Joan as anything other than a figure to measure and a form to fit. When Joan raised her arms the first time, though, Mrs. Simmons's eyes fell on the scar there, the one from when a fell beast had grabbed Joan. Mrs. Simmons stopped, tape measure dangling from one hand.

Joan had prepared her explanation of a fall when she was young onto a piece of broken glass. She braced herself for the question.

It never came. Instead, Mrs. Simmons looked past Joan and met Rose's eyes. Neither of them spoke for a moment.

The scar didn't say *glass* to them or *tentacle*. It said *whip* or maybe *rope*. A sudden, knowing sympathy crossed both women's faces for just a second before they bent back to the task at hand. This world had its cruelties as well.

Then the dress went down over Joan's head. It felt like a tent and weighed a ton, but she relaxed a little. At least her marks were well hidden now. "Did Mr. Grenville give any, um, specific instructions?" she asked.

"Yes, miss." Mrs. Simmons kept measuring while she talked, moving with the swift purpose some men had when they fought. "Blouses and skirts mostly, he said, plus the other, er, essentials. The corset'll take some time, but I should have the rest within a few days."

They'd told Joan about corsets before they sent her.

She fought back a wince and told herself that it couldn't be worse than a broken rib. "Thank you."

"Yes, miss. Will this do?"

Mrs. Simmons gestured toward the mirror, and Joan stepped forward. The skirt swung against her legs, heavy enough that she knew her reaction time would suffer. She felt like she was walking through water. Also, if she had to kick anything in this costume, she was screwed.

On the other hand, at least she'd have plenty of places to stash knives. And, for what it was worth, the dress didn't look half bad. Hell, it made her look better than she had at home most of the time, though being clean and rested went a long way too. Plus, it was warm, whole, and softer than either canvas or leather.

"Good," she said, stepping back. "Thank you."

Mrs. Simmons bobbed a curtsy. "I'll send a girl when the other things are ready, miss," she said, and headed out.

"If you don't mind, miss," Rose said, "Mr. Grenville's expecting you in the library. Shall I get you ready?"

"Sure," Joan said, not sure how much more ready she could get.

Chapter 7

THE DRESS WAS HARDLY FLATTERING. SIMON WAS NO judge of female fashion, but even he could see that it had been taken in and that dark brown wool and severe lines did nothing to disguise the wire-over-bone look of Joan's body.

Normal clothing made her less strange, though. Before, she'd been so far outside Simon's experience that he couldn't even have thought of her as pretty or plain. The flash of beauty he'd seen on the walk from the forest had been like the beauty of a thunderstorm or a wild animal, something he couldn't conceive in terms of feminine appeal. Now he could evaluate her, at least superficially, as if she'd been any other woman of his acquaintance.

She had good bones, even if she needed more flesh on them. Good posture too, and a certain primitive grace. Her mouth was firm and well shaped, and she had good teeth, from what he could see. Now that it was clean, her hair was actually a rather pretty sort of dark blonde—a bit dull at the moment, but there was doubtless some feminine art to fix that, or perhaps enough good meals would do the trick. And her hazel eyes were really quite striking.

As he watched her take an unasked-for seat in the chair opposite his desk, he had an idea. It was a scandalous and perhaps entirely immoral one, but a way forward all the same.

At the same time, Joan lifted her eyebrows. "See anything green?"

Simon didn't recognize the phrase, but the meaning was clear enough. "My apologies," he said. If she'd been another woman, he might have offered a compliment to mollify her, but he didn't think Joan would welcome that. "I was wondering what your plans were."

"I don't know yet," she said. "We didn't get much more than his name and the date."

"And they threw you through time with only that?" Nice considerate way to treat a woman.

Joan shrugged. "They knew I was competent. I can think of a couple things off the top of my head."

"Oh?"

"One," Joan began, holding up a finger. "I break in. I've got black clothing and the equipment I need. If I can find his house—"

"You'll have the law on you. Reynell spends most of his time in London. That's probably where the manuscript is, and he lives in a *very* good part of town. The police would show up, and they'd probably catch you."

"Possibly before I burn the book," she said, grimacing. "All right. I pose as a servant."

"He's not hiring, and you don't know how to act like a servant."

"You could teach me. And I could say that the real one got sick. Bribe her or knock her out and hide her somewhere, though that complicates things either way. I'll need enough time to search the house too, so I'll try to get some information beforehand."

"And that's all you can think of?"

"Right now? Yes. Give me a little while, and I'll come

up with something better." Joan leaned forward, putting her elbows on the desk. Incredibly, a hint of a smile touched her mouth. "He doesn't know that I'm here, and he doesn't know why. So I'll take my time, learn the place, learn his habits. Eventually I'll see an opening."

"I think," said Simon, "I know a way we can make one."

"Really?"

"It's not precisely, um…" He cleared his throat. If Joan had been a woman of his world, Simon would have been about twenty seconds from getting slapped. He still wasn't sure he was safe. "I don't mean to insult you by this, and—"

Joan rolled her eyes. "What's the idea?"

"When Eleanor and I return to town, you come with us. You'll be a friend of my family's. That will admit you to our social circles, and from there, you can cultivate an acquaintance with Reynell."

"Seduce him, you mean," Joan said matter-of-factly.

"Or merely spend enough time around him to learn where he goes and for how long."

"Hmm. You think he'd go for it?"

"Alex has always competed with me," Simon said, keeping his voice even. He remembered evenings out and friendly rivalry over women and cards. He'd thought it was friendly, at least. "He'll want revenge as well now, and seducing someone close to me will seem like an easy way to get it."

"Sure of himself, isn't he?"

"He's always had a way with women. And a hard time resisting the beautiful ones."

"I'm not beautiful," Joan said easily. "Not to you people. I might not ever be. What then?"

"You will be. There are people in London who can see to it, if necessary."

"All right." Joan drummed her fingers on the desk. "So. I get close to him, and he either invites me to his place or arranges to meet me somewhere. I don't know how they do things here."

"He'll probably have you to his house. He could hardly seduce you under my roof, and I've never known him to use a hotel. Our earlier agreement still holds," Simon added. "Perhaps it would be better if he did suggest a hotel. I could confront him there while you disposed of the book."

"Yeah. Maybe." Joan gave him a long look. "Do you have any plans?"

"One," he said. "There are *geasa*—spells of binding— in old books. I don't have any myself, but if I can find one, I can make sure that Alex harms nobody else. I can even get him to leave off his study of the occult."

He regretted even that, in a way. There was much he never would have discovered in his youth if not for Alex's damn-the-odds enthusiasm for the latest ritual, the next source of information, the newest avenue of amusement. In another life, the man might have been a great asset to the world.

It didn't matter.

"Got any leads?" Joan asked.

"A few hints. Are we pressed for time?"

"Unless a rock falls on my head or something, I've got about forty years. I don't know the people Reynell's fucking with, though. If they matter to you, you might want to be speedy about this."

"Thank you for that," he said.

He knew Alex was capable of ruining men at the card table and ladies in the bedroom, of exposing innocent girls to evil far beyond the petty sins of this world, of willful and deliberate murder. Perhaps he'd gotten in over his head, perhaps he was sorry now...but most likely he was acting now as he always had, and people were suffering for it.

On the other hand, Simon knew two other magicians. Both were outside the country, and one was quite elderly. Just now, he and Joan were the only people in the world who knew Alex's path and could stand in his way. If they ran instead of walked and fell by doing so—

In the end, he stayed as close to the middle path as he could get. "Give me until we go to London. That should be time enough—it'll take a month or two to get you ready."

The look Joan gave him was so searching as to be, from another woman, entirely indecent. From her, though, it was just evaluation: *Can you do what you say?* Simon half expected her to look at his teeth.

"I'm in," she said. "Where do we start?"

"With you." Ideas began to fall into place like tumblers in a lock. "We'll say you're from America, one of the Western states. That'll explain why nobody's heard of you, and it'll cover what we can't fix."

"Fix?" she asked, dryly amused.

"Fix. You'll have to learn to act like a lady. At least in public."

"Damn, I thought so. Lay it on me."

"For one thing, ladies don't curse. No profanity, no blasphemy, no vulgarity."

"No shit?" she asked, quirking a grin. Simon had to laugh in response. "What if I'm, um, angry?"

"Ladies aren't supposed to get angry most of the time," he said, and wasn't surprised to see the face she made. "If someone makes improper advances or swears around you, or so forth, then you should be very cold and correct. Or faint."

"Faint. Yeah, I don't think that'll be happening. Not unless it gives me a major tactical advantage."

"Oh, it does."

Joan smiled again, impishly, and suddenly Simon didn't think he'd have to worry about her being pretty enough. He shifted in his chair, trying to ignore his body's response.

Her question didn't help either: "Were you an innocent bystander or the one making the improper advances?"

"That," he said, "depends on the occasion."

"Mmm. Anything else?"

"Quite a bit. There are a number of rules you'll have to follow…while implying that you'd be willing to break some of them for the right man."

Joan sighed. "I couldn't have just had to shoot things a lot, could I? You'll be training me?"

"Some. But you'll have a better guide—my sister, Eleanor." Both amusement and incipient arousal vanished. Simon sat forward, holding up a hand. "She knows you're from elsewhere. She doesn't know you're from our future, and you're not to tell her. Nor are you to try to recruit her for a more active role in this scheme. She's neither a soldier nor a spy, and she's not well."

"All right," said Joan. "I get it."

"I hope you do."

———

It was a good beginning. At least Eleanor looked at Joan with more interest than she'd shown in anything over the past few weeks and forgot to flinch at the sound of the closing door. She bowed gracefully to Joan, who pulled back the hand she'd extended and made her own attempt. It wasn't as bad as Simon had feared.

"It's good to meet you," Joan said when Simon had made the introductions. "Thanks for agreeing to teach me. I'll try to learn quickly."

Eleanor, who shrank from her acquaintances these days, was surprised into a smile. "I-I'm sure you'll be a pleasure to talk with."

"I'll do my best, but I should warn you that I'm pretty ignorant. I *can* read, though, so if you want to get me out of your hair a couple hours a day, just push a book in my direction."

Eleanor tilted her head to the side. "Out of my hair— I'm sorry?"

"Don't be. I meant if you want your privacy." Joan grinned at her. "Please do give me a weird look if I say something that doesn't make sense. It'll help me learn."

"Oh," said Eleanor. "Well, I'll certainly try, if you'd like."

"I would. But don't worry too much about it. I'll pick up vocabulary, and I'm sure you have plenty of other things to teach me."

"Yes. Simon, I'm sorry for asking, but—"

He laughed gently. "Part of the reason I asked you is that I don't really know, myself. You can assume, though, that she knows nothing a young lady should."

Eleanor's eyes went wide and she looked swiftly, half apologetically, over at Joan, only to relax a little when she saw that the other woman wasn't upset. Eleanor frowned a little, forehead wrinkling, and then tentatively spoke. "Dancing, of course, and proper forms of address, and table manners. General etiquette, but you'll probably learn that out of a book and only practice with me." She added slowly, "History and literature would be nice, though not essential."

She was too polite to say what both she and Simon knew. Most young ladies in Society knew no more of literature than the latest novel and no more of history than the last scandal. Eleanor was interested in those things, though, so Simon said, "I think those would be quite useful. And we're hardly pressed for time."

"I'm very glad to hear that," said Eleanor, and thought a moment longer. "Riding, though I admit I'm quite unskilled there. It would be good if you could play or sing, though there are alternatives."

"Can't play an instrument or anything," Joan said, "but I can sing decently. At least, nobody ever told me to shut up. I don't know any of the songs here, though."

"Easy enough to remedy," said Simon, "and one of the grooms can teach you to ride."

"I'd be glad to teach what I know," said Eleanor, "only please don't consider my word final. I'm hardly the most fashionable girl in England."

"That shouldn't be a problem," said Joan.

"I'll leave you for a few hours," Simon said, "since I have some business to deal with. Do make the house your own, Miss MacArthur, by all means, and the grounds as well. Ellie, I'd consider it a great favor if you'd show her about, since I'm a rather negligent host at the moment."

Another smile appeared on Eleanor's face. "It'd be my pleasure," she said, and sounded as if she meant it.

As Simon went out into the hall, the light seemed more golden, the air warmer and clearer than it had in months. Perhaps he was only imagining any improvement. Perhaps the novelty of teaching Joan would wear off, or she would be too strange for Ellie to really like. Perhaps this would all come to nothing. He'd not dared to hope once since he and Eleanor had come out to Englefield.

But now he couldn't help it.

Chapter 8

"So," said Joan, trying to figure out how to begin with this girl, now that Simon had gone. She glanced out the window, stalling for time, and the view gave her an idea. "Why don't we head outside?"

"If you'd like, of course."

"We can stay in if you want."

Eleanor took a breath. "No," she said. "It's only that I haven't done much exploring around here myself."

There was something to this girl after all, beneath the nerves and the trauma. Joan smiled. "We can get lost together then. Got a spool of thread with you?"

"Oh, do you know that story?"

"Some version. Ariadan, right? The goddess?" It wasn't exactly the right term, but she didn't know what they called the Watchers here. "Angel?"

Eleanor led Joan out into the hall, talking softly as she went. "Not quite, not here. A princess. Ariadne. Her father, the king of Crete, kept a-a monster in a maze and fed youths to it."

"Nice dad," said Joan. "Your royalty doesn't do that kind of thing, right?"

"No, not at all." Eleanor gave a half-shocked laugh at the thought. "Nobody civilized would—"

She was starting to stare at Joan, and Joan, remembering Simon's lecture, didn't tell her that feeding youths to monsters would've been fairly standard behavior among the Traitor Lords. "What happened to the girl?" she asked instead.

"Well, Theseus, the son of Poseidon—sorry, that's the Greek god of the ocean—came to kill the monster. Ariadne fell in love with him, and she gave him the ball of thread so that he could get back through the labyrinth afterward. What's the story like where you're from?"

"There's a princess there too, but she's a different woman. She gets cursed and falls asleep for a hundred years. A maze of thorns, or sometimes fire, grows up around her. Ariadan gives the hero a ball of magic thread. It rolls ahead of him and shows him what path to take."

They stepped outside. Sunlight washed over Joan, and she turned her face up to it, closing her eyes and feeling the heat against her skin. A deep breath brought her the smell of earth and grass.

When she opened her eyes again, the lawn she'd seen from her bedroom window stretched off before her with a wide road looping around it. A narrower path, though it was still big enough for two or three people to walk side by side, led around the house, flanked by a row of tall trees. Eleanor had taken a few steps in that direction but then paused. She was politely looking elsewhere.

"Sorry," said Joan. "Been a while since I saw the sun, you know? Where do these roads go?"

"The large one goes out to the village," Eleanor said. "It turns off halfway, and there's a path to the woods. This other one will take us to the gardens and the stables." After they'd gone a few feet, she added, "I'd heard some of your story before too. The princess and the curse, I mean."

"Oh, there are a million of 'em," Joan said. "And the *dratted* prince never gets the job done himself either. Something always shows up and helps him. And then he gets the reward. Nice in stories."

They turned a corner. A large brown building stretched out in back of the house, and Joan saw horses in a corral near them—they were huge goddamn things even from a distance, and she was glad she didn't have to learn riding right off—while another path led away, down between two lines of trees. As they walked toward it, Eleanor was silent, and she didn't look at Joan.

"Sometimes it works out," she finally said, not much louder than a whisper. "Sometimes, someone comes before things get too bad."

"Yeah," said Joan, clearing her throat. "Sometimes, yeah."

If she got the chance, she'd kick Reynell in the balls a few times before he died.

Trees gave way to low hedges bordering green grass and low banks of flowers in bright red and blue, yellow and white. A little farther on were rosebushes with rich spots of red and yellow and white against their shining, dark green leaves. Joan tried to drink it all in as she walked, the color and the light and the sweet smell in the air. It was a few minutes before she looked over at Eleanor.

The girl was putting up a fairly good front, or maybe a fairly good fight, walking along with her head high and her face mostly calm. Her eyes kept flicking to the shadows and back, though, and her breathing was too quick, like a trapped animal's.

"By the way," Joan said, turning away reluctantly from the flowers, "where are we, exactly?"

Englefield Hall, she learned, and Queen's Engle was the nearby village. They were half a day from London, more or less, if you caught the train and had a good coach. When the weather wasn't so fine, Eleanor said, perhaps Joan could look at some of the atlases, and Joan eagerly agreed. She'd never seen a map of the world in this time; she hadn't really seen a map of the whole world at all. High Command had one, but it was mostly guesswork. She didn't tell Eleanor any of that.

As Eleanor spoke, she seemed to calm down a little. By the time they reached the house again, she was even smiling once in a while. She did keep looking at the shadows, though, and that made Joan think about security.

The subject was still on her mind that evening when she sat in what Eleanor had called the drawing room and tried to make sense of the rules in a book of etiquette. Footsteps, when she heard them, were a welcome distraction.

Distraction didn't explain the way her pulse leapt when Simon came through the door, though. It was the first real opportunity she'd had to look at the man without considering tactics or trying to get her bearings, and she couldn't deny liking what she saw. The tall athlete's body that his clothes outlined, the hint of something not so stern about his firm mouth, and the crisp black hair that fell across his forehead—there was plenty to like.

He seemed a little surprised as he looked at her, and Joan clamped down quickly on her thoughts. No good ogling her allies too blatantly—the last thing she needed was Simon getting awkward around her. "Evening," she said, and tried to make her smile casual rather than lecherous.

"Good evening," he said, and looked from her face to the book that was now closed in her lap. "Did you hear me coming?"

Joan stifled a grin. "Were you trying to be quiet?"

"No, but the hall is carpeted in this part of the house."

"I noticed," Joan said and shrugged. "Carpet's not air."

"You hear very well, then."

Now she couldn't resist. "I do a lot of things very well." Joan let herself grin this time and then moved on. "Eleanor's gone to do some reading, but she seemed to be all right this afternoon. Showed me around the gardens and everything."

"That's…more than you realize. I'm glad to hear it." Simon dropped into a chair next to the sofa where Joan was sitting, crossing one leg over the other. "I hope you enjoyed the tour," he added.

"Yeah, it's a great place you've got here." She didn't actually want to describe how great it was, not with his eyes on her. She had no desire to sound sappy around this man. "I was assuming," she said quickly, "that you'd have warned me if it wasn't safe out there. After yesterday, I mean. If I was wrong, though, or if you hadn't thought about it—"

One corner of Simon's mouth quirked upward. "That's astonishingly diplomatic of you. Not simply asking if I'm a complete idiot, I mean. I'm pleased to say that my protections should cover you both, and I doubt Reynell can manage a demon or a spell to break through them."

"So any threats should be basically mortal?"

"Yes, and I can't imagine you'd encounter many of those as long as you stick to the grounds and the village.

I may not keep as close an eye on my household as Alex does, but I expect people would notice an assassin around here."

"Some would," said Joan. He knew the place—but if he was wrong, she didn't think one assassin should give her much trouble.

"All the same, I'd like you to keep an eye out. For Eleanor, especially." Simon leaned toward her as he spoke, putting one hand on the arm of the sofa, and it was suddenly hard to look away from his eyes. "I know it won't always be possible, and I hardly expect you to sleep across her threshold or any such thing, but where you can—"

"I'd be glad to," Joan said, and couldn't keep laughter out of her voice. The man sounded like he was asking her to break into one of the great fortresses or to find a living elephant or something. "It won't be a problem at all," she said. Without thinking, she reached over and touched his hand.

A rush of energy came with the momentary contact, along with a sudden awareness of what seemed like every inch of her skin, especially where the cloth of her dress lay against her breasts.

Did he feel the same heat? Joan's fingers were calloused, she knew, and she wasn't anywhere near the way a woman should look in this time. Still, she thought she saw his eyes widen a little, and there could have been more color on his face.

Better not to think too much about that.

"Thank you," Simon said. "That's at least one weight off my mind." He smiled at her—a damn nice smile too.

Chapter 9

THE NEW CLOTHES ARRIVED TWO DAYS LATER, MRS. Simmons and her daughters having more than earned their payment. Joan came down to her first practical lesson in a blue serge skirt and a snowy blouse embroidered with small blue flowers. Her hair was done as simply as ever, she wore no jewelry, and neither good food nor plentiful sleep had more than begun to take effect. Still, her face was softened and her eyes were brighter. She could have been called pretty.

Rising to greet her, Simon suspected she'd go well beyond that in the end.

She returned his look with a questioning glance of her own, and the corners of her mouth turned up just a little. "Mr. Grenville," she said, mindful of the servants still setting up the tea things. "Eleanor says she'll be in shortly. We were looking at the atlas, and she wanted to look something up, but she said I should come and tell you."

"Thank you," he said, and then smiled and went as far as polite society would allow. "You look very well today."

"That's very kind of you. I'm…very much obliged."

Simon winced. Of course, "Miss MacArthur" had been in dire straits. Of course, sending a dressmaker to her in this one instance wasn't at all like giving a gift of clothing would have been otherwise. The servants understood that, and they'd known he was giving her clothes. Even so, he shook his head at her very slightly.

Joan was just beginning to look puzzled when Eleanor stepped in. She still wore the plainest of dresses, and she was still very thin and pale, but she'd spent the last two days walking with Joan in the gardens, and now she was having tea in the drawing room with them, a small miracle in itself.

"Ellie," Simon said, smiling, "I hope you're well."

"Oh yes, thank you. And you?"

"Quite so, thank you." He was relieved to see the last of the footmen put down his tray and walk out, the door closing quietly behind him. "Shall we?"

"Please," said Joan. "I'm pretty hungry."

"No, you're not," Simon said.

Joan blinked. "Ladies don't get hungry," she said then, her voice highly skeptical.

"No. You don't mention that you're uncomfortable in any way. Besides, saying you're hungry says that your host hasn't done a good job of providing food for you. You also don't mention gifts in front of strangers, especially not gifts from men."

"Is there anything you do mention?"

"How nice everyone looks," Simon said. "And how lovely the weather is."

"What if it's not?"

"Then you don't mention it. Rolling your eyes is also not done in the best circles. Now, say that we'd just been introduced. Follow me." He bowed slightly, keeping his eyes on hers, and smiled. "A pleasure to meet you, Miss MacArthur."

"A pleasure, Mr. Grenville." Joan bowed as if she had a poker in her spine. When she looked up into Simon's face again, she sighed. "What?"

"Military precision isn't quite in fashion. Try again, please. Less rigid this time." Her second bow wasn't as stiff, but it made her look like a tiger ready to spring. "Better," Simon said. "We can work on that."

"Wonderful."

He helped Joan and Eleanor to their seats, noting briefly that a footman would do so at any real party. "Leave your elbows off the table," he told Joan, "and don't let your back touch the chair." Then he asked Eleanor, "Am I missing anything?"

"No, not at all." She added to Joan, "You'd take your gloves off and leave your hat on, but that's a bit academic at the moment."

"I've been down to the village lately," Simon said, pouring the tea and trying to remember how to start proper conversation. "Things seem to be going well."

"I'm glad to hear it." Eleanor lifted her teacup carefully, took a sip, and then took a breath. "The rain we had the other day should do a great deal for the farms, shouldn't it?"

"Yes. The dry weather's been a worry lately. I hope this rain eases the farmers' minds." He added to Joan, "Lift the cup, not the saucer," and racked his mind for a new, less insipid topic of conversation. "I understand you've been reading Edward Bellamy's book, Ellie?"

"*Looking Backward*? Yes, it's quite good. Very unlikely, of course, but you do almost believe in such things when you're reading it. Have you read it?"

"Yes." It had been a few months earlier, before Joan. Back then, he'd thought about utopian philosophy, talked over Bellamy's ideas at his club, and wondered about socialism and about America. Now he thought of two hundred years in the future and tried not to glance at Joan. "I preferred some of his earlier works myself, the ones that didn't get much attention. But it was quite well done."

Eleanor nodded. As Simon passed the tray of cucumber sandwiches, she took one but left it on her plate, and her approach to the pastries seemed just as much form. They fell into a conversation about books, though, almost as light and easy as such had been in the old days, and Simon rejoiced that Eleanor listened and smiled and even told one short story about a strict teacher she'd had.

By the end of the tea, he'd begun to feel a bit like that teacher himself. He'd told Joan to keep her arms at her sides, to take smaller bites, and to hold her teacup by the handle. He'd warned her against letting her eyes drift from the other people at the table, letting her expression grow too serious or too bored, and taking more than one sandwich or scone at a time. Simon chose not to address the fact that she'd eaten five sandwiches and two scones with cream. They could talk about that when she wasn't quite as thin.

Joan followed his instructions precisely. He never had to warn her twice, and she didn't complain or even speak, just nodded quickly to acknowledge a point. Toward the end of the meal, though, her smile was beginning to resemble a grimace.

Afterward, once Ellie had taken herself off to read in the study and the servants were clearing the table, Joan stood looking out the window. The parlor had a good view at times, but the day was bleak. The sunset was lost behind the clouds, and Simon doubted Joan had any desire for natural beauty just then. As the door closed behind the last of the footmen, he stepped forward, close enough to speak but no farther. Alarming her would probably be unwise.

"I'm a dead shot with any weapon I can name," Joan said. "I can survive for ten days in the wilderness. I've killed things that would make you run away screaming. I've led men on missions where we knew we all could die, and I've brought most of them back whole. And I've been through rituals. Never put a foot wrong either."

"I—" he began, and didn't know how to go on.

"I get that I have to do this. I'll learn. But everything I just talked about had a point. That?" One hand gestured to the now-empty table. "That's about showing that you're fragile. There is no point, and it's stupid. Just so you know."

"It does serve a point, I think," he said, and then laughed, careful not to seem like he was laughing at her. "But I couldn't explain it. I'm afraid I'm not a very good teacher."

"You didn't make your world. You didn't set its rules." She sighed then, as if letting a great weight go, and turned to face him. "And don't worry. You always want to punch your instructor. It passes. You're a damn sight nicer than most of mine were."

"Really?"

Now she laughed. "I was a soldier, remember? I was thirteen when I started training, and I don't think the corporal who had charge of us ever used anyone's name—waste of time with perfectly good words like 'maggot' and 'dipshit' around. You haven't left a tenth of the bruises he did either."

"Lord," said Simon. "I'd bloody well hope not!"

"Oh, he wasn't a bad guy. Had to toughen us up, you know? And he knew most of us did better when we had someone to hate."

"Did you hate him?"

"For a while. Then we went out in the field. Those of us who came back learned to like him after that."

"I hope it doesn't take such drastic circumstances this time," he said, half joking.

Joan stepped forward and put a hand on his arm. Her palm was warm and firm, and her hair smelled like roses now. "I don't hate you," she said. "I'm not good at this, and all my other training happened when I was a kid, around other kids who were as bad or worse, and I hate that. It's not your fault, though, and I'm not thirteen anymore. I might get pissed off, but I'm not going to hate you."

"I'm glad to hear it."

"Hey," she said, with a shrug and a resigned smile, "I signed on for this. You didn't. I'm a bitch sometimes, but I can remember that much."

"You're not—" he responded automatically, and she waved the protest away, shaking her head.

Her hair shifted a little, a curl falling against her neck. What would it be like, he wondered, to run his hands through that hair now? What would her skin feel like under his hands?

"I should get back to my research," he said, hoping his voice wasn't hoarse. Clearly he'd been in the country too long.

Chapter 10

"WE WON'T HAVE TO LACE IT VERY TIGHTLY AT ALL, miss," Rose said cheerfully. "It being an informal occasion, and you still so thin and all."

"Wonderful," said Joan, looking down at the corset and trying not to sound too sarcastic. Her stomach couldn't expand, so she was breathing from her chest and feeling like a panting dog, and the whalebones managed to prod her in the side and the breasts at the same time. If this was loose, they'd lace the damn thing tightly when she was dead. "Does it always take this long to put on?"

"Not at all, miss. Won't take hardly any time in the future, now that it's properly laced."

Hardly any time, Joan had learned over the past two weeks, meant about half an hour, at least when it came to getting dressed. She made a noncommittal sound and let Rose slide the dress over her head and start buttoning.

If Eleanor hadn't blushed bright red and told her that yes, people really would notice her going corset-less under a dancing dress, Joan would've said to hell with the whole thing. She had to wear it, though, which meant she should start getting used to it, and today was the first waltzing lesson.

It was also the first day in weeks that she'd really see Simon, since neither Eleanor nor the maids could be her partner. Simon had spent the past two weeks mostly shut in his library or the study upstairs. Joan had passed by a couple times, felt the dull heat behind her ear that meant magic, and decided not to bother him. Not that seeing him mattered, really, Joan thought, but she wanted to impress him with her competence at something since table manners had been a bust. She was also looking forward to the lesson itself. The quadrille had been sedate, the grooms were still tentative with her riding lessons, and she wanted to *move*.

"Have a look, miss?" Rose interrupted Joan's thoughts. There were twenty or so little gray buttons at the back of Joan's dress, and Rose had just finished buttoning them without swearing or fumbling once. Back home, Joan would have sent her down to sniper training ASAP.

She turned toward the mirror, blinked, and blinked again.

The dress was pretty: deep rose cotton trimmed at the cuffs and hem and collar with silver-gray ribbons. When it arrived, Joan had thought it looked good. Now she barely noticed it. She was too busy staring at her breasts.

Great Powers, it's like puberty all over again.

The corset pushed up what she had and padded what she didn't in a way that stood out even under the relatively modest dress. Joan had never minded being small up top—easier to run and shoot that way—and the corset was still a whole new level of impractical in a world that was full of impracticalities. Still, she could see now why women wore the things.

The human mind adapted quickly. It was a bit sad sometimes, but everyone started taking things for granted eventually, no matter what they were. After two weeks, dinner was good but not mind-blowing, and most of the rooms at Englefield didn't make Joan stop and stare anymore.

The ballroom was still stunning. The walls were gold, or looked like it, though that was probably just fancy wallpaper, and darker gold curtains hung at the windows. Except for a black piano in one corner, the room was bare, and the wooden floor had been polished so much that it shone. Joan caught her breath as she entered. Then she heard Simon catch his.

He'd been standing by one of the windows, talking quietly with Eleanor. Both of them had turned when Joan opened the door, but Joan met Simon's eyes first and saw the look on his face—surprise, followed closely and unmistakably by lust.

Heat swept over her, a wash of sweet white fire that pooled in her groin and left her speechless as Simon walked toward her. He moved smoothly, she noticed, not like a warrior but with a more unhurried grace. He'd be good in bed. Agile. She could imagine his body beneath hers, rising to meet her in smooth, liquid thrusts, his lips closing around one of her nipples—

Joan breathed out in one unsteady rush. This was bad. She shouldn't be thinking this way now. Maybe in her bed later, but not right now. She tried to remember the signs of radiation poisoning. Those were disgusting enough to turn anyone off.

"Miss MacArthur," Simon said, and bowed. "It's always a pleasure."

"Good to see you, Mr. Grenville." She wasn't panting, at least, or drooling. "What do I do now?"

"Give me your hand," he said. His voice was lower than usual, more intimate, and the instructions sounded suggestive instead of annoying. "Fingers out—good." Simon took her hand gently, bowed again, and raised the back of it to his lips.

Oh, God. The kiss was very brief. It shouldn't have been a big deal. She'd had much more contact with men back home, men she would never have thought of sleeping with.

It was a bigger deal here. Maybe that was why she wanted to throw her arms around his neck and really kiss him, among other things that she wouldn't let herself think of right now.

She cleared her throat. "Will everyone do that?"

"Probably," said Simon. "It is gentlemanly behavior, after all."

"I'm surprised nobody's lips get chapped. Can anyone just come up and say hello that way?"

Eleanor actually giggled at the thought. It was the first thing like a real laugh that Joan had heard out of her, and Simon's face visibly brightened when he heard it. For a moment, Joan forgot her desire in a mixed wave of relief and pity. Eleanor went on. "You'd have to be introduced first."

"Who introduces me?"

"Any previous acquaintance," Simon said. "You can hardly avoid the process."

The setup had potential. There were lots of toxins you could probably apply to gloves. Sad that she hadn't brought any with her except for the stuff on the darts. Maybe a ring would work or a hidden needle—

"If you'd care to begin the lesson," Simon broke in dryly.

"Sorry," Joan said. "How do we start?"

"Well, it's a box step," Eleanor said, and shyly demonstrated.

Joan followed her movements, back with the right foot, back and to the side with the left, and bring them together. "Does this get tricky somewhere?"

"The rhythm," said Simon, "and the partner."

"Then we'd better practice those, hadn't we?"

"Precisely. Your hand?" He took it again and stepped forward, closing the distance between them. Up close, he was very big and warm, his hand smooth around hers. "Put your other hand on my shoulder, and keep your arms firm. I'm going to put my hand on your back."

There was pressure just above her waist. She couldn't really feel anything else through the dress and corset, and that was probably good. "What now?"

"Follow my lead." Simon smiled. "As difficult as that may be."

His eyes really were very bright blue, and the lashes were thick and dark around them. And there was an interesting curve to his otherwise thin lips. Joan dropped her eyes, which didn't help. It just meant she was staring at his chest. "So," she said, a little faster than she'd have liked, "lead."

Dancing was surprisingly easy—of course you retreated when the other guy advanced, and vice versa—and fun, maybe because it was the closest thing to fighting Joan had done since she'd arrived. You had to wait and watch, alert to the subtle changes that told you what your opponent was going to do next. You had to be ready, moving at a moment's notice but never too early. Like in a fight, there was energy in the back-and-forth of a dance, of the movement and tension between you and the other guy.

Then, just when the dance started getting a little predictable, Eleanor began playing the piano. Now there was a third party to think about, something bigger than a person and with different cues to follow, and she and Simon were working together against it—or with it—as much as they were playing off each other. Sometime during the second song, she laughed from the sheer thrill of it.

Simon lifted an eyebrow but smiled himself. "I somehow thought you'd enjoy this."

"You were right. You're not going easy on me, are you?"

He shook his head. "You catch on very quickly."

"Compared to company manners? You bet. I do better when there aren't a million little details—here everything relates to each other, and I can see the shape of it. Besides, I've always been good at physical stuff."

Her thoughts shot immediately to one or two specific kinds of "physical stuff," and she felt her nipples harden against her corset. By the way Simon's eyes darkened, she knew his mind was in the same place.

"Do they dance at all where you're from?" His voice was thick.

"Yes. But not like this."

There'd been one room in the tunnels, one dark room with a string of tiny red lights and music as loud as you could get from a dying tape player. One-Eyed Charlie ran it, and he'd sell you booze or stronger things when the raids went well and you had something to trade. She'd gone there to drink, but sometimes she'd danced too.

"How?" Simon asked.

"Less formal. Faster. And you don't have partners. Well, not always."

With another rush of heat, she remembered writhing forms pressed against each other, legs clamped around thighs, the smell of sweat and perfume and rotgut like an aphrodisiac. There were a lot of ways to release tension. Sometimes dancing had been one. Sometimes it had been a prelude, and not all that *pre* either.

Simon swallowed. She watched his throat move. "Ah."

Back home, she'd have made him an offer, they'd have gone off to her room, and this crazy tension would've ended. It was just excess energy, really, and the presence of an attractive man, both easy enough to deal with back home. But here they assigned some sort of crazy meaning to sex, and she had to work with him. Even back home, she hadn't slept with anyone in her squad.

If a mission had ever been critical, this one was. She wouldn't put it at risk to scratch an itch. No way. No matter how much she was tempted.

Chapter 11

AT FIRST, KEEPING BUSY HAD BEEN EASY. THERE HAD BEEN the business of the estate, for one. As much as Simon had tried to keep up with things when he'd been in town, some matters really did demand his personal attention, and enough of them had piled up to keep him occupied for some time. He'd had to answer correspondence from his acquaintances in town as well and handle affairs there. And he'd certainly had plenty of research to do.

Simon had welcomed all of it at first. In the days since Joan's arrival, he'd felt the need to face the future with as much information as possible and with his affairs laid in order as best he could. He'd also wanted to build a wall out of fact and footnotes and duty, a wall between him and rash actions or unwise decisions, or simply to keep from looking too long at the task ahead of him.

Joan had been part of what he didn't want to look at. He was thankful for her presence with Eleanor and fascinated by the things she mentioned about her world, but when he spoke to her, he felt as if the world whose solidity he'd always taken for granted was as fragile as an eggshell.

He retreated from that feeling to his books and his accounts, but the strategy didn't quite work, because he found himself thinking of Joan anyway. When he read about breaking spells with salt, he wondered if her

people had tried that. When one of his books described a
man being turned into a dog, he imagined her remarking
that it wasn't really that much of a change. However he
tried to blot her from his mind, she wouldn't go.

On a sunny morning, after he'd exhausted his own
books and then posted discreetly pleading letters to magicians miles away, Simon discovered two things. First,
he had nothing more to do. The accounts had been sorted
and the tenants visited, and he'd searched every book in
his library for references to *geasa*. Second, he was restless and utterly tired of sitting in small rooms reading or
making respectable conversation with strangers.

He dressed for riding. Then he went down to the dining room and joined Eleanor and Joan for breakfast.

When he came in, Eleanor turned away from Joan and
stopped whatever she'd been saying in mid-sentence. It
stung to see that, but young ladies didn't want to discuss some things with men, even their brothers. Besides,
Eleanor looked decidedly improved. She had more color
in her cheeks, her eyes were brighter, and the plate in
front of her was well filled. He could certainly be content with that.

"Good morning," he said.

"Good morning," said Joan, and grinned. "I'm glad
to see you still exist."

She was quite altered. The hollows in her cheeks
were much less pronounced, and her face itself seemed
brighter. Her hazel eyes sparkled, and her lips were dark
and sensuous. And with good food and Rose's attention,
her hair had become a gleaming reddish gold. She was
still thin, and probably always would be, but she looked
closer to slender than starved now.

When she saw him looking, she smiled a little, knowingly, and Simon flushed.

I'm just...noting changes, he thought, *not—*

And then he *was*, because he saw her hair spread out over his pillows like a golden storm and thought of the way her face would look transported by passion. His cock jerked, hardening. Simon dropped quickly into his chair and hoped nobody had noticed.

"I—hope you're both well," he said, collecting himself.

"Very well, thank you," said Joan.

Her table manners were almost acceptable now, though absolutely mechanical. A little crease of concentration showed between her eyebrows whenever she held a fork or a teacup. Hopefully, that would pass with time.

"Eleanor and I," she went on, "were talking about riding. I believe they'll let me head out on my own today. She was kind enough to suggest some routes."

"I see you're going to go out as well," said Eleanor. "Perhaps—if it's not too much trouble—you could accompany Miss MacArthur? You do know the land better."

She looked back down at her plate after she spoke and not at Simon, but he smiled at her anyway. "I'd be glad to, Ellie. Will you come with us?"

"Oh—no, no thank you. If you don't mind, I have a few letters to write this morning. I've been very remiss about it, and my friends will be wondering." She picked up her teacup and took a sip.

"Then," he said, "it would give me great pleasure to ride with you, Miss MacArthur."

~~~

When he came out to the stables, Joan was already there, a tall figure in dark blue, her hair brilliant gold in the sun. From a distance, she cut quite an elegant figure, though it would have been better if she hadn't kept raising her hand to push at the brim of her hat. The gesture was appropriately equine but not quite appropriate to a lady.

"It won't fall off," Simon said, as she turned to face him with a skeptical look on her face that set him grinning. "Really."

"You sure?" she asked and then shook her head. "I mean, are you certain?"

"If Rose did her job properly, you have nothing to worry about. And it's not as if you'll be galloping or jumping."

"Mmm," she said, looking down at the skirts of her riding habit. "Not in this anyhow, I'd hope. I like my neck whole."

The grooms led out the horses then, Aladdin and another gelding, a gentle, fat chestnut. Joan stood still for a moment looking at them. She concealed her feelings well, Simon thought. Even he didn't know for certain whether she was nervous, and he alone knew that she might have reason to be.

"You've been riding Gareth," he said into the silence. "There's a gray around here called Gawain. I'm afraid I was in something of a romantic phase when I named them."

Joan looked over her shoulder at him, lips curved a little. "How old were you?"

"Fifteen, or thereabouts. My father wrote me at school and asked me what I should name the foals that year. I think he hoped to make me take an interest in the estate. Or in horse breeding. Something practical."

"Did it work?"

He laughed. "As well as anything else did. It certainly gave us a generation of interestingly named horses. There's a mare named Deirdre here, named for a tragic Irish heroine, and the most placid little thing you could imagine."

"Fate loves thwarting youth," Joan said, pausing only briefly to substitute "thwarting" for whatever profanity had been in the original. "They'd be, what, ten years old now?"

"More like twelve. Quite free of the storm and strife of youth, such as it is where horses are concerned." He swung up onto Aladdin's back and heard a whuffling sigh from Gareth as Joan mounted. "We'll just take a short ride around the grounds today, I think. Nothing too strenuous."

"Worried about me?" It was a challenge but a playful one.

"Worried about the horses."

It didn't take long to get away from the stables and onto one of the paths that led around the lake. "It's just women who ride this way, huh?" Joan said then, giving the sidesaddle a dirty look.

"I can't imagine that a man would need to. It'd be immodest for a woman to sit astride, you see."

"Mmm," she said, unsurprised but dubious. "But it's modest for you." She looked down at her own skirts, then at the line of his legs, and he felt a brief but intense heat follow her gaze. Simon swallowed and looked between Aladdin's ears, concentrating on the landscape ahead.

It was a lovely day: clear, blue, and windy. Perhaps that was why Joan didn't say half the things Simon knew she wanted to. When he got his urges back under control and looked over at her, she was studying the gardens off to the left. She was smiling too, a softer smile than he'd seen on her face before.

"What are all those?" She didn't let go of the reins to gesture, just jerked her chin. "I keep meaning to ask."

"Flowers," said Simon, following her gaze. "I'm afraid I couldn't tell you the names for most of them. There are roses, I'm sure, and larkspur and such. Other than that, you'd have to ask Hobbes. The gardener."

"Do they do anything? I mean, do you eat them or build with them, or do they protect against—things?"

"Some of them, I suppose," he said, startled. "White roses are good against demons, I hear, and there are herbs and such for different spells. But that's not why people grow them. They're just flowers. Pretty, you know."

Her eyes widened. "But there are so many."

There it was again, the sense that the world was very fragile and that darkness lurked just ahead. But it was a pleasure too to see how Joan reacted to such things and, through her eyes, to see them again as if they were new.

"It's the country," he finally said. "Nearly everyone has something growing about the place, I'm sure."

"Oh," she said, and looked at the gardens for a long few minutes before she finally touched her foot to Gareth's side. "Would it be all right if I went in the gardens alone sometimes? Not to abandon Eleanor or anything, but—"

"Good Lord, go wherever you want. We've no secret rooms at Englefield."

"No madwomen in the attic either?" Joan asked, one side of her mouth quirking upward. "Damn."

"Ellie has you on Brontë, does she?"

"Among other things."

"And what do you think?"

"Brontë's good when people are committing arson, but the bits about religion were really dull. Stoker's better, if a bit too close for comfort. I liked Tennyson," she added. "In parts."

"Which parts?"

"The ones that aren't about drippy girls dying of love. 'Charge of the Light Brigade' was pretty good," she said thoughtfully, "and 'Ulysses' was great. I knew one of the lines already. I just never knew what it was from."

"Oh?"

"'Though much is taken, much abides.' They'd painted it above the main armory." She looked off into the distance. "I always liked reading it. I like it more now. There's such hope in that poem, in the face of everything."

Reverie softened Joan's face and strengthened it at the same time. For a moment, it was as if she stared into a bright light and didn't flinch. "That's why we have our names," she added.

Simon wanted to hear more. Mostly he wanted her to go on talking. "Names?"

"The names of heroes. People took them after the end and passed them down to their kids." Joan took a deep breath. "You know who you're named after. You know the stories going back as far as you can, and you tell them on the holidays."

Daughter of Arthur and Leia, he remembered. The second name was strange, but he knew the first well enough. "They live on in you?"

"Sort of." She was sitting up straighter now. "The world's dark. It's easy to fall into that darkness. So everyone has someone to live up to. A reason to keep fighting, even if it's just fighting to stay who you want to be."

That future was still a path he never wanted to take. There was more than fear around that bend, though, Simon realized, and not all the shapes that lined the way were twisted and shadowed.

Some work of noble note may yet be done.

"You suit your name well," he said.

Chapter 12

RAIN CRAWLED DOWN THE DRAWING-ROOM WINDOW. It had been falling most of the day in slow sluggish drops without the excitement of a real downpour. Joan stood at the window and glared at the empty lawn outside. Behind her, her newspaper waited on the couch. She should pick it up again, she knew. It would help her disguise considerably if she was even remotely up to date on current events.

She wondered when she'd started thinking about anything in terms of "helping considerably."

Good to know she was blending in, she supposed. Good for the mission, at least.

Joan tapped her fingers against the glass but realized she was doing it only when she caught motion out of the corner of her eye and saw that Simon had looked up from his book. "Sorry," she said, and lowered her hand.

"All I ask is that you don't break my windows until the weather's better," he said.

"When the weather's better, I won't have a problem."

Simon lifted an eyebrow. "Won't you?"

Joan's first impulse was to snap back that she obviously wouldn't, since she wouldn't be stuck indoors reading about some countess getting married and practicing what to do on social calls. But Simon wasn't stupid. Nor was he sarcastic to no purpose. She bit her tongue and thought.

Yes, she'd spent most of the day silently cursing

the rain, the busybodies who'd have noticed and com-
mented if she'd gone out in it anyhow, and the endless
need to give a damn whether a bunch of idiot civilians
thought she was weird. No, she wouldn't be in *as* foul
a mood—and there it was again, "foul" instead of the
word she'd have chosen a couple weeks ago, even in
her head—if she could have gone walking or riding. It
wouldn't have been as bad.

She'd been shut up before in worse circumstances
and for longer than a day. A different kind of rain had
fallen for weeks back home, and nobody with human
skin could set foot outdoors. She'd had to recover from
injuries, and once, she and two men had spent three
days holed up in an abandoned store, waiting for the
not-quite-mindless-enough things outside to get tired
and move on. She'd never gotten surly then.

She'd never needed to exhaust herself then. The
world had always been very good at doing that for her.
Now she had more energy and less to do with it than had
ever been the case at home.

That part was easy to think about.

Simon was still watching her, not intensely but
enough to make her aware that she hadn't replied. Joan
shrugged one shoulder. "I just…" she began.

She'd planned on saying something about too much
rest and good food. Those were basic physical facts, no
real trouble there. No need to think more.

"I wish I knew we were going somewhere."

The man was too damn easy to talk to. Still, her
thoughts were out so she might as well go on. Better to
voice problems at the beginning of the mission, right?
Even if she didn't know exactly what the problems were.

Joan took a breath and tried to find words for what she'd been trying to ignore, what had been easy enough to ignore when she'd been surrounded by things she'd never seen before and struggling to master the basics of life in this time. "We've got this plan. It seems pretty good."

"I certainly thought so at the time," said Simon, but he was frowning up at her. "If you're having second thoughts, though, or if you've spotted a problem—"

"If I'd seen anything that concrete, I'd tell you," Joan said. "I haven't seen any problems we haven't discussed. It's not that."

"Then—"

"We have a saying back home: no plan survives first contact with the enemy." Joan raised her hand and then yanked it back before she could run it through her hair and dislodge the million-and-a-half pins. "You make a plan, sure, but then you start carrying it out, and you get feedback, and you adjust."

"Feedback?" Simon was giving her the look that said, "You just used a crazy made-up word." She'd gotten to know it fairly well by now.

"Like…say you want to get into a building with five guards," she said. "So your plan is to first set a fire and draw out some of the guards, maybe into a trap. Then you shoot the others, take whatever opens the door off one of their bodies, and head in. But you need at least two of the guards to leave before you start shooting, and you'd really like three."

"Right," said Simon, smiling. "I think I had this problem back in my school days—that or it was two trains leaving Harrow."

Joan laughed. Explaining the problem was actually

helping a little. She didn't want to pace or hit things as much, though she was tempted to ask for some paper and a pen. "Okay," she said. "Maybe it takes me a couple days to come up with the plan, if we're planning way in advance and I'm really dumb. But as soon as I set the fire, as soon as I put the first part in motion, I'm already finding things out. Maybe I'm lucky and four guards leaves rather than three, or I find a fuel line and blow them up. Maybe I'm not lucky and only one guard goes, or they can put fires out at a distance. But either way, I know something more. I can change what I'm doing."

"You're not getting that now."

"No. This stuff I'm learning—you think it's the way forward, and I think you're right, but…I don't know. If I'm not good enough—"

"You will be. You're nearly there."

He thought so, maybe, and so did Ellie, Joan thought, but they'd been around from the beginning. Easy enough to see victory when they were comparing who she was now to who she had been—and she found she didn't want to think too deeply about that. "Well, what if Reynell doesn't give a damn about me when I show up?"

Simon shrugged. "I'd imagine we'd try something else. That plan of yours with the servants, perhaps. It's riskier in its way," he admitted, "and Reynell may well have wards up against uninvited guests, but those can be dealt with. Or we could find a new plan. We're both intelligent people."

"After wasting all this time."

"I was under the impression," Simon said calmly, "that you had forty years or so."

Joan blinked and then found herself laughing again. "Right. Nice memory."

"I've found it useful on occasion." He gestured, not to the couch with the boring paper on it but to the chair nearest him. "We are making progress, you know," he said as she sat. "Honestly. I doubt we'll be here much longer. But even if we do have to revise our plans… what you're learning here will be valuable. It's how my world works, after all, and I have to imagine you'll need that knowledge if you're going to try anything but a, mmm, direct frontal assault?"

"Wouldn't work," Joan replied almost automatically. "I've got two targets and no explosives, and blowing up buildings is tricky anyhow, especially if you don't want to kill bystanders." As Simon's eyes widened, she added, "Which I don't here. And I get your point."

"I take it you don't have many long-term campaigns?" he asked.

Joan started to relax into the chair, feeling for the first time that afternoon the warmth of the nearby fire and the soft cushions under her back. "No," she said. "Too hard to predict the Dark Ones in advance. And I'm not high up enough for strategy, mostly. Only plan I've been in on more than a week or two in advance was…"

"Coming here?" Simon asked, and his gaze was both sharper and sadder as he looked at her.

"Yeah. That."

Chapter 13

My friend, the letter began, in Sangupta's neat, round handwriting,

> I cannot even guess at the events that prompted you to seek such information from me, and I feel certain, from the vagueness in your earlier letter, that you will not disclose them. Therefore, I will not trespass upon your privacy or presume on our friendship by pressing the matter.

> Let me, however, warn you. *Geasa* are no light matter. It is, in a way, easier to kill a man with magic than to compel him to act against his will, just as it is in the real world, and any attempt to command a man's obedience often comes back on the caster.

> To change a man's nature for the rest of his life takes power seldom seen today, and the ways of shaping that power are themselves secret.

> There was a book written by one of your countrymen a few centuries ago, *The Wisdom of Raguiel*. It is difficult to find, as are all sources of real power, but I was fortunate enough to read a copy in my youth. From what I remember, it may have what you seek.

When I read this book, it was in the hands of a
scholar in London, a Doctor Gillespie. He is a private and a very strange man, but you may be able to
persuade him to let you see it.

Whatever your quest might be, my friend, I can only
trust that you pursue it out of the best of motives and
that you do so with all the wisdom and judgment
I know you possess. Thus, I wish you the best of
fortune; may all the Powers and the Secret Masters
attend you in your endeavors and keep us both safe
until we meet again.

Sangupta

Simon folded the letter and sat back at his desk,
tapping his fingers on the mahogany surface. Leaving
Englefield for a few days would not be such a disaster
now. The threats he'd feared when he'd left London had
shrunk. Between the warding spell and Joan, Eleanor
should be quite safe. She seemed happier too, more
involved in life. Surely there were no more grounds for
the other fear, the one Simon hadn't quite been able
even to articulate.

Leaving Joan behind should present little problem as
well. On her own, she could probably keep from making
herself conspicuous. She'd be fine with Eleanor's help.
Between riding and reading and walking in the garden,
she'd keep herself quite content without him.

The thought didn't please him. Perhaps that was another reason why he should go. That and Alex himself.

No further attacks had occurred since Simon had set

up the wards, or at least none that he knew of. Nobody had reported mysterious creatures skulking around. It was quite possible to believe that Alex had given up. Whatever dedication he was capable of in the service of his own gratification, he was easy enough to distract.

Simon almost hoped Alex was using his absence to plot some grand and complicated scheme. Better that, in a way, than to believe that Eleanor's misery or the attack on his own person had been the whims of a moment or that the world might end because of a spoiled schoolboy. And if a scheme was in the works, it would be best if Simon wasn't away from London for too long.

He told Mathers to begin packing.

"I'll be three days," he told Eleanor. "Four at the most."

She nodded. Then, as silence stretched out between them, she swallowed and spoke. "I hope that you have a safe journey. And that your business goes well."

Not too long ago, simply having her speaking on her own initiative would have been a triumph. But she'd laughed and joked with him, if quietly, when Joan was around. Now she sat with folded hands and huge eyes.

"I'm sure it will," he said. "If you feel, ah, up to it, you might have a few of the village girls up to tea. With Joan. As a trial, I mean."

"Thank you," said Eleanor. "I think she's more than equal to the task now. And—"

"And out here, gossip doesn't travel as fast. At least it doesn't get back to the city quickly," Simon finished for her, watching her blush. He rose, looked down at her, and cleared his throat. "Well. Take care of yourself."

"And you," said Eleanor.

When she'd bowed and left, Simon turned to the window and stared out for a long time.

━━━⁓⁓━━━

Walking in, Joan didn't quite slam the door, but she definitely closed it more loudly than the servants did. It gave Simon time to compose himself before he spoke.

"You wanted to see me," she said. She didn't sit down.

"I'm leaving for a few days."

Joan met his eyes. "Progress?"

"Possibly. I wouldn't—" Simon shook his head. "I wouldn't jinx myself by being too sure. I know that sounds a bit ludicrous."

"Nope." Joan grinned. "But then, I never knew a man who'd light three on a match."

"Three on a match?"

"Bad luck. Especially for soldiers."

"Ah," he said, and waved her toward one of the chairs. "Eleanor was thinking you might meet some of the village girls while I'm gone."

"While you're safe in London, you mean?" The grin reappeared. Despite his mood, Simon found himself answering it with one of his own.

"Chivalry forbids me to say. Ellie's much better qualified to manage such a meeting, anyhow. You've certainly picked up enough." He added, "And you're looking well," understating the case considerably and trying not to be aware of it. "A credit to my cook, I think."

She half winced and then laughed at herself. "Thanks. Sorry. Old associations."

"You weren't that thin on purpose, were you?" he asked, horrified into tactlessness.

Joan snorted. "Hardly. We do as well as we can. But there's only so much food to go around, unless…"

"Unless?"

She didn't even look upset. He'd carry the memory to London with him, the look of calm acceptance on her face. *This is the way the world is*. *It's too common to be worth crying over*. "The Dark Ones are very good to their pets. Or their livestock. And if you don't want to sell out to them directly—"

"I think I can guess," Simon said. A term floated through his mind, one he'd read long ago in a pirate story, *long pork*. He grimaced.

"Yeah." Joan made a face and then shrugged. "Anyhow. Most of me knows this isn't that. Physically, I feel great. But it's hard to shake what you grew up with."

It took a moment for Simon to find the thread of his conversation. "Tea," he said. "I think you'll enjoy it."

"I think you're wrong," she said, but cheerfully.

"Look at it as a challenge."

"It'll be that, all right." She raised one hand and then stopped before she could run it through her hair and scatter the pins. "Besides, if Ellie suggested it—"

Simon nodded. "That's what I thought. And she seems to enjoy your company." His best efforts couldn't keep a hint of bitterness out of his voice.

"That's what you wanted."

"I know," he said, and looked away, turning back to the window. "I'm sorry."

From behind him, he heard Joan's footsteps. He couldn't see her, but he knew that when she stopped, she was just out of arm's reach. "I don't think she blames you."

It was what he hadn't asked. Hadn't dared to. "She barely speaks around me. She's never been alone with me since we came to Englefield unless I've requested it. You're a stranger, to say the least—"

"That's probably why," said Joan, and the mundane steadiness of her voice was soothing. "I'm not part of your world, and I don't have its standards. Also, I wasn't there to see her possessed—I mean, hell, I'd be jumpy around anyone who saw me that helpless. And, I wasn't some kind of father figure to her."

Some of Simon's black mood lifted. *I should have said something before*, he realized. Joan wouldn't shy away from a subject because it was personal or improper, and neither would she lie to spare his feelings. Of course, she could be wrong, but he felt as if he'd put out an unsteady hand to catch himself and found a rock underneath it.

"A bit hard for you to manage, yes," he said, his voice light with relief.

"I could always fake it."

He turned and looked at her. The skirt and blouse did little to hide her body: slim, yes, and strong but gracefully curved now. "You'd have to deal with a blind man for that," he said.

"Thank you," she said, startled and amused, but not only that. Her breasts rose and fell a little more quickly now, pushing gently at the white cloth of her shirt.

If he cupped them in his hands, Simon thought, probably only that cloth would be in the way.

And cloth ripped so easily.

Arousal was so quick that it left Simon no time for thought. One step brought him close enough to reach out, to raise his hand to Joan's cheek. Her skin was like warm silk beneath his fingers. "Thank *you*."

"For what?" Her eyes were dark now, full of heat.

She wants me, Simon thought, and knew it to be more than vanity. When he spoke, his voice was thick. "Many things."

Joan's laughter was low and sensual. "Things that already happened? Or are you thanking me in advance?"

Slowly he slid his fingers down her cheek and then across to trace the curve of her lower lip. "Which would you prefer?"

A knock at the door made them both jump. Joan's right hand, Simon noticed in a sort of delirium, still went to her waist when she was startled. "Yes?" he called out, and hoped that he sounded at all like himself.

"The carriage is ready, sir."

"I'll be out directly," he replied, and only then turned to face Joan. He could still feel her skin against his fingertips, warm and smooth. If he'd ever known what to say in such a situation, he'd forgotten. "Ah. Well."

She smiled easily enough—with a shade less warmth, and the smile could almost have been mocking—but her face was flushed, and she too was breathless when she spoke. "You'd better go."

"It seems I'd better," he said, and fought back the urge to step toward her again. Instead, he dropped his hand back to his side and bowed formally. "Be well."

Joan met his eyes, serious now and with all the playful sensuality gone from her face. "Be careful."

─⁓⁓─

London was as Simon always found it in the summer—

hot, noisy, and crowded. He'd given no notice of his arrival. Fortunately, he'd given no notice of his departure either, so the servants had not shut up the town house completely. He lived out of a very few rooms, but that was no great hardship for he spent very little time at home.

Discreet inquiries among his more occult acquaintances turned up Gillespie's address, a flat a fair distance from the fashionable part of town and a much shorter distance from several booksellers. The good doctor was known to deal, on occasion, in rare books. He was not known to deal with people, or at least not particularly well.

Simon wrote and sent a brief letter, communicating his connection with Sangupta, the recommendation of Gillespie by the same, and the urgency of the matter in question. *I beg for your discretion and aid, sir,* he finished. *I fear that more than one life may hinge upon my business.*

The rest of the day fell under the broad heading of "reconnaissance"—dinner at his club, followed by the theatre. Many of his friends asked about Eleanor, and Simon found their concern unexpectedly touching. It was good to be reminded that the world was bigger than him and his problems, and to be reminded, perhaps, of what he and Joan were fighting for.

Nobody mentioned Alex. But then, most people wouldn't. Society at large didn't know about the possession or even that Eleanor had been alone in a room with Alex, but it knew that the two of them had been often seen together and that Alex had sported a black eye around the time that Eleanor had "taken ill." Whatever people assumed, it wasn't the sort of thing they wanted to discuss around Simon.

The rumors had Alex gaming more profligately and more luckily than ever, though fewer and fewer men would sit down with him. They mentioned a few liaisons, though none of them was doing as badly as the baker's daughter who'd spurred Simon to confront Reynell in the first place. Otherwise, they were silent. Business as usual.

That night, he dreamed of Joan, a not uncommon occurrence of late, but this was an extraordinarily vivid dream. They were at the circle of stones again and this time had neither rain nor cerberi to worry about. It was high summer with the sky arching blue overhead, and Joan was naked. A breeze blew her loose hair around her, showing him teasing half glimpses of her small firm breasts and flat stomach, of the golden patch of hair between her legs.

It was no surprise to find that he was naked too, or that his cock was flushed and erect. The very feeling of the air brushing his skin was arousing, almost electric, and he moaned as he looked up.

In the circle, the dream-Joan met his gaze. Her eyes were brighter than he'd ever seen them and full of a joyful excitement that was almost as arousing as her naked body. She smiled, the slow, teasing smile that she'd given Simon before he left, and held out a hand. "Well?"

He woke aching then, and when he wrapped his hand around his cock, he found the head already damp with arousal. *Ah, God*, he thought, dazed with sleep and lust, *this is a dangerous place where I'm going*.

It didn't matter. When he closed his eyes, he saw

Joan's face turned up to his, lips parted a little. He heard the hunger in her voice and saw the warmth in her eyes like a living flame.

If he'd drawn her to him, kissed her—

It took only a few strokes to make him spend. The force of it was stronger than anything he'd ever felt—by himself or with a woman.

The next few months, Simon thought as he came back to himself, *are going to be a challenge*.

Chapter 14

JOAN STILL WALKED TOO FAST.

She didn't notice it much, most of the time—she moved a lot slower than she'd done back home, now that she had lots to take in and no need to run—but on the way back from the village, walking next to Eleanor, it was hard to miss. Ellie glided. Joan strode.

As they walked back to Englefield, Joan halfheartedly tried to work on that, but she suspected it'd take more time than she had. Maybe more time than she'd have even if she lived here for the rest of her life. This was a world in the summer of its time, and the people here moved and talked like leaves on the wind. Someone probably had to be born here to learn how to relax in that way. Even Ellie, who never really relaxed, had something of that air about her.

She walked along now with a parcel under her arm, a perfect leisurely gait, and a tight, nervous look on her face.

"Those books looked interesting," Joan said, to take Ellie's mind off things. "Mind if I have a look when you're done?"

Eleanor looked up, surprised. "Of course, if you'd like. It's more mythology, and some history and politics. You're not expected to know anything about it, though. Most girls don't."

Joan snorted. "Most girls sound like a pack of damn fools."

For a second, Eleanor looked like she wanted to protest, but she just laughed a little, disbelievingly, and shook her head. "What are women like where you're from, then?"

"People."

They'd passed out of the village a while ago, walked up the road past fields and farmhouses, and now were on the road leading uphill to Englefield. Nobody was around—the farmers were small figures behind them—and the world seemed fresh and new and sunlit.

It reminded Joan of her first day there, and realizing that she'd arrived only about six weeks ago made her uneasy. Her time there felt like a lifetime. More than that, it felt like her only lifetime. As her manners improved and the face she saw in the mirror got more like the ones around her, her memories of home felt like they belonged to someone else.

Maybe they did. Maybe travel wasn't just a matter of space and time. Maybe you went from self to self, leaving who you were behind. If she was far away from what she'd known, maybe she was far away from who she'd been as well.

She shivered and spoke hastily into the silence. "What happened to Ariadne, anyhow? In your version, I mean? Did she marry the hero or what?"

"No," Eleanor said, returning from her own distant thoughts. "He left her on an island instead when she was sleeping—there are arguments about whether or not he meant to—and she cursed him. He'd set off with black sails and told his father that he'd come back with white ones if he was alive, but Ariadne made him forget. Theseus's father saw the black-sailed ship returning, and he killed himself."

"So she punished his dad for what he'd done? Sounds unfair."

Eleanor shook her head slowly. "Theseus was the one who had to live with the guilt. Killing him might have been kinder. Once you're dead, I suppose you don't feel things as much." She had a thoughtful look in her eyes, and she was paler than she had been.

"Once you're dead," Joan said sharply, "you don't do much of anything until you're born again. And then you have to grow up and get trained all over. Shi—I mean, it's really a waste."

"They believe in reincarnation where you're from?" Eleanor asked, but absently.

"At least until you've done everything you're supposed to."

"Oh."

"Yeah."

Eleanor took a deep breath. "Do you know what business took Simon to town?"

"Not specifically, no," said Joan slowly.

They walked on in silence for another few paces, their boots crunching against the gravel path. When she spoke, Eleanor's voice was almost inaudible. "Does it have to do with Mr. Reynell?"

She didn't want to lie, Joan realized. That had never bothered her before, but she didn't want to lie now, not to this girl. "He—"

Eleanor stopped, put a hand out, and caught Joan's arm. Her face was white. "Simon's not going to challenge him! Please say—"

"No. He's not. Calm down." On firmer ground now, Joan went on. "If Simon wanted pistols at dawn or whatever else you go for here, he'd have done it already."

The fear left Eleanor's eyes, and her taut body slumped. She looked down, away from Joan. "You know what happened, don't you?"

"Yeah. Simon didn't want to tell me, but I was pretty insistent when we met. Wanted to know how he knew Reynell."

"Then…you know Mr. Reynell."

Joan nodded, wincing inwardly. "He's a common enemy," she said, and tried to divert the conversation. "Anyhow, don't blame your brother, and I'm sorry if this bothers you."

"No—I mean, it does, a bit, but—well, I'd thought for a while that you might know. You have been very understanding. And someone who didn't know would've asked before—why I'm like this, I mean."

"Someone who didn't know would've thought it was none of her business, if she wasn't a total…witch."

"Oh," Eleanor said. It looked like a new thought. She started walking again, going faster than Joan for once. "Do you talk about it often?"

"No. It doesn't come up much."

"Oh." A few more feet, with her hat and dark hair bobbing briskly. Then: "Is he very angry at me, do you know?"

This time, Joan stopped first, her first thought stunned dismay: *Oh, hell. I wasn't* trained *for this!* "No," she said as calmly as she could. "Why would he be?"

"I—well, it's my fault that he's out here. And that he's angry at Alex." Eleanor looked down at her hands. She didn't seem to notice that she'd used Reynell's first name. "They used to be the best of friends, and I—perhaps I presented too much temptation. If I'd refused his invitations or his suggestions, if I hadn't been so quick to believe what he perhaps never intended to suggest—"

Joan caught Eleanor by the shoulders and swung her around. "That's bullshit," she said, "and you know it."

Eleanor cringed, eyes wide.

"Sorry," Joan said, and stepped quickly back. She'd never talked to sheltered young girls back home. There hadn't been any. "It is, though."

"Wh—what do you mean?"

"It's not a crime to be innocent. Especially not when your whole stupid world tries to keep you that way. And there's nothing wrong with…liking someone or wanting to believe he likes you when he acts like he does."

"He might not have meant to," Eleanor said softly.

Joan rolled her eyes. "Oh, he damn well did. He had a grudge against Simon, for one thing. Also, he's ten years older than you are. He's been dealing with women for a long time. Don't you think he knows how to avoid sending that sort of signal?"

"I—I don't know." Joan read guilt and hope and fear all mixed in Eleanor's face. Fear of the hope itself, because sometimes guilt was better. Guilt at least meant you hadn't been helpless.

"I do. Reynell wanted to get back at your brother, so he did a horrible thing to you. That means he's a son of a bitch. It doesn't mean anything about you except that you're hurt now. And that's natural."

"I wish it wasn't." Eleanor closed her eyes. She wasn't quite crying, but her voice cracked when she spoke. "I wish I could forget about it for more than an hour at a time. I wish I could turn out the light without being afraid—or look at Simon without wondering if he hates me."

"He doesn't hate you." Joan sighed. "God, he's as torn up about the whole thing as you are, and he thinks you hate him. Your society is just great at communication, by the way. And the other stuff…it'll get easier. It has a little, hasn't it?"

"Yes. A little. But," her voice dropped, "I keep thinking I feel *it*. Looking at me."

That, at least, was familiar territory. "Well, it's not."

"Are you sure?"

"Pretty sure." The dermal sensor might not pick up something watching from another plane. "Anyhow, Simon would know. And he could probably show you. You should ask."

"Oh, no. I don't want to bother him. Maybe he thinks I'm better."

"He does not. I mean, he knows you've been getting better, but you haven't been fooling anyone." Joan raised her hands, stopping an apology before Eleanor could start it. "And you shouldn't be. If you'd broken your leg yesterday, would you be trying to run a race right now?"

"Well, no."

"And you wouldn't be going around pretending that everything was fine, right?"

Eleanor shook her head. "But this is different."

"No, it's not. I mean, people here don't believe in what happened to you, but people here are wrong about so damn many things I don't even know where to start. So." Joan started to count off on her fingers. "Point one:

if there's any chance something is hanging around you, we need to know. You can tell Simon when he gets back, or I will."

This time, when Eleanor flushed, it was at least partly with anger. Good. "I'll do it," she said. "What's your second point?"

"This isn't a small thing. You're not malingering. You're not slacking off. You've been trying to get over it—I've seen you, and so has Simon—and you're doing a whole hell of a lot better than anyone else I've seen. But you're not just going to tell yourself to be fine and do it. You've been hurt. Healing takes time. That's, um, physics."

"Biology, I should think," said Eleanor, with a very faint smile.

"Whatever. Keep trying. Stop beating yourself up. That's my point."

Joan stepped back, letting everything sink in and hoping she'd done right. For a moment or two, they were silent again, and then Eleanor took a deep breath. "We should keep going," she said. "They'll have dinner started at home."

Good girl, Joan thought. She took Eleanor's arm. Together, they started down the road again.

"You said anyone else you'd seen," Eleanor said, after a minute or two. "Have you seen other people like me?"

Don't try to recruit her, Simon had said. But this wasn't recruitment, and Eleanor had been lied to quite enough. "I have."

Eleanor bit her lip but went on. "This happens often in your world?"

"Yes," Joan said, "it does."

"It's a…a bad place, then?"

"Yes," Joan said, "it is." She kept her eyes on the road ahead. It blurred a little in front of her.

Chapter 15

THE NOTE CAME ON THE THIRD MORNING WITH THE paper and what little there was of the post. Gillespie wrote in a thin, spidery hand with elaborate loops and flourishes, but he came to the point quickly enough: *I will be at home this afternoon.*

That was all.

Simon took a hired carriage to the building where Gillespie kept his rooms, an anonymous redbrick square spotted with small windows, like a hundred or a thousand others in the city. Knocking on the door brought a small gray woman who looked at Simon somberly and didn't speak.

"Dr. Gillespie, please."

She nodded and turned. Simon followed uncertainly up a flight of narrow, dim stairs and through a hallway that smelled strongly of cabbage. They stopped in front of a plain, slightly warped door, and the landlady—or whatever she was—knocked more loudly and briskly than Simon would've thought her capable of doing.

"Pray come in," said a low voice. The woman shrugged and gestured toward the door with one hand, then took her leave.

Inside, the room was surprisingly well lit and comfortably appointed, mostly with bookshelves. They lined each wall, and all were stuffed full. There was a small fireplace with a row of crystals glimmering on the mantel and a black statue in one corner. Kali, Simon recognized after a moment, and a chill went down his spine. Perhaps it was truly a coincidence, but it made him think, nonetheless, of patterns and of fate and of the weight of invoking great powers.

In this state of mind, he saw a figure rise from one of the chairs in front of the fireplace.

Gillespie was a tall man, half a foot taller than Simon, and very thin indeed. Had his nose not been so prominent, nor his bones so small, he would have looked skeletal. As it was, he gave the appearance of a large wingless bird. Unbound gray hair fell to just below his shoulders, and he wore wrinkled linen.

His green eyes were startlingly vivid. Cat's eyes almost.

Simon cleared his throat. "Dr. Gillespie, permit me to express my gratitude for allowing this intrusion. I know that we have not been introduced, and ordinarily I would not have dreamed of presuming—"

"From the content of your letter," Gillespie interrupted, "it is not the presumption that bothers me but the danger. Yet if our Indian friend thinks the matter serious enough to recommend you to me, I cannot but trust his judgment, at least so far. I had a letter from him, you see, a little less than four days ago."

"I'm much obliged to him, then."

"Obligation is the currency of our world. Do sit down."

Gillespie returned to his own seat, folding himself into it with a heron's grace. Simon took the chair at his right. The black upholstery, he noticed, was battered but very comfortable. Gillespie might be unaware of appearances, but he was no ascetic.

The old man turned toward Simon. "You want the book," he said. "*The Wisdom of Raguiel*."

"Er," Simon said, "yes, actually. Or at least to see it."

"Why?"

Simon had prepared the answer in his room that morning, even rehearsed it, but now the words came sluggishly to his lips. "I need to stop an evil magician. A murderer, and worse."

"Do you want to kill him?" Gillespie cocked his head to look at Simon, his eyes bright and curious.

"No. That's why I'm here. I'd like to give him a chance to redeem himself, but I'm not such a fool as to accept his word alone."

A year ago, he'd have taken Alex's word for anything without a second thought. *Plus ça change*...he thought, weary. The more things change, the more they stay the same.

Gillespie's thin gray eyebrows went up. His regard was almost gentle now, but when he spoke, his voice was brisk and matter-of-fact. "The loss of innocence, of course, is very much a part of the human condition."

There had been no way for Gillespie to tell that from Simon's face. Someone unusually good at reading people might have inferred it from his conversation, but Simon didn't think so.

"The human condition, sir?" he asked. "Is it something with which you're familiar?"

"As much as many a mortal man or woman, Master Grenville. Particularly one who asks such daring questions." A smile played around Gillespie's narrow mouth. "For which I thank you. Far better to have the questions asked and in the open than to sense them lurking around the edges like rats."

Let it be bluntness, then. "Can you read my mind?"

"'Reading' is not the word I would use. It's a precise art, reading. Words are very exact things. I knew that you mourned what had been. I knew that you wondered—and wonder still—whether I am entirely human. The details escape me. I assure you I am human enough."

"Ah," said Simon.

"It's rather like having a cat brush against you in the dark. Or, in some cases, an elephant. Your feelings are rather more disciplined than most, Master Grenville, which has made this meeting so far more bearable than I'd feared. You will be so kind as to continue that trend, I hope."

Simon swallowed. "I'll do my best, sir."

"You very rarely, I would imagine, do anything else." Gillespie leaned back into his chair, and his shining green eyes traveled over Simon again. "Indeed, you seem a very driven young man. The wards around you would provide quite enough safety from most magic unless you did something foolish. Either you are very altruistic or the man facing you is much less a *man* than you think he is."

That was a frightening suggestion. Even knowing Alex from childhood couldn't banish entirely the unease Simon felt. It was due to Gillespie, he knew, and the room and the statue that stared at him with a slight smile on its onyx face. He shook his head. "Let it be altruism, then, if you will, sir. Or vengeance, perhaps. I make no claim to sainthood."

"Good. Saints are well enough in their place. Men with aspirations to that place are often tedious. But I don't believe that it is vengeance. You don't want him dead, after all. Perhaps you want a worse fate, but I would not, so far, believe that of you."

"I've had my moments," Simon admitted.

Gillespie smiled. "But they've been moments, have they not? You're going to great lengths here. I do have to wonder why. Dark magicians often destroy themselves. They burn out pursuing power or rot with decadence. Why not let opium or the French disease accomplish your end for you?"

"Because I can't," said Simon. He was about to go on, but Gillespie recoiled, holding up a hand.

"Lord God, defend us. Armageddon." His lips were white. "The Scriptures promise the end of the world and in a none too pleasant fashion, but—"

"They don't say that we'll lose." Simon took a breath. "This isn't St. John's Revelation, Doctor. If I fail, what happens to humanity will make that look like a garden party."

Gillespie passed the back of one thin hand across his mouth. "Not only humanity, I'd imagine," he said faintly, "though we'll get the worst of it by far. But such things always spread. I'll get you the book, Master Grenville, and I hope you're on the right path."

The Wisdom of Raguiel was fairly slim as occult books went, which meant that it only nearly crushed Simon's knees. The cover was supple blue leather, but the pages were yellow and fading. "I mean to copy it one of these days," Gillespie said when he handed it over. "One of many projects."

The book was full of spells. Spells for protection, many of them, as well as spells for learning the truth, for finding thieves, and for knowing if your wife or servants were faithful. There were no love spells, nor spells to keep old men young, as he'd seen in other books, but there was a spell to keep dogs watchful and one to keep guards from leaving their posts. If the matter hadn't been so urgent, simple scholarly curiosity would have kept Simon reading for days.

Then, about a third of the way from the end of the book, he found what he was looking for.

Bye Which A Manne May Bee Helde To Hys Worde.

Simon stopped, putting his finger in the book to mark the place. He looked up—Gillespie had taken a book of his own off the table and was reading as placidly as if Armageddon had never come up—and took a breath. Then Simon read on.

The spell wasn't actually that difficult, as spells went. Three drops of the caster's blood, three from the man swearing the oath, and a fairly long incantation full of all the horrible things that would happen if the spell's target broke his word. The target had to speak most of it.

Simon must have made some sort of sound, for Gillespie looked up from his reading. "Is something amiss?"

"No," Simon said, coming up slowly from his reading, "not at all." And then, because Gillespie didn't look as if he believed him, he added, "It's just that he'd have to actually participate."

"Of course." Gillespie closed his book and fixed Simon with the stern look of a schoolmaster. "You'll find no bindings in there that don't require such things, and I would be most reluctant to give you one. Most reluctant indeed."

Simon blinked. "Why?" Suspecting he had a great deal more to fear than being thrown out if he angered Gillespie, he hurriedly added, "I'm not complaining, just a bit surprised. After all, I'm trying to find this spell so that I don't have to kill the man."

"And is slavery any better than death? Even slavery in a good cause?"

He saw Eleanor, her eyes dull and her body floating above the sofa, and he flushed with mingled shame and irritation. "We put men in prison when we must, and you'd meet few men who'd call that immoral."

Gillespie's lips tightened. "Few, yes. But prison confines a man's body, Master Grenville. It cannot touch his spirit. Not directly."

"Being confined for years would have some effect on a man's soul."

"What in life doesn't? But such things can only influence. They cannot compel." Gillespie was sitting forward now, watching Simon's face.

"It would compel only a very minor part of him— turning it to what it should have been in any case. Wouldn't you agree?"

"With what it should have been? Certainly. But it doesn't matter." Gillespie spread his hands. The fingers were long, the joints thick. He was human enough for arthritis, it appeared, and that was vaguely reassuring. "Our Lord gave us free will, the ability to choose good or evil. He could have compelled us from the start. He did not. Not even at the greatest of costs. Who are we to contradict him?"

It was all very quiet. Very civilized conversation in a warm, well-lit room with books lining the walls and the smell of beeswax coming from the candles. Nonetheless, Simon had the same sense of will he'd gotten when he'd stood and argued with Joan on the rainy road to

Englefield. He might batter at the walls of Gillespie's convictions, but he would not get through.

"I suppose," he said, "that you also think I would do better simply to kill him."

Gillespie's eyes widened, and he shook his head gently. "Not at all, Master Grenville. Where there is life, there is hope—the hope of redemption, the hope that each man has a role to play in the greater part of things and that any role might yet be for good. And to kill a man without doing all you can to offer him that hope would be, indeed, a thing to regret.

"But redemption means choice. You may offer, yes. You may hold him to his word, once given, as only a fool would not, but you cannot force his hand. Only evil will come from that."

Simon looked at Gillespie again and saw that he was younger than he seemed at first—there were no lines on his face, no tremors in his body—and that the look in his eyes was very old. He had been far and seen much, Simon knew in that moment, and whether he was right or not, he spoke out of more than abstract principles.

"Will you help me, then?" he asked. "You know what will happen if I fail."

"I would if I could." Gillespie sighed and looked down at his hands. "Do not mistake me for Oberon, sir, or for Merlin. Ancestry is no guarantee of ability, and ability itself is a sad and temporary thing. I have no power now, save to pick up the thoughts men fail to guard. And I would be of no use as a spy. Around many people, I am crippled. Almost mad, at times. I will give you the book, Master Grenville, and I will pray for your success. That is all."

Chapter 16

ELEANOR WAS ALREADY IN THE DRAWING ROOM WHEN Joan came in, standing near the table and looking out the window. Eleanor wore pink today, trimmed with brown, and someone had done her hair in an elaborate nest of curls. It all looked nice but alien. More alien, Joan realized, than *her* clothes had felt in a week or two. Maybe more.

"You look good," she said, crossing the room.

Eleanor spun around, raising a hand to her throat. "I—oh—thank you."

"Sorry. Didn't mean to startle you."

Eleanor composed herself and smiled, but there was a blankness underneath her expression. Her back was a rigid line. "Quite all right. You look very nice too."

"Good dressmaker," said Joan. She was glad of the crisp yellow-and-blue print blouse and the flowing serge skirt. They felt like armor.

"Oh, yes." Eleanor glanced back toward the window and then down at herself. "I should have been eating better these past few weeks. Does it show terribly?"

She was thin. She was also pale. But she'd been thin and pale the whole time Joan had known her. "Hard to say. But they know you've been sick, right?"

Eleanor bit her lip. "Yes, of course. But I do hope they won't ask too much about it. It makes me feel dreadful to lie. And I'm horrible at making up details."

"What details? You had a fever. You came back, you're recovering, and you're getting better. It's not like they'll ask how high your temperature got. Will they?"

"No, of course not." Eleanor's smile had a little more warmth in it this time. Then she sighed. "I suppose I just think they'll know, somehow."

"Hey, if they know, we've got a whole lot more to worry about than a tea party, right?"

"There is that."

—— ᴡ ——

There were footmen this time, or at least a footman. He came in with the Misses Talbot, introduced them, and pulled out chairs so that they could sit down. Then he stood around waiting. It must, Joan thought, be one of the more boring jobs anyone could do. On the other hand, he was indoors and nobody was trying to kill him.

The Misses Talbot—Rosemary and Elizabeth—were both a little taller than Eleanor and both on the plump side, even for this time. Both were also brown haired and brown eyed. Rosemary was wearing white. Elizabeth was wearing light green. Joan made very sure that she remembered that.

They did, thank the Powers, seem to know how hard it was to tell them apart. "We're not actually twins," said Rosemary, laughing lightly as she sat down next to Joan. "I'm two years the older. And it was much easier to tell us apart when we were younger, of course, because we were of different heights. Nowadays, it's awful. Papa threatens every so often to have our initials embroidered on all our dresses."

"Though we could always switch," said Elizabeth.

"So it's really quite pointless, yes. Poor Papa. We're a dreadful trial to him." Rosemary sounded happy about it.

"Do you have brothers or sisters, Miss MacArthur?" Elizabeth asked.

Joan shook her head. "I have no family living, I'm afraid."

Both sets of brown eyes widened. "But how awful!" said Elizabeth. "I'm so sorry."

"No, don't worry about it." Joan said. "It was a long time ago. But when Miss Grenville offered to let me stay with her, I jumped at the chance for company."

Rosemary smiled approvingly. "Dear Eleanor is everything kind. Anyone who's made her acquaintance knows *that*."

"I deserve no such praise," said Eleanor, blushing. "Miss MacArthur is wonderful company. It was only natural that I invite her."

"Only natural for you, you mean," Rosemary replied. And then, that particular dance concluded, she took the first few steps of the next. "We were so relieved to hear that you were seeing callers again, Eleanor. It must have been very hard for you, but Papa says that illness is quite common in town, particularly in the summer."

"With so many people, it could hardly be otherwise," Elizabeth added.

Eleanor took a swallow of tea and then entered the fray. "Yes, it is quite crowded. It was all very new to me, of course, but I still don't know how everyone manages such a crush."

"Very sharp elbows," said Rosemary, and giggled. "But you must have been there long enough to have some of the news. We hear nothing at all out here, and you know that the papers don't print anything that's really interesting. Worried about panic in the streets, I suppose."

"Even if we don't have many streets. Or many people to panic in them." Elizabeth sat forward. "So please do tell us everything."

Eleanor managed a smile. "That's quite an order," she said, and took a comically deep breath, which made both the Misses Talbot giggle again. "There was no great cause for excitement, I'm sorry to say, or if there was, I was informed of it no more than you were. Nothing like the Jubilee last year."

"But then, what would be?" Rosemary laughed. "An event notable enough for Papa to take us up to London comes along…perhaps once in a lifetime. If that."

As they talked on, Joan slowly ate a slice of lemon cake and tried to absorb their conversation. It was harder than she'd thought it would be. Eleanor had taught her well, but a person could do only so much with bare facts. Every time she spoke, she felt like she was crossing an abyss, jumping from one slim foothold to another, knowing that even the footholds wouldn't have been there two weeks earlier.

It wasn't just men and fashion. Oh, there was that— they talked about sleeves for ten minutes, while Joan resisted the urge to play with her fork—but there was more too. "Have you heard anything from your family? Papa says that the situation abroad…"

"…but they're saying that times will be much tighter next year, and we'd best start economizing. Something to do with the wheat crop, I think…"

"The thing is, I'm not sure at all that I want to be an officer's wife. Not unless I know he'll be posted somewhere in England…"

"Oh, I don't think we have anything to worry about in His Royal Highness. You know what rumors are. And besides, Her Majesty's not in very bad health…"

It was confusing, but it was familiar. Strip off the names and the ranks, and anyone back home might have asked the questions underneath. *Who's going to be leading us next year? Will they do a good job? Will we have enough? Will we have to fight?*

Fighting back home was never a question, though, and while the war the girls talked about might hit them where it hurt—Rosemary's sweetheart, Eleanor's parents—they'd never see combat themselves or have to run from armies in their homes. If their queen died, they'd get a ruler who might have had a mistress or six but who wasn't promised to a Dark One, power mad, or just plain crazy—and who couldn't have done anything much if he had been. Royalty here couldn't have people impaled for impertinence or test weapons on the peasants. The queen couldn't even raise taxes.

In the traitor lands, there were sacrifices every new moon, and you were lucky if the lord slit your throat before he gave you to his master. Even in the caves, leaders had cracked. Joan listened to the three girls discuss "character" very seriously and tried not to laugh or roll her eyes. *You idiots*, she thought. *Does it matter where your prince put his hands? There's no blood on them.*

Except that they did care because they could. Because they'd never known anyone worse. Tyrants were hazy figures from history. If this was a land, maybe a time, in the summer of its life, these were women in the summer of theirs. Their voices held no desperation, no need to hurry, no real fear. Earnestness, yes, and lots of it, but they gave a damn because they chose to, not because they had to.

Even Eleanor was like that. After she'd started talking, the rigid nervousness had left her. She didn't actually say a lot, but she listened intently. When she did speak, her words were earnest, thoughtful, and unrushed. At ease.

She belonged here.

Joan didn't. She could live here a hundred years, she thought, and never manage that easy grace. If the other girls had seen her when she arrived—but was she really that woman now? Now that she could dance in a corset and ride a horse? Now that luxury no longer instantly put her on her guard? Was she really Joan, daughter of Arthur and Leia, when she didn't answer to that name anymore?

In the polished silver of her knife, she saw her own eyes in what should've been a stranger's face. But change was gradual. She saw nothing alien looking back at her, nothing unfamiliar, not the likely traitor she'd have seen a month earlier. Not that it mattered: this was her world now. There was no point in worrying about who she'd been before.

"You seem very quiet, Miss MacArthur," Rosemary said in the sudden silence that happened sometimes in conversation. "I do hope we're not boring you."

"No, not at all," she said, and the voice came reflexively now. "I was just thinking about…human nature, I guess."

Rosemary laughed, but the sound wasn't an unfriendly one. "Truly? How Papa would like you! Have you figured it out, then?"

"I've only confused myself," Joan said, and sipped her tea.

Chapter 17

SIMON HAD PLANNED ON DEPARTING LONDON IN THE late morning, after taking care of a few genuine business affairs, and arriving at Englefield by supper time. His business took longer than he'd thought, however, and then, walking past a row of shops on his way home, he thought of Eleanor and Joan.

When he did depart, it was after two. He brought with him *The Archipelago on Fire* for himself, a set of pink-and-blue enameled combs for Ellie, and *King Solomon's Mines* for Joan, the last after much frowning deliberation in the bookseller's. It was a dashed tricky thing to buy presents for women you hadn't grown up with—for respectable, unrelated women, anyhow.

Not that Joan would know or care, and not that he hadn't already supplied her with half a wardrobe full of dresses. But that was different, and he would know. For all that he'd spent his youth racketing around with bohemians and socialists, for all that the lady herself thought nothing of stripping off before a strange man, something in Simon quailed at the idea of approaching her as he might one of the demimonde.

Well, of course, he told himself, *she's bound to find out about that sort of thing later, if Ellie hasn't already made her aware. And then she'd question* my *motives, and it would all be quite awkward. Sensible enough, really.*

Besides, she is *practically a stranger. No man of*

sense would give anything elaborate to a woman he knew so little.

And she'd probably laugh, anyhow. Such things are dreadfully impractical.

It was all very logical when he thought about it. Yet perhaps Joan wouldn't laugh if he brought her something more luxurious. She might be amazed, as she had been when she first saw the flowers.

He had become used to arousal when he thought of Joan. This other, more affectionate impulse was new. And the way one led into the other was decidedly uncomfortable. Breathless now, Simon closed his eyes. That didn't help—he could see Joan all the more vividly in his mind now, flushed and eager—and he wasn't sure that he really wanted it to. If the heat rushing through his body was unsettling, it was also intoxicating, and frustration itself had its own strange appeal.

But infatuation, he reminded himself, could not be helpful here. There was far too much at stake. Lust was a distraction, though perhaps an inevitable one. Any serious attachment could only cloud his mind further.

Simon made himself open his eyes and look out the window. *When I get back, I will see her for what she really is: human, imperfect, no more compelling than any other woman in the world. I'll note those flaws that might ruin our plan, and I'll carry on with removing them.*

She's only a woman like any other.

Simon arrived past ten at night. The rain had become a downpour by that time, and he was glad to see what few lights remained in Englefield's windows. All were on the lower floors. Here in the country, only the servants would be awake at such an hour.

Simon hurried inside, handing damp cloak and wrapped parcels off to the appropriate people. He kept *The Wisdom of Raguiel* in his own arm, though. It would not be for the general library. In part, that was why he sent Peggy back to the servants' quarters and took the candle himself.

In part, but not entirely. There was an appeal to walking the dark halls, a sense that he was reclaiming Englefield that he'd never before felt. Perhaps it was that he had just never been there long enough before; perhaps it was that such strong spells as he'd cast upstairs bound him, in some sense, to the place where he'd cast them.

Or perhaps it was that the world outside was so much less certain now.

The candle cast dancing shadows ahead of Simon. He caught sight of his reflection as he passed a mirror, wavering and alien in the dim light. Half-remembered children's tales came to mind, none of them pleasant. He looked away quickly.

A line of light caught his eye then: dim light, not much more than his own candle, coming from under the library door. Eleanor, he thought, and shook his head. It was too late for her to be awake, even if she had been in town. If she'd been having trouble sleeping and had told neither him nor her maid, that was not a good sign. Simon straightened his back, assumed his sternest look, and opened the library door.

He had only a moment to see the woman at his desk, to observe that she was bent forward with her face in

her hands, to catch sight of red-gold hair in the candlelight and know that he'd been very much mistaken.
Only a moment.

Then Joan sprang from her chair and whipped around
to face the door, grabbing at the desk. She raised her
hand, and the letter opener gleamed in it.

They'd done their best, Simon thought, he and
Eleanor. On the surface, they'd even succeeded. Below
that, they'd made no impression at all. Joan's eyes were
narrow, her teeth bared, and her body poised to strike.
The ivory dressing gown didn't matter. She was every
inch the savage he'd met in the circle of stones. But she
was beautiful now.

Simon thought, in a stunned second, that a month of
good food and a few civilized clothes couldn't make that
much difference. Not really. *If I saw her in leather and
blood now, I'd still want her.*

Even as the realization shook him, she was relaxing.
"Sorry." She lowered the letter opener and flashed a
smile nearly as sharp and thin. "Jumpy, I guess. But the
servants knock, and—anyhow, I'm sorry. Hope I didn't
wake you up."

"Not at all. I saw the light and was curious. I hope I
haven't intruded."

Joan shook her head. "Don't worry about it."

A candle sat on the table, but even that and the one
Simon held revealed only a little redness around Joan's
eyes, a slight flush on her cheeks. If he hadn't seen that
one unguarded moment, he might never have known
that anything was wrong.

It might be best to pretend he didn't. Joan would
never mention the incident; quite probably she would

rather he didn't. Or at least, Simon thought, she would be embarrassed if he did. Not quite the same thing. Perhaps thinking that it was had led, in part, to all his earlier trouble with Ellie.

Simon thought of the moment before Joan had known he was there, of the way she'd looked in that small patch of candlelight. Sad, yes, but more importantly, alone.

"Joan," he said, stepping forward, "tell me what's wrong."

She hesitated for only a second. "What? Nothing. Thanks, but I'm fine."

"No, please," Simon insisted. "I must know. Is something wrong here? Has anyone been uncivil to you— were the girls—"

Improbable—impossible—for Joan to be crying over what a bunch of village chits thought or said or did. He knew that even before Joan shook her head. "No. It's nothing you did. Nothing anyone here did. I just—"

She stopped and looked up at Simon, then swiftly away again at the desk and the opened book on it. A flush crept up her neck and over her face. "What the hell," she said in a tight voice he'd never heard from her before. "If I'm going to act like a six-year-old anyhow, *I want my mother*. And my dad and my friends and the world I knew. It was a shitty world, but it was mine, and everyone I love is there. Was there."

At the last, her voice cracked. Joan spun around to face the bookshelves, but Simon saw her face before she did, stripped of control at last, a study in weariness and fear and stark bleeding grief. The pain there made his own look like a stubbed toe. "Oh," he said, sounding awkward and insufficient to his own ears. "But—won't you see them again?"

"No."

It was just the one word, as flat and uncompromising as a funeral bell. There was no room for *but if*, no possibility of bargaining, no holding out for one last chance. Just knowledge, cold and dark as the night outside.

"There were rituals," Joan said. "I'm cut loose from time. That's how I could come back, and I guess it lets me survive any changes I make by being here. But that's just me. If I succeed...there'll be a different world two hundred years from now. Mine won't be there any more."

"And if you fail?"

"Then everyone I knew dies. Horribly." She shrugged, quickly and almost mechanically. "At the end—just before I came—the Dark Ones had broken in. My people might have fought them back that time, but...we were losing."

Joan laughed humorlessly. "I'm not a priest or a philosopher. I don't know what the difference is between dying and never existing at all except that dying probably hurts more. The kind of death they were facing? There's no question."

Simon remembered the cerberus's teeth and pictures he'd seen in books and shuddered.

"So you see?" Joan scrubbed the back of her hand across her eyes, quickly and roughly. "I'm doing them a favor. And it's—it's not like they'll miss me."

Perhaps, somewhere, Simon thought, but he couldn't say it. It might be true—he thought that the soul persisted, in some shape or other—but he didn't know, Joan wouldn't believe him, and it didn't matter in the end. Whatever might survive outside of time, it wouldn't be her world or her people.

There was nothing he could say. He stood and looked at her instead. The cream silk of her dressing gown was the brightest thing in the shadowed room. Her shoulders were stiff, her posture military.

It would be good to take her in his arms. It would also be highly improper, and Joan wasn't one to cry on a man's shoulder in any case. Still, he ached to touch her. To offer something when words had failed. Simon jammed his fists into his pockets.

Joan took another rough swipe at her face and then took a deep breath. "Anyhow, I didn't mean to disturb you. Couldn't sleep—came down to read for a little while." She gestured to the open book.

Simon, following her gaze, recognized the title on the spine. "The Greeks? Eleanor has been an influence."

"She's got good taste." Joan shrugged again and cleared her throat. "I knew some of the stories. The details changed, but my dad used to tell me the one about Icarus."

Quite a story for a child, Simon thought, but he held his tongue.

"I think that was humanity, for him. We'd had all the warnings. We ignored them, and we fell. My father wasn't a very optimistic guy. But he was proud when I volunteered to go, like maybe I could change the old stories. Reading that book, I could hear his voice."

She swallowed hard. "It's late. You've had a long day, and none of this is really your problem, is it? I didn't mean to throw it all on you."

It's not your business, Simon heard in her voice at

first, and it was that he first responded to. "No, not at all," he muttered, and took a step backward, hesitating. Hesitating because there'd been something else in her voice, just as there'd been in her face earlier. And if he was fumbling in the dark again, perhaps there was no other way to find a light. "I hope—"

Again she turned to face him, almost as fast as she'd done when he first opened the door. Her eyes were fierce, all the more so because they shone with unshed tears. "This is just a moment. I'll get over it. I'm not falling apart. Don't think any less of me."

What remained of Simon's self-control vanished on the spot. "Think less of you? I—" Before either of them knew what he was doing, he'd taken her by the shoulders. "Most men I know would be mad in your shoes. Gibbering. Think less of you?"

Touching her had been a bad idea. There was perhaps half an inch between their bodies now. Simon was quite aware of that and of how little she was wearing. It was quite an improper position to be in. It was quite an *exciting* position to be in. It was a position in which no gentleman would remain for very long, not with a woman he wasn't paying. But he couldn't move.

If Joan had spoken or pulled away herself, the spell might have broken. But Simon's words seemed to have caught her as off guard as hers had him, and she was silent. Her shoulders were warm beneath his hands, and her hair fell over them. Simon's desire was almost blinding, a sweet hot ache not just in his groin but, it seemed, all through his body, as if his skin itself hungered for the woman in front of him.

I should move away, he thought.

He had only a second to think it.

Then Joan slid her arms around his neck. Simon thought he'd never felt anything so arousing. "You're a good guy," she said. "I hope you know that."

She leaned upward just a little but enough to close the rest of the distance between them, to press her body against Simon's from shoulder to knee. Her lips pressed against his, hot and sweet. Then they parted, and Simon lost himself.

Chapter 18

SIMON DIDN'T KISS LIKE JOAN HAD THOUGHT HE WOULD.
She'd imagined it a lot over a week of hot evenings,
sliding her hand between her legs and thinking that she
was just scratching an itch only to have it come back
over and over again. In all of those fantasies, he'd been
graceful like he'd been when he danced and rode. Careless, even.

Not now. He held back for a second, surprised,
shocked, or maybe trying to resist as Joan had done for
all those long nights. But it was only a second.

Then Simon's lips were hot against hers and his
open mouth was urgent. Desperate, even. Hard enough
to bruise, but hell, Joan wasn't complaining. Not at all.
Simon's grace and control had been exciting because
they were new. Violence wasn't. Neither was hunger.
Joan knew them both very well, and neither was less
exciting because of it. The ache between her legs bore
that out.

She pressed up against Simon, crushing her breasts
against his chest. If she had been less turned on, the
pressure might have hurt but now it only made her groan
into his mouth. He made his own muffled, incoherent
noise, low in his throat. Even that little, intangible thing
sent heat running through Joan's body. When he twined
one hand in her hair, pulling her mouth up to his, there
was only heat. She cried out sharply.

And Simon stopped for just a second. *He thinks something's wrong*, Joan realized, a dim thought half buried in the red haze of lust. *Better convince him otherwise*.

Before Simon could disentangle his hand from her hair or raise his head to ask a question, Joan slid her tongue into his mouth. Simon groaned again. His hand clenched in her hair once more, and his other hand, at the base of Joan's spine, tightened as well, pressing her against him. She went willingly, parting her legs a little so his hard-on could rub between them.

Bright Powers, it was so good that he was tall. And big in other ways as well, Joan noticed. She circled her hips, rubbing against him, and moisture soaked the ludicrous things they wore for underwear in that time.

Simon cried out this time. His hand slid lower, cupping her buttocks and then squeezing hard. Joan arched into him in response. Her fingers were probably digging divots in his shoulders, but he didn't seem to care, any more than she cared about the bruises she'd have on her ass tomorrow.

When Simon lifted his mouth from hers, Joan almost protested, but then his lips were on her neck. He kissed her hard and then bit, and she was writhing against him, hips pumping, oblivious to anything but the desperate hunger of her body. *Want*.

Joan sought his neck with her mouth, trying to return the favor—or just desperate to taste him—and found only cloth. They wore too damn many clothes in this time. She couldn't even wrap a leg around him properly; the damn nightgown was in the way. Joan snarled in frustration.

When Simon slid his hand down out of her hair to cup one of her breasts, she snarled again. Not in frustration, though. At least not entirely. The world was made of white heat, of warm hands and a warmer mouth, and if she didn't feel more of both soon, she would scream.

Somewhere around here was a desk. That would work. She just had to remember where it was.

Simon flicked his thumb over her stiff nipple. Once, then again—then he took it between finger and thumb and pinched lightly.

To hell with the desk. There was a floor. There was a wall. Either would do fine.

Joan dropped her hands. One went to Simon's chest, pushing him away just a little. She hated to do it, but she needed the space. Her other hand went downward, brushing past Simon's waistband and over the hard bulge of his cock. Unable to resist temptation, Joan closed her hand for a moment, very gently.

"Ah, *God*." Simon sounded like he was as close to howling as she was. Felt like it too. His cock had fairly leapt in her hand.

Good. Very good. Now—buttons. Joan tugged at the first of them with clumsy fingers and then yanked.

Simon closed his hand over hers. "Wait. Stop."

The teachings of her childhood rose up through her arousal. *Do you know how much those things* cost? *You have been here too long if you've stopped noticing.* Joan shook her head. "Sorry. You do it, then."

When Simon shook his head, it was like a sign in an alien language, a gesture that might have meant anything from "I come in peace" to "I spit on your mother." Because it couldn't mean what it usually meant. Not the way he'd just been touching her.

Simon took both her hands in his and stepped back.

He was panting and flushed, and his eyes were dark with passion, but he shook his head again. "I'm sorry. I fear I'm no gentleman at all—but I'll do what I can, at least."

"Huh?" She stared at him openmouthed, looking more than a little stupid. Feeling more than a little stupid, like she'd just been hit over the head. Her sex was still hot, still pulsing; her breasts ached for his hands. "Wait—what?"

"I won't take advantage of you," he said roughly. "I've done too much of that already, I think."

"*I* kissed *you*."

"Because you were tired and upset."

"Yeah—wait, no. I mean, yeah, I was, but so what?" She shrugged. "There are worse ways to take the edge off, and I wanted you anyhow. Still do."

Simon flushed again, and his hands tightened on hers. "Don't tempt me."

"Why not?"

"Because it's not right. You're my guest. You aren't thinking clearly."

"If you're thinking clearly during sex," Joan said, and this time she couldn't keep the edge from her voice, "you're doing it wrong."

Simon laughed. His laugh was short and breathless, but he was definitely amused. "There's that. But"—and his face grew more serious—"there are consequences, you know."

"I won't get knocked up. We took care of all that long ago." She remembered the ceremony, the sharp smell of herbs, the heat just above her pelvis.

"Not just that," he said slowly. "We have to work together. Getting involved with each other—"

Dammit. He had to bring up the objection she'd spent the last couple weeks trying to keep in mind. Hearing it was like a bucket of cold water over her head. "Yeah," she said, shoving her hair out of her face. "Okay. I'd better get to bed, then."

The good thing about arousal was that it was easy to deal with, at least for a little while. A few quick strokes of her fingers under the covers and the stupid nightgown sent Joan over the edge. She bit her lip hard as she came, since noise would attract the servants. She tried, and failed utterly, to think of anyone but Simon. It was his face that she saw in her mind's eye as her orgasm hit, his muffled groans that she heard.

What the hell, she thought sleepily, turning her face into the cool pillow. *There are plenty of men to distract me in London.*

In the morning, though, the memory of kissing Simon was still with Joan. It heated her blood and set up a familiar sweet ache between her legs. She groaned and pulled the pillow over her head for a second, but she couldn't deny what she felt. The only option left was to fight it.

The physical came first. That morning, Joan threw herself into the practice with even more energy than usual. Then she splashed her face with cold water and scrubbed it as roughly as if the rose-scented soap were the eye-stinging stuff she was used to.

It helped. A little.

When Rose came in, Joan picked out the plainest and most severe of her new dresses. It was dark gray, like the sky just before a storm, with just a trace of navy-blue ribbon for ornament. The neckline was high, and the sleeves were long. She hadn't worn it much before. It had been too confining. Now a little confinement seemed like just what she needed.

There was a note on the breakfast tray from Simon, recommending that she spend the day reading some books he'd left on the library table, saying that he'd spend most of the day in the private study, and requesting her company at dinner. Clearly, Joan wasn't the only one taking protective measures here. She wouldn't have expected anything less. It was very sensible.

She wasn't disappointed at all. Really.

Chapter 19

"MIGHT I SPEAK WITH YOU?" ELEANOR ASKED.

It was after dinner, with the last red beams of the summer twilight still coming in through the long windows. To Simon's mind, the meal had been rather stilted. He was very much aware of what had happened in the library the night before, and though Joan was fairly adept at subterfuge, he thought that she was as well. When Eleanor spoke from behind him, his first thought was that she'd noticed.

He cringed inwardly but nodded. "Of course."

"Would it be very much trouble for you to cast a spell?"

That was the last thing Simon had expected. "What sort?" he asked, wondering if she'd somehow fallen in love with one of the village boys or wanted her fortune read—but Eleanor had never been one for such feminine silliness.

"Something to see into...other places? Or perhaps things that are invisible here." She drew a breath and then spoke in a rush. "I want to know if that thing is anywhere near me."

"It's not," he said automatically. The wards would carry over into other worlds. If something was watching her from there, it did so impotently. "But there's no harm in making sure, if you'd like."

"I would," she said firmly. "Please."

By the time Eleanor knocked at the door of his

private study, Simon had put most of the preparations in place. The smell of cloves was thick in the air, the paper and ink were out and waiting, and on the floor, in the middle of the paper, was a large mirror. He could already feel the power building. It wasn't the sensual heat that had accompanied the protection spell, fortunately, but rather a coolness that never became *quite* cold enough to be uncomfortable.

Eleanor's face, when she saw him, was a study in surprise and uncertainty. Understandable enough since Alex had made the "experiments" she had seen in evening dress, not high ceremonial garb. "Er," she said, eyeing his tunic nervously, "must I—"

"Not at all. Even I don't have to, strictly speaking. It's just a good idea." He smiled, trying to put her at her ease.

As he'd hoped, he saw curiosity overcome her fear. "Would this be less likely to work if you didn't?"

"Harder for me to control, rather."

"Oh. Is there anything I should do?"

"Stand here." Simon gestured to a spot just north of the mirror. "And try not to move at all."

She took her place and watched, wide eyed, as Simon knelt by the paper and began the spell proper. This time, the ink was blue and silver, and the characters far more familiar: Gabriel at the westernmost point, Apollo to the east, Neith to the south, and Freya to the north. He wrote the characters requesting sight into other worlds and then those, less familiar, asking to see all enemies and evil spirits around Eleanor.

As Simon completed the last stroke, he saw a flash of pale blue from the corner of his eye and heard Eleanor stifle a gasp. The double ring of characters floated in the mirror, glowing with blue fire—the same sort that had appeared between the stones when he'd met Joan. Around it, the mirror was black.

Slowly, a pale shape took form inside the ring: Eleanor's face. The light was wrong and the angle impossible, but it was her staring back out of the mirror with what Simon knew to be the same half-alarmed, half-fascinated expression that he'd see if he looked over to where she stood. The light crawled over her, flickering its symbols across the pale expanse of her forehead and down her cheeks, moving like a living thing.

The darkness vanished, and the mirror reflected the room again—behind Eleanor now, not the view from its real position—before shifting to a clear, pearly gray. Strange shapes moved behind it. Simon couldn't make out the whole of their outlines, and he rather thought he didn't want to. They didn't seem bad, not precisely, but neither were they shapes that the human mind was meant to take in. And yet the eye wanted to linger on them, to trace the impossible curves and the unlikely angles—

Bright light shone out from the mirror, banishing the gray. Bright green light with strands of gold shot through it somehow. Eleanor gave a cry of delight, and Simon felt much the same impulse. Whatever this place was, it was one of joy, strange though that joy might be, and peace, even if it was a peace foreign to humans. In a second, that too was gone. It went quicker than the others, as if the searching light had a mind and seemed to grasp that the Dark One was very unlikely to be in a place like that.

Next came a skyline where twisted rust-colored

buildings raised strange heads to a murky violet sky and shapes as tall as they were moved ponderously among them. The backgrounds flickered faster: a snowscape under three golden moons, a bloody forest where the trees opened gaping mouths to greet them, a hillside that might have been autumn anywhere in England. Faster and faster, worlds spinning past behind Eleanor's face— and finally, darkness.

At first, Simon thought that the journey was over, that the mirror had gone back to its starting point. But the ring of blue light hadn't vanished, and the darkness, when he looked into it, wasn't complete. Flecks of light swam in it, a dull, rot-green light that was utterly unlike the joyful radiance they'd seen so briefly. When he'd banished the Dark One from Eleanor, it had given off just such a glow.

This was its home.

Eleanor made no sound. In the mirror, her face was dead white and her teeth firmly set in her lower lip, but she didn't whimper, and she didn't move.

The flecks of light drifted past her image with a lazy, predatory grace. Their movement spoke of things that could have been from the bottom of the ocean, things that existed only to eat or be eaten, terrible enough in their mindless innocence. These were worse. Malice flowed off them like a scent.

Yet they passed Eleanor's image without wavering. Not one of them stayed by her. Not one even seemed to linger.

Simon let out a slow breath. "Be done," he said to the mirror.

It went blank. The power lingered, as it would until

he cleaned the room, but Simon had no trace of the energy he'd felt after the protection spell. He was weary instead and chilled, and he very much wanted a bath. Somewhere in there was a dim species of relief, but it was a feeble thing indeed.

"You're all right," he said. Eleanor stood like a statue, watching him. "It's like I thought. Nothing's taken any particular interest in you."

Now she closed her eyes and let her shoulders slump. "Thank God," she said, and sounded almost like her old self. "And thank you, Simon. I don't mean to be a bother, you know."

"You're nothing of the sort."

"Hardly the classical younger sister, then." She smiled faintly.

Laughter, even his brief harsh laughter, seemed to take a great deal of effort. "Perhaps the ancient masters were wrong on a few points."

"One or two." Eleanor opened her eyes and looked at him again. "Did I do all right?"

"Wonderfully, Ellie."

"Good. It was interesting in its way, you know. Bits of it, at least. Do you—do you think I might learn more?"

Simon's first impulse was to forbid it. His second was to ask how, after Alex, she could even think of such a thing. But her face held such tentative hope—and it was the only thing she'd really asked of him in the time since they'd left London.

"A little more," he finally said. "Nothing dangerous, mind. I'll send up a book you can begin with." He still had one or two of the notebooks he'd used in his school days. Protective charms might actually help, and the bit of candle lighting and fortune-telling in the notebooks was far too minor to hurt her.

Eleanor had never, in all the time he'd known her, been demonstrative, and she was less so now. All the same, the sudden light in her eyes and the tone in her voice were unmistakable and slightly embarrassing. "Oh, thank you!"

"It's probably for the best," Simon said, clearing his throat. "After all, my business takes me to the city on a regular basis, and Miss MacArthur will quite probably come with me next time I go. If you feel up to it, of course, we'd like you to join us."

"Even if I do," Eleanor said thoughtfully, "I'd imagine she'll have to spend a great deal of time away from me. It would be horribly inconvenient otherwise, wouldn't it?"

She knew.

"What did Joan tell you?" Simon asked, managing by sheer force of will to keep his voice even. *By God, the woman had no right—*

"Nothing at all important," Eleanor said, and while she didn't meet Simon's eyes, her voice was unexpectedly firm. "Only that Mr. Reynell was an enemy of hers, and she only told me that because I asked. I'm sorry, Simon. I didn't mean to pry, but I couldn't stand not knowing."

"You don't need to apologize," he said.

"I—I don't think that she does either. You'll forgive me for saying it, I hope, but I thought your business in town was something to do with him even before Joan said anything. I was worried."

"A duel?" He'd thought of it and cursed the fact that

he'd been born fifty years too late for such a measure to be anything short of ridiculous. But he hadn't thought Eleanor had any idea.

She smiled a little, sadly. "You're my brother, Simon. And you're a good man. Yes, I thought something like that. I didn't want to believe it—I prayed I was wrong—but when you left for London, I was almost certain."

"You didn't want me to go through with it?"

"No," she said, her reticence falling away on that one intense syllable. "Not ever. They'd hang you for that. And if they didn't, it would have haunted you."

"Maybe I deserve to be haunted," said Simon. "You—"

Eleanor shook her head. "I'm hurt. I'll get better. People do. It's not worth losing you."

Simon stepped forward and put his arms around her. She was taller now than she'd been the last time he'd done that, but she leaned her head against his shoulder as she'd done then, and she didn't pull away. "I'm sorry, Ellie," he said.

"It's not your fault."

"It is, in a way." Simon braced himself. "Reynell chose you because he hated me."

"Not really. Or not entirely."

"What do you mean?"

Eleanor closed her eyes again. "That night was the first time I'd done anything, really," she said, "but not the first time he had. That thing—" She broke off, tense but not still. Rather, she trembled like a small animal before a predator. Simon stroked her hair and her back, but he didn't speak.

"It knew him," she said finally. "Knew him like I

know you. I wasn't the first girl to host it, Simon, and I don't think I'll be the last. And nobody, *nobody* ever mentioned the ones who came before."

"Oh, God." Simon sent a silent and hasty prayer of thanks to Lieutenant Carter, wherever his spirit might have gone.

"I think he gave himself to darkness long before you knew," Eleanor said. Her voice shook. "I think the other girls were practice, and I hope—I pray—that he paid them to disappear afterward. I don't know anything for sure, or I would have said."

"I know you would," Simon said. He tried to sound reassuring, but he didn't think he succeeded. His mind was whirling, and a cold and certain fear had settled at the pit of his stomach. Girls went missing all the time. Not girls like Ellie or her friends—children of wealth and breeding, with protective brothers and worried parents—but in the slums of the East End, girls vanished every day, and there were spells that wouldn't just use them as mediums.

"God," Simon said again, and his arms clenched more tightly around Eleanor.

She looked up at him. "So, you see? If it hadn't been me, it would have been someone else. Some other poor girl. And would that have been better?" She swallowed hard. "I try not to think so. She might not have gotten away. I did. You saved me. And you—and Joan—are going to save the rest. Aren't you?"

"Close enough," he said, and heard his voice crack.

Chapter 20

ANOTHER FAMILIAR THING: WAITING FOR THE INEVITABLE. Not like right before a raid when you were nerving yourself for the moment when everything started and the world went all cold and clear. It was like waiting for orders, instead, orders that you and everyone else knew would come. Those were the times when you played poker, trying to keep your mind on the cards and not on what the old men in the inner room were talking about.

There were no cards now, but the feeling was the same. Joan sat at the dinner table, remembering to use the right fork and not pick up the wineglass by its stem, but she could have been back home watching the pile of ragged-edged cards grow in front of her. *London* wasn't just a word. It was a weight on all of them. *Reynell* was another.

"How are you enjoying your reading?" Eleanor asked. She'd calmed down considerably since Simon's return. She wasn't exactly outgoing, but she'd lost a lot of the stiffness and the scared-rabbit look.

Joan hadn't asked what had passed between Eleanor and Simon, any more than she'd asked about the small leather-bound book that Eleanor had been reading. She'd seen Simon's handwriting in it once, and that was enough for her.

"Spiritualism?" Joan shrugged. "Interesting once you get the language sorted out. And they're not entirely wrong, I think, even if they're not seeing things the way I do."

"Oh?" Simon asked, lifting his eyebrows.

"They think that the universe is a friendly place," she said. "And that people are basically good."

Simon nodded. "And how do you see the universe, Miss MacArthur?"

Like an outhouse the morning after a hard party, Joan thought at first. It was the way she would've answered back home. Not what she actually believed, though. "Like a lion. Not bad exactly, but unless you're good at what you do or really lucky, it'll probably rip your throat out and go on its way."

"That makes a good deal of sense," said Eleanor.

Simon had given Joan a sharp look and then turned to watch his sister, but now he relaxed. "I suppose it does. Though the best society doesn't discuss that sort of thing at dinner, you know."

"Doesn't it?" Joan asked, only a little sarcastic. *Ellie will not break. She's read novels with worse,* Joan thought as she looked at Simon, hoping he'd pick up her thoughts from her face. "Oh, drat."

"Most of the books you've been reading would say that humans make the universe friendly, or not," he said, not taking the bait.

"Why? Even if we all lived in peace and harmony"— Joan couldn't keep from rolling her eyes as she said it—"there'd still be disease and famine and, oh, people getting eaten by real lions."

"That's one view. Excuse me." Simon beckoned one of the footmen over and said something quietly to him. The footman bowed and then went to speak to the other servants, and Simon turned back to the table. "Some people say that the world at large mirrors what human beings choose, even if the connections aren't obvious."

"So if everyone's nice to each other, we'll stop getting sick?" Joan asked.

"'The lion will lie down with the lamb, and the wolf with the sheep,'" Eleanor quoted.

Joan blinked. "Bad luck for the lion and the wolf, isn't it? Or do they become vegetarian?"

Eleanor smiled. "I think that's the general idea, though I admit I've never been particularly clear on that verse."

The servants headed out of the room as they talked. When they'd gone, Simon looked back and forth between Eleanor and Joan. "We should travel to London in a week's time," he said, "or less. We'll be able to catch the rest of the Season then."

"Should I pack—"

"All you have and more," Simon said dryly. "We'll get you proper ball gowns and so forth once we're there, of course. I've already sent ahead for appointments."

"*More* dresses." Joan sighed. "I can be ready to go in a day or so, then. Anything else?"

"I, um, was wondering," said Eleanor. "You said you'd like me to go with you?"

"If you feel up to it," Simon said, smiling at her gently. "If you don't, then by all means, don't force yourself."

"But if Joan—Miss MacArthur—is traveling alone with a man—"

"I'll have a maid."

"If necessary," Simon said, "we'll also hire a companion. I'm certain we can find someone discreet."

Across the table, Eleanor lifted her chin. She was pale

again, and her hands had vanished below the table. Joan knew that she had been clenching them in the fabric of her skirt. "My presence would be helpful, though."

Joan looked at Eleanor as she would have any newbie who wanted to come on a raid, weighing intelligence against fear, knowledge of the enemy against vulnerability, another body and mind against further complication. Then she nodded. "We don't need you. But it'd help."

"Then I'll begin packing."

Chapter 21

IF ELEANOR GRENVILLE'S SUDDEN DEPARTURE HAD turned her from a bluestocking nonentity into a subject of brief interest, her return to Society fanned the dying flames almost at once. When she and her brother made their first public appearance at an afternoon lecture on spiritualism, half the crowd turned its attention from metaphysical theories to another kind of speculation altogether.

Miss Grenville had returned too soon for the worst and most interesting of the rumors to be completely true. She was definitely thinner and paler than she had been. Some people held that up as proof of genuine illness, while others pointed out that unrequited passion had been known to have the same effects. Still others, of considerably lower mind, mentioned that there were many sorts of disease. And a few, mostly those who'd been in Alex Reynell's inner circle back in May, wondered about less worldly causes.

Then there was her brother. Society knew that Simon's interests were eclectic and his friends not quite respectable. It also had known since May that he could be provoked into violence on occasion. Theories about his return ran from a desire to settle accounts with Reynell to a need to help his sister brave the scandal to the simple wish for a good time. Nobody knew for certain. And nobody knew anything about the other woman he'd brought, the tall one with hazel eyes and golden hair. A relative, perhaps, but she didn't resemble any of the Grenvilles. *Maybe* a cousin by marriage. More likely something else.

Whoever she was, she strode easily along at Simon's side, chin high, and met all stares with cool detachment. *Most unfeminine*, sniffed some of the older women and a few of the younger ones. *Bold as brass*.

Near the front of the lecture hall, Alexander Reynell let his gaze travel lazily up and down the stranger's slim body and decided that she was the one promising thing in the whole damn situation.

He'd been dismayed, of course, when his hellhounds hadn't done in Simon. Not as dismayed as he had been when his former friend had turned Puritan on him, though, nor as outraged as when he'd woken up to find his jaw aching and Simon's insipid little sister gone. The High One hadn't been at all pleased by the exorcism either, and it had been weeks before Alex had been able to get its attention again, even with the proper sacrifices. He'd taken a certain joy in killing Carter, partly because of that, and a greater joy in setting the hounds on Simon.

Bad enough that Simon had survived. Worse that he'd come back to London, in the face of all Reynell's power. Worst of all that mouse-faced Eleanor had also somehow found the nerve to return. Not that any of them could hurt him, of course—he had more knowledge tucked away in his study than Master Grenville would be able to collect in a lifetime—but it was rather a slap in the face.

In the woman, he saw his chance to hit back. Whoever she really was, Grenville at least trusted her in his sister's company and quite probably in his bed as well. Simon might have told her a few stories about Alex, but he couldn't have possibly told her all of them. No sensible woman would believe stories of possession and magic. Alex could pass the rest off as a horrible mistake or the vagaries of an overprotective brother.

Perhaps he could turn her against Simon. This wouldn't be the first time in history that a pretty woman could achieve what brute force couldn't. If not, Alex could still have the satisfaction of taking something away from Simon and proving, once and for all, that he was the better man.

As Alex had expected, the lecture was insipid, full of angel children and floating tables, the sort of thing that he (and, he'd thought, Simon) had grown far beyond but that comely young women drank right up. So did a surprising number of powerful men. Therefore, once Alex had gotten a good look at Simon and his women, he cultivated a properly rapt look and waited out the rest, listening just enough so that he could drop a few key phrases on demand.

Afterward, he slipped through the crowd to the small ring of people on one side of the hall. He didn't push his way past anyone—no point in showing his hand right off—but he looked into the center of the ring with cool interest that he didn't bother to conceal.

Of course, he couldn't approach them directly. Simon had planted a facer on him, and after that sort of statement, a man rarely feels obliged to make introductions, even in the best society. Nonetheless, Simon couldn't bar Alex from a public place nor from a crowd who, at least in part, looked on Alex as something of a pet and believed that Simon had overreacted. Some of them would have done so even if Reynell hadn't touched their minds with magic.

So Alex stood a little way off and watched. Eleanor met his eyes and flinched. That was an eminently satisfying moment but not nearly as interesting as Madame Mysterious and whatever Simon was saying about her. A quick exercise of magic tuned out the buzz of the crowd around Alex and let him hear the introductions as if he were standing next to them.

"I'm extremely glad to be back, of course," Simon was saying to a tall man whose bushy blond mustache made him look like an overgrown walrus. "Archie, may I introduce you to Mrs. MacArthur?"

~~~

"You need a husband," Simon had said.

Joan had been looking out the train window, watching the landscape change. They'd been passing a lake just then, and it had sparkled in the summer sunlight like someone had dropped a golden net over it. "Sorry," she said absently. "Forgot to pack that."

Eleanor giggled. The sound blended well with Simon's laughter. "Not a real one. We'll make up a name and kill the poor chap off as well. A widow has about as much freedom as you can get."

"Particularly a wealthy widow," Eleanor added, "and *most* particularly a foreign one."

"How do either of you know that?" Joan asked. Simon was looking at Eleanor curiously himself. On second thought, Joan was fairly sure how *he* knew. He sure hadn't kissed like a virgin.

The memory made her want to squirm in her seat and

press her legs together. She quashed it quickly, as best she could, and looked back at Eleanor instead.

She was blushing, but she shrugged. "Oh—well—everyone knows that. At least everyone who reads."

"I'm surprised girls don't just invent dead husbands all the time," Joan said. She leaned back and put her feet up on the seat across from her. A four-person closed compartment was especially good with three people. "Okay—how do people die these days?"

"I'll think of something," Simon said.

"A mountain lion," Joan said, and raised a handkerchief to her eyes. "I don't much like to think about it."

The small ring of people made various sympathetic noises. Two of the women exchanged one sort of look—*oh, the poor brave thing*—and three others another type entirely. A married woman might be an interesting acquaintance for them, but a young, good-looking widow was a different kettle of fish. At least one of the young men confirmed that by directing his attention toward Joan more intensely than before.

"Oh, I'm terribly sorry," Archie said. He was brick red now, looking away. "I had no idea—please do accept—"

Joan shook her head. "Of course, Mr. Petersen. Don't worry about it for a moment. " Then she added, squaring her shoulders, "After all, it's been three years. And he's in a better place."

Doing great things for the Montana soil, Simon thought, and bit the inside of his cheek. He wished he and Joan hadn't spent so much time going over her responses. Every sarcastic thing she'd said was coming back to him now.

One of the more sympathetic women tactfully changed the subject. "Indeed he is. After all, isn't that what we're here to learn about? And it's a great comfort for all of us that such advancements are being made and that we gain bright young students like yourself, Mrs. MacArthur."

"Yes," said one of the other young men, a chap named Donald who Simon had always thought looked more than a little fishlike. The resemblance had never been quite so striking before. "Quite a step forward for civilization, don't you think?"

The conversation shifted to a bright new dawn, an age of spiritual understanding and similar topics. Simon had heard them all before. Back when he and Alex were young, they'd have met each other's eyes across such a conversation and would have been hard pressed to keep from laughing. Alex had done a remarkable imitation of the female spiritualist devotees a few times, complete with fluttering gestures and uplifted palms.

On the heels of that memory, he saw Alex's face.

At first Simon thought that it was just memory. Another look dispelled the idea, though. Alex was there, half buried in the crowd, not trying to get anyone's attention. For the moment, he seemed content just to watch.

Simon saw him clearly, perhaps more clearly than he'd ever seen anyone before. Alex was a tall man with dark brown eyes and pale blond hair. Well dressed, after the latest fashion and in the most expensive fabrics. Languid. Unbothered.

His friend once. A murderer now, and worse. Humanity's downfall in the end.

A fluting, feminine voice spoke from behind him.

"Mrs. MacArthur, you must come and have tea with me. I simply insist."

It should have been a triumph, just as Alex's interest should have been. Simon felt only the desire to take Joan and Eleanor and leave, to flee before Alex did something or before his mere proximity tainted them all. He half saw, half imagined the layer of corruption that lay over Alex now, like rank blood around a spider's maw.

Something of Simon's disgust must have showed itself on his face. The people facing him looked away and then behind themselves, not wanting to believe that they had inspired such an expression. When they saw Alex, doubt became clarity and relief…and then anticipation. All of Society knew of Simon and Alex's quarrel. If its members were divided in their opinions, they all at least knew to expect scenes when the two principal actors met.

Alex Reynell met Simon's eyes and smiled. Slowly. Pleasantly, even. It was the smile of a good sport admitting defeat. *All right,* it said, *I fouled up, and I know it. Mistakes happen, old man.* As if betrayal and pain and God knew what else were nothing more serious than losing five pounds at the racetrack.

In that moment, Simon could have turned to Joan and told her to go ahead with her plan—and to Hell with any notion of redemption or honor. He could have pulled a pistol and shot Alex himself. Three rounds through the face would have removed that smile quite well.

But Simon had no pistol. The crowd was thick. And there was Eleanor to think of: Eleanor, who would be prey to every unscrupulous fortune-hunter for miles if her brother went to jail for murder. Eleanor, who was in no state to see bloodshed and whose face, even now, was white with strain and shock.

So Simon lifted his chin and met Reynell's gaze, letting his face show none of his rage but all his disgust. *You were better than this once,* he thought at the other man. *What's wrong with you?*

Then he turned away.

Chapter 22

London was huge.

Joan had been in a city before. She didn't know its name, but scavenging had been good there for those who could defend themselves, so she'd taken a squad through a couple times a year. The place had been mostly empty, though—empty of anything living, at least. The Traitor Lords, or the Dark Ones themselves, owned the cities with people in them. You didn't go there much, not if you wanted your skin to stay on.

She'd stuck to the abandoned cities. Now she realized that they hadn't been cities at all. They'd been shells. Sometimes you got gangs of cultists or packs of beasts there, but at the most they'd taken up a couple streets. They'd talked big and *fought* big, but the space had dwarfed them. In the end, there'd been rusting buildings, old cars, bones, and the wind blowing down empty streets. Those were the big things. People were tiny.

Not here.

There were people everywhere in London: rushing down the narrow, winding streets; pouring in and out of the redbrick buildings; forming clumps on the street corners by the flickering gaslights. At first, Joan hadn't even been able to see individual figures, just one flowing mob. Now, looking out of the carriage on the way to the dressmaker's shop, she could make out individuals but only for a moment each.

"How many people live here?"

Eleanor looked up from her book, blinking. "I'm afraid I couldn't really say. Perhaps a million. It's difficult to tell because so many people come and go."

"A million."

Joan wanted to laugh. *Come on, Eleanor. You aren't fooling anyone. How many really?* Except that Eleanor didn't lie, and she wouldn't joke like that. Plus, she'd sounded sincere, even casual.

A million.

Maybe a couple hundred people had lived in the caves. More in the past, when the casualties hadn't been as bad and people had had more babies. More in the controlled cities, of course. There had to be, since the Traitor Lords and their masters bred people like cows. They'd said there were ten thousand in Chicago. Joan hadn't believed it.

There might have been a million people in the whole world back home. Maybe. If you went to Asia and South America and a bunch of places nobody Joan knew had ever seen.

She swallowed. "Oh. Got it."

Eleanor was looking at her with kind surprise. "I suppose it is a little, um, intimidating. I've never been very good with crowds myself."

"Intimidating." That wasn't the word Joan would have used. *Rich*, maybe. Or *vital*. Maybe just *alive*. She'd never have used the word about a city before. Cities were bunches of buildings. They didn't live.

Outside, people flickered past: short women with elaborate hats, tall men with mustaches, men in military uniform, women dressed as servants. Some strode down the street in a hurry to get somewhere. Others waved through the crowds, hailing friends, and stopped to talk. Everyone was moving. Everyone was speaking.

Alive.

She'd read books. She'd heard about cities before. But she hadn't been prepared. She didn't think there was any way she could have been. It was the difference between seeing a picture of a tiger and then coming face-to-face with one. The picture didn't show the play of muscles under the beast's skin as it moved—or the razor points of its teeth when it yawned.

A thousand thousand people in one city, crowding the streets and packing themselves into buildings. A thousand thousand eyes that could be watching. A thousand thousand hands, and each could be holding a knife. You'd never see it coming. A single person could get lost in this city. He could slip out of sight, submerge himself in the mass of people, and then surface behind you.

Any one of the people on the street could be a killer.

Or all of them could. Get them angry enough or scared enough to rise, and this many people could be a wave that drowned anyone standing before them. There'd been hangings after the end, and riots. Joan had never been able to picture them until now.

Intimidating, Eleanor had said. She didn't know half of it.

How did you live in a place like that? How did you walk down the street without watching your back, without jumping at every movement? How did you not wonder if the man beside you was going to pull a knife? You didn't know him. You couldn't trust him.

But the people on the street, most of them, just walked.

Some of them were worried, sure, but about other things. They didn't look around, and they didn't flinch when someone jostled them. They weren't all worried either. Plenty looked angry, happy, or even bored.

Some of them were kids. Grimy, some of them, and clearly on their own. Others were out with adults, though: girls in frilly dresses with big bows in their hair, boys in short pants and flat caps, and infants in carriages with fussy blankets and awnings. Most walked with older women who wore severe clothes and held the children tightly by the hand, but those women looked pretty frail, and none of them were armed. Civilians.

Joan stared for a long time as the carriage rumbled through the London streets. She watched the crowds moving and the people moving through them. None of them looked to the sky. Nobody carried weapons. They went where they needed to go, and whatever might wait for them when they got there, they knew they'd arrive.

Another word rose up in her mind: *free*.

"Um," Eleanor said. "I hope this isn't too...I mean, perhaps we should have had Mr. Allen come to the house instead. We didn't think a great deal about it, but I know this isn't what you're used to."

"It isn't." Joan realized that she was smiling, fierce and hot. "It's not what I'm used to at all. But I'm glad I saw it."

Joan had been expecting another dressmaker to be like Mrs. Simmons, brisk and businesslike. Mr. Allen, though, was old and plump, with a long white mustache and a sleepy smile. He welcomed them to the shop and

offered them tea and biscuits with the same dreamy ami-
ability. "I had your measurements already, of course,
Miss Grenville, and as you were kind enough to send
Mrs. MacArthur's, there's nothing left but the selection.
But then, that's the best part, isn't it?"

He chuckled at his own joke and poured out the tea,
while a woman about twenty years his junior came out
with a thick book and set it down on the little table.

It was full of pictures of women with their hair
curled high on their heads and their chins lifted, staring
flirtatiously out of the pages. They wore frothy dresses
that someone had colored in by hand using bright con-
trasting shades. Joan looked over at Eleanor, asking
silently for help.

Eleanor met her eyes and nodded. A small crease appeared between her eyebrows as she thought, and her
fingers tapped slowly against the creamy china of her
teacup. "Two ball gowns to start, I think," she said, "and
an evening dress. I won't speak to colors—besides, I'm
sure that Mr. Allen has a number of lovely new fabrics
I haven't seen yet."

"You're too kind, Miss Grenville," Mr. Allen said
absently from behind them. "Please do excuse me for
a moment."

He drifted off toward the back room. Joan took that
opportunity to lean across the table toward Eleanor.
"What about money?"

"Oh—I shouldn't worry about it." Eleanor looked
awkward. "We don't really talk about that sort of thing,
you know. But I can't imagine you'd spend enough here
to worry Simon at all."

"Anything I should avoid?"

"Bright red, of course. Otherwise, you're a widow so you don't have the same rules I do, but I'd take a pale color for at least one. And nothing terribly heavy. Ballrooms are quite warm, generally, and you'll be dancing a great deal."

"You're pretty optimistic."

Eleanor smiled and shook her head. "You made your mark quite admirably at the lecture. I shouldn't think you'll want for partners."

"Thanks," Joan said, looking through the book. Nothing low in the back and sleeves long enough to cover the scar on her arm. Gloves would cover the place where she attached the flashgun, at least. The skirt was probably a lost cause, but if she had to run or fight, she could always cut it off.

"You're quite pretty," Eleanor said matter-of-factly. "And, well, I don't mean any offense, but more importantly you're new and foreign and a little bit mysterious."

"That's putting it mildly."

"The *ton* is dreadfully fond of novelty. That's why scandal goes around so fast," said Eleanor. A flush crept up her face. "And why it ideally gets forgotten quickly. They do grow bored."

Eleanor was reassuring herself, Joan knew. "People forget things. We're good at that." She smiled and gestured to one of the pictures. "Do you think this would work all right?"

By the time they'd picked out the requisite three dresses, Mr. Allen and the woman—who turned out to be his wife—had made several trips to and from the back room, bringing out cloth and trimmings. There were silk and satin that caught even the gray sunlight from the windows, and there were spools of lace and ribbon, papers of buttons, and bunches of feathers. All of it went on a long table, into a heap like dragon's gold. Joan tried not to stare too much.

For herself, Eleanor had picked out a relatively modest dress with few of the frills and bows that were on the other ones. "I'd like it in something not very bright, please," she said, and looked down at her teacup again.

"Lovely," said Mr. Allen, but with a less sleepy look than usual. He looked over at Joan again and then nodded once in vague approval. "If you ladies are done, then, we can get started."

Fittings, as always, involved standing very still. This time Mr. Allen and his wife draped bolts of fabric over Joan, eyed them, took them away, put others on, and eyed *them*. Then, more often than not, they brought the first bolt back. Sometimes they muttered things. Very rarely, they asked Joan her opinion.

In the end, she thought they decided on silk, ice blue and dark rose-pink, for the ball gowns and dark green satin for the evening dress. There were dark blue ribbons and white ribbons and lace, but Joan didn't really know which went with what.

Then there were a few more measurements, this time with her corset laced more tightly than was really comfortable—though Joan drew the line well before the Allens wanted her to and held firm there—and a bit of discussion. And then they were out.

Back in the carriage, Joan finally relaxed. Eleanor saw it and bit her lip. "Was it...bad...for you?"

"Huh? No. They were very nice. It just makes me nervous. Undressing."

"Oh." Eleanor didn't ask. Nice girls, shy girls, didn't ask about that. But her eyes went to Joan's arm, and Joan knew she'd noticed the scar.

"Because of that. I have others, but they're easier to hide. Don't worry," she said, seeing Eleanor blush and look away, about to apologize. "I don't expect you not to notice. Noticing things is good."

At least it was good for Eleanor to notice things. Eleanor was on her side, and Eleanor was quiet. Hopefully, nobody else would be so observant, but then, Joan wasn't planning to undress in front of anyone else. If she did, she could always turn the lights out. Maidenly modesty was a pretty believable cover here. Nothing to worry about.

Except that Joan couldn't help wondering what Simon would think if he saw her naked. She remembered the way he'd looked in the library and when she'd come in for her dancing lesson. Would his eyes widen the same way? Would his lips part and his breath come faster? Or would he draw back, revolted by her scars and tattoos, used to the unmarred white skin of the women here?

It didn't matter. She was never going to sleep with him. They'd decided all that already. If Joan woke up hot and aching from dreams where they'd gone further, where she'd opened his pants and he'd taken her against the wall—well, that didn't matter either.

And she didn't want to punch walls over it.

Nope.

"So," she said, yanking her mind back to the carriage and Eleanor. "What happens next?"

Chapter 23

"DO YOU PEOPLE EVER TALK ABOUT ANYTHING BUT THE weather?" Joan dropped, with a deep and exasperated sigh, into one of the chairs by the study's fireplace.

Simon closed his book and studied her face. She looked irritated but not badly so. He flattered himself he was familiar enough with her real anger to recognize it. So he answered lightly, "I take it your visitors haven't been to your liking."

"Oh, not at all," Joan said. "They're very informative. If you want to know that it's been unexpectedly fine this year. I'm very well aware of that right now. And it's been nice of them to ask how I am so frequently. Next time, I'm going to tell them I've broken something. Or cut my own toes off with a carving knife. It'll make a nice change."

"You're going to cut your own toes off? Lord, Joan, don't you think that's a bit extreme?" Simon smiled over at her.

Joan rolled her eyes. "You don't have to sit through it."

"Thank God for that. I've danced with Miss Thomson—there's only so much suffering one man can endure in this life."

"Which one is she?"

"The pale little thing who called on Monday. Spiritual girl. Poetic. Or likes to think she is."

"Oh. Her." Joan closed her eyes, leaning her head back against the chair. "She expressed her 'unutterable sorrow' about my husband. I always thought that 'unutterable' meant you couldn't talk about something at all, let alone for five minutes straight. But I also thought it wasn't in good taste to say you don't know how you'd live if you lost a husband, the implication being that I should've jumped off a building."

"Oh, I don't think she meant to imply that. Suicides are such messy things."

Joan snorted and then opened one eye to look at Simon. "And how do you know she was here on Monday? The butler said you weren't here."

"I hid," Simon confessed, looking down at the cover of his book.

"How manly of you."

When Joan grinned, Simon wanted to forget everything he'd said at Englefield and kiss her again. Now that he was in town, without the reminders that he was supposed to play the responsible country gentleman, stopping that night in the library seemed more and more like a bad idea. Their mission was going well, and Eleanor was looking much better. At times like these, sober responsibility began to chafe.

Careful, he told himself, but careful was the last thing he wanted to be just then. He wanted to pull Joan onto his lap. He wanted to undo her blouse and take her small, firm breasts in his hands again, this time with nothing between his fingers and her skin.

But the bonds were still his to bear. "She hasn't set her cap for you."

Joan needed a moment to figure out the slang. Then she started laughing. "Oh. Oh, God. Poor guy. I take it back. But can't you just tell her you're not into her?"

"A gentleman doesn't do that sort of thing. Not if he has any sense of honor at all."

Joan stared at him. "You can't even tell her gently? You know, 'I like you as a sister' or something?"

"Not unless she confesses her feelings openly. And no lady would do such a thing. Certainly not Miss Thomson."

"What do you do, then?"

"Suffer."

That made Joan laugh again. She did it quietly, Simon noticed, one hand over her mouth. Not like Society ladies did, but rather like a woman used to close quarters and the need for stealth. Would she cry out, he wondered, when she made love? Or stifle her sounds in a pillow—or a man's shoulder? He quickly crossed one leg over the other, hiding his growing erection.

Then he cleared his throat. "It's, ah, a little easier for a lady, if only because a gentleman will declare himself at some point. And there are so many ways by which a gentleman may be made to declare himself without meaning to."

"And then you're stuck with a girl for life? Even if she's a vapor with eyelashes like the Thomson chick?" Joan shuddered. "This place screws men over almost as well as it does women, doesn't it?"

"Worse, I'd say." Simon ignored the way she'd put it. These days, in fact, he found it absurdly flattering that she did say such things in front of him. She trusted him enough, at least, to drop the façade when they were alone. "We protect ladies. Which means they can take shocking advantage of us if they're so inclined and we're unwary."

Joan's mouth quirked again. "When you chain a dog, you shouldn't be surprised if it barks."

"You do have a flattering opinion of your own sex."

"Women are people," she said calmly and cheerfully. "People are bastards. And someone who's caged—no matter how pretty the bars are—is going to get bored and restless and go for the only entertainment she can. Even if that's catching men."

"'Confined, then, in cages like the feathered race, they have nothing to do but to plume themselves and stalk with mock majesty from perch to perch,'" Simon quoted Wollstonecraft absently. The firelight played over Joan's face, casting her eyes into shadow. "I've heard the arguments before. I even sympathize, though they make me no more willing to play the fox. But most women don't seem unhappy."

"Most women don't know what they're missing. And I don't think you've exactly taken a survey."

She said it with enough good humor, but she was good at hiding her emotions. *It was a shitty world…but I had a place there. I wasn't wrong.*

"Are you unhappy?" he asked. "Really unhappy, I mean? I know the calls can get tedious."

"Not really. Frustrated, mostly."

The word had several meanings. Simon couldn't keep from thinking of the others. From the way Joan's color rose and her eyes widened, he didn't think she could either. She swallowed once and then slowly licked her lower lip, drawing it into her mouth slightly. Simon watched, hypnotized.

Absurd, really. He'd asked a serious question, and she'd given a serious answer. But he couldn't even talk to her in private without being distracted by other things. It was like being a schoolboy again, with all consciousness centered on one thing.

He could see the pulse in her throat, a rapid flutter. If he set his lips there—

Unwise, Simon thought, and at first the word was without meaning. His cock pulsed, aching pleasurably. He needed every iota of the control he'd learned as a magician to ignore the sensation and meet Joan's eyes again.

When he did, he thought that might have been an equally bad idea. Her eyes were golden hazel in this light, and her gaze was knowing, warm, even eager. Simon had to swallow hard and clench his fists on the chair. Even that gave him only momentary control. In a second, he'd move toward her—

Then Joan looked off to the side and took a deep breath. "What I mean," she said roughly, "is that I haven't even met Reynell yet."

Her comment was cold water to the face. They'd both needed it, but that made it no less of an unpleasant shock. "It'll happen. We don't receive him these days, of course, but you'll meet someone who does. Will you be happy then?"

She lifted her eyebrows. "I wouldn't say happy, exactly. I have a mission. It's something to do. If I wasn't working on that? Yeah, I might be unhappy."

"If you weren't risking your neck?"

"If I didn't have a purpose." Joan shrugged and lifted her chin. "Life kills you sooner or later. You might as well go out doing something worthwhile. Otherwise, you're just meat."

Whether she knew it or not, she'd come into the library out of more than simple boredom. And out of more than the desire for his company, much as Simon would have preferred otherwise. He heard the thwarted energy in her voice. "You should ride," he said. "In the mornings, I mean."

"To work off my...tension?"

"To meet more people. You can say that I sleep late," he added regretfully, realizing his absence would be necessary, "and take a groom with you. It's a public place, so your reputation should survive well enough."

―――∾∾∾―――

Even at nine in the morning—well before most wealthy city-dwellers got up, Simon had said—there were plenty of people in Hyde Park. "Hardly anyone around" meant something very different here.

But Joan could see why Simon had said it. There was room out here. The park stretched brilliant and green around her, the road was wide, and there was plenty of space between her sedate gelding and the agitated horse of the man in front of her.

She could probably pass him, Joan thought, tempted to nudge her horse into a trot. It would have been great to feel herself moving with some speed again. She was still too new to riding, though. With people around, speeding up would've been asking for an accident. Besides, she was here to see and be seen, and walking would serve that purpose best.

So Joan kept her horse to a sedate walk. It was still more exercise than she'd had in a while except for what little practice she'd been able to do in her room. She could feel the play of muscles in her thighs and the effort it took to keep her back straight. Not great effort, not anything Joan would have noticed if she hadn't been used to paying attention to her body, but it was there.

Strange that she could miss something after only two weeks, but she had—and she hadn't realized it until now. Part of it was being outside, she thought, and on her own. There was pale morning light out here, and there were bright flowers against thick green grass. She could lose herself in these things, away from the crowds and the endless fussing, chattering callers.

Not entirely, though.

A high, feminine voice called her name, and Joan turned quickly. She saw Thomson standing a little way off with another girl and two men. "Mrs. MacArthur!" she repeated, waving a hand.

She had come here to meet people. Joan reined in her horse and moved slowly toward the little crowd, looking them over as she approached.

Both girls were blonde, Thomson ashy and her friend almost silver. Both wore white, like most girls did around here, with their hair done loosely. It was probably supposed to make them look romantic. It did make them look ineffectual, which was the same thing as far as Joan could tell.

One of the men was tall, slender, and blond. The other was shorter and dark, with a well-groomed mustache. Joan did a quick mental flip through the people she'd met in the last few days and couldn't place either of them or the second woman.

"Morning," she said, smiling as she reached them. "Miss Thomson, it's good to see you again."

"Divinest chance," said Thomson, wide eyed as always. "I was just telling my friends about you, and they're all very eager to make your acquaintance."

"Desperately so," said the blond man. You could hear

sincerity in his voice if you were looking for that. You could also hear sarcasm, if you wanted, or lust.

This one is good.

"Must be destiny, then." Joan dismounted, hitting the ground even as the men were stepping forward to help her. She saw the blond's eyebrows go up but not, she thought, disapprovingly. "I was looking for company myself."

That was even true, in its own way.

"Please permit me to introduce you." Thomson stepped back a little and gestured to the dark-haired man, who smiled and bowed. "Mr. Cunningham."

"Mrs. Cole." That was the other woman. Up close, Joan could see that she was five years or so older than Thomson. Probably a chaperon, then, whatever else she was.

The blond man was watching her during the introductions, undressing her with his eyes and then evaluating what he saw. He was subtle enough—anyone else would've missed it—but Joan felt his gaze like she hadn't felt anyone else's in this time. Simon's had come close, but that had been simple lust. The way this guy sized her up was predatory.

Joan met his eyes, narrowed her own, and lifted her chin even as she smiled. There was no reason to make a scene, but she'd be damned if she'd let some over-dressed primitive get away with looking at her like she was meat for grilling.

He smiled back, looking a little surprised but mostly interested.

Well, thought Joan, *we can deal with that too.*

"Mr. Reynell," said Thomson.

Chapter 24

REYNELL BOWED LIKE A TREE BENDING WITH THE WIND. As he rose, he met Joan's eyes and smiled—knowing, sensual, and conspiratorial. *We know something they don't*, his expression said. *How nice for us.* "How do you do, Mrs. MacArthur?"

A red cloud passed across Joan's vision. She saw herself lunge forward, grabbing the knife from her sleeve while the others drew back, their faces blank with horror. She saw one hand settle in Reynell's hair, yanking his head back for the knife.

This is for Eleanor, you son of a bitch. And this is for everyone else.

She felt his blood spray over her hands.

In her whole life, she'd never wanted anything more.

But she couldn't do it. Not here, not in front of everyone. Too much could go wrong. *If I don't take him down with the first strike, he'll know something's up. And if he knows—if he even suspects—*

Besides, I need to find the book.

"How do you do?" Joan said, through half-numb lips. "It's a pleasure to meet you all."

She couldn't see any of their faces properly. The red cloud obscured them, like the shadow of the Earth on the Moon. Joan fought it back. She needed to know too much: Was Reynell suspicious? How much had she given away?

Little enough, it seemed. Reynell was still smiling at her, the smile that suggested they were in this together and nobody else understood. It made her teeth itch. She hoped he was just thinking of sex.

What had he heard about her?

No way of knowing.

At least her training seemed to have held up and she'd hidden her feelings well. Nobody was staring, and nobody had backed away. Thomson, in fact, had stepped forward. "Do *please* join us. Unless—well, are your hosts expecting you? Or are they about?"

Nobody could have missed the hopeful look on her face. And nobody could think it referred to Eleanor. Sad, really. Joan shook her head. "Mr. Grenville and his sister don't care so much for riding in the morning, I think. I brought one of the grooms with me, but he's waiting at the park entrance."

Thomson's mouth fell open a little, and she raised one gloved hand to it. "How very brave of you to come all this way alone."

Oh, very. Really dangerous park. Is it my independence that bugs you, or are you just disappointed that you can't drape yourself over Simon?

"I'm used to doing things by myself. Comes of growing up in the country, I suppose."

"I daresay they do things differently in…America, is it?" Cole asked.

"Montana," Joan said, nodding. "I'm afraid I'm going to make more than a couple mistakes while I'm here."

"Hardly mistakes," said Reynell smoothly. "I'd say, rather, that you'll probably show us several fascinating things about ladies from your home."

Again the voice that could be sincere or anything but. "Thank you," said Joan, keeping hers equally neutral. However, she dropped her eyelids, smiled, and took a closer look at Reynell from under her lashes.

He *was* handsome. High cheekbones, full lips, and big brown eyes with long lashes. He moved smoothly, he *talked* smoothly, and he practically oozed sex. Joan stopped her hands from clenching.

"I'd love to join you," she said, "but I'm not sure what you do about horses around here."

"Oh, that's no trouble at all," said Cunningham. He raised one hand and beckoned, and an older, plainly dressed man came over from where he'd been walking. "Meadowes, take Mrs. MacArthur's horse. Which direction did you ride from?" he asked Joan.

"Over there a bit. But I don't mean to impose. I can take him back myself."

"Not at all, dear lady, not at all," said Reynell. "After all, that would deprive us of your company, wouldn't it? And surely it would be more of a problem to injure so many than to make Cunningham spend a few moments without his man."

"Truly, it's no inconvenience," said Cunningham. He didn't look at Reynell. Clearly, something in the other man's voice had made him uncomfortable.

"Thank you, then," Joan said, and relinquished the horse's reins to Meadowes, squelching the urge to thank him as well. "Do you always take walks here in the morning?"

"Oh, yes!" said Thomson, her face lighting up again. "I find the morning very inspiring. Don't you, Mrs. MacArthur? It seems as if the entire world is made new.

And the light at this hour—it must have looked so in Eden itself!"

Joan bit the inside of her cheek. "Morning's one of my favorite times, yes," she said. "Especially with a place like this to ride in."

"Do you ride often?" Reynell asked.

"When I can," Joan said. "I'm not very good at riding in the city yet, but I hope to improve."

"If your hosts will permit," said Reynell, "I'd be very glad to go riding with you."

Now the double meaning was clear. Joan fought a shudder and cursed herself for being a wimp. If things went well, she was going to have to do a hell of a lot worse than listen to the man. She'd better start getting used to it now. *Besides, if Simon were saying these things, you'd be getting pretty hot.*

But this wasn't Simon. It wasn't any of the other men she'd met in London, from whom innuendo would probably be fun and, at worst, be nothing she hadn't heard before. This was Reynell, the man who'd thrown an innocent girl to the Dark Ones, who would destroy the world, and who would kill, in the end, half the people she'd grown up with. Her stomach clenched.

None of that mattered. "I'm sure they won't object," she said, "and I'm sure I'd love company." She smiled again through gritted teeth.

Walking wasn't nearly as much fun as riding. A woman couldn't take proper steps in a riding habit, just little mincing half steps that made Joan want to rip the damn skirt up the side before they'd gone more than a few feet.

It might have been all right in decent clothes. Or in decent company. Thomson was burbling about some poet she'd seen at someone's house, Cole and Cunningham were making the same polite comments Joan did, and Reynell was chiming in with the occasional not-quite-sarcastic aside about how lady poets of that stature were so very rare these days. Mostly, though, he was watching Joan.

He wasn't obvious about it. Joan had to give him that. She'd met plenty of men who couldn't keep their eyes from her chest or her ass and who hadn't bothered to hide the fact. Reynell wasn't like that. If Joan hadn't been aware of him, alert to every movement of his hands and every shift in his pace, she might not even have noticed where he was looking.

It might have been easier if he had leered. Joan was used to that. She could dismiss him then as just another drooling monkey-boy. But he looked at her subtly and, as he'd done before, with the cool, focused perception of a predator. It made Joan want to hit him. It also made her nervous.

He's good, she thought again. *Shit.*

"I beg your pardon?" said Reynell, sounding both surprised and irritated.

For a hideous moment, Joan thought that she'd spoken aloud—or that Reynell could read her thoughts. Everything went cold.

"I'm sorry," said Cunningham, "I'd asked if you were acquainted with the works of Mr. Stanford. Mrs. Cole and I would very much desire your opinion on the subject."

He was talking to Reynell, but he met Joan's eyes as he did, just for a second. It was long enough for her to see the concern in his face, though. She wasn't the only one who'd noticed Reynell's gaze. Joan wished she could have thanked Cunningham, maybe said something reassuring.

As if there were anything reassuring to say.

Reynell said that he wasn't familiar with the man. He didn't have time to develop the knowledge of music that Cunningham and Cole had. It was a source of great sorrow to him, but he had to stay an interested amateur.

"But perhaps," said Thomson sweetly, "that makes you the most valuable sort of person there is. After all, by coming innocent to a work, don't you open yourself to the purest of sentiments, untainted by prejudice or popular opinion?"

"A lovely sentiment. Beautifully put." Reynell turned a slow smile on her.

It made Thomson blush violently and look down. "You're too kind, sir."

Watching, Joan wanted badly to smack the girl in the back of the head and even more badly to shove her out of Reynell's sight. She was a babbling moron, yes, but she didn't deserve him.

"Celia mentioned that she met you at a spiritualist lecture, Mrs. MacArthur," Cole said. "Do you often take an interest in the unseen world?"

You'd be amazed.

"Oh, not in any organized sort of way," Joan said, "or I haven't until now. We didn't have many lectures in Montana, and I've been traveling too much, until recently, to attend any. Miss Grenville lent me a few books, though."

Reynell lifted his eyes to her face again, and this time

they were keen with another sort of interest entirely. "And what do you think, now that you've had the lecture as well as the reading?"

"I think I'd like to know more," Joan said, "before I develop any solid opinion. After all, it's such a large field, with so many new discoveries happening—"

"Oh, indeed!" said Thomson. "Do let me recommend that you pursue such studies further, Mrs. MacArthur. There's such a wealth of knowledge, and better than knowledge, understanding."

The beauty of ignorance, evidently, was only for things Reynell was ignorant about.

"It sounds worthwhile indeed," Joan said, and then sighed as she saw the entrance to the park ahead. "Unfortunately, this is where I have to leave you. It's past time I was getting back. The Grenvilles will worry if I stay out too long, and I'd hate to cause them any trouble."

"That would be unfortunate," Reynell agreed. Cunningham and Cole exchanged glances at the silky note in his voice. "But I hope to have the pleasure of seeing you again quite soon. As, I'm sure, do my friends."

"Since it seems like fate that we ran into each other, Mr. Reynell, I'm sure we'll do it again before too long."

"So am I," he said. "How fortunate for us all."

Chapter 25

INDEED, IT DIDN'T SEEM THAT JOAN WOULD GO LONG without seeing any of the people she'd recently met. She would never be the belle of the Season or the most sought-after guest at any particular party. She wasn't young enough for the former nor well-known enough for the latter. But she was pretty, intelligent, and startlingly unconventional, while still observing enough of the proprieties to be polite and, most importantly, a new arrival in a Season half over.

"You're quite a success," Simon said, opening one envelope in a thick stack of invitations.

Sitting in front of the fire with her feet up on the hearthstone, Joan made a face. "Yeah, like a two-headed dog."

Simon looked down at the heavy cream paper in his hand, an invitation to a dinner party. This one was from a man he knew, one who'd previously enjoyed some notoriety for his collection of Egyptian relics. "I wish I could tell you otherwise."

"Don't worry about it," Joan said with a low chuckle. "Better to be honest. Anyhow, it's not like it matters. I'm not really here to make friends or get married or…fit in, really. I'm glad to be a freak if it gets me what I want."

"Most freaks aren't nearly so attractive," Simon said without thinking.

He got a smile in return that brought swift heat to his face and a tightening somewhat lower. "Thanks," Joan said. She leaned forward, peering at the pile of papers on his desk. "What've we got, anyhow?"

Simon set the dinner-party invitation on the "maybe" pile. It was for two weeks hence, and they had more immediate concerns. "Tea with Lady Fairfax Wednesday afternoon. Tea with Mrs. and Miss Greenwood Friday afternoon."

"More weather," said Joan, disgusted.

"Not necessarily. Lady F. has a bee in her bonnet about spiritualism. If you're from America and you know anything about it, she'll probably ask if you can get an Indian brave to guide her through the underworld."

"What the hell do Indians have to do with America? Indians were from"—Joan waved a hand vaguely in the air and continued—"the East. Near Tokyo."

"American Indians are different. Lots of, ah, hunting. And spirits. They're great believers in spirits, I hear."

"Smart of them. She'll be disappointed, though. I can't summon one." Joan frowned, tapping her fingers on the arm of her chair. "Well, maybe I could, but I'd have to have a chicken or something to kill. And we'd probably get eaten anyhow."

They said that Lady Fairfax was always in at the end of the hunt, and that she went regularly to the bloodiest plays the theatre could show. "Tell her that. She'll be all the more impressed."

"As long as she doesn't make me do it. If I switch the details around a little, I can probably make her hair stand on end." Joan grinned. "What other gauntlets do you have me running?"

"Dinner at the Stancliffes'. That'll be a large affair. I'll brief you on the guests beforehand so all you should need to do is ask questions at convenient times. A small private dance at—oh Lord, the Coles'. Which means I'll be trying to dodge Miss Thomson the entire time."

"Oh?"

"She's Mrs. Cole's sister." It came out as a groan.

Joan snickered. "Should I be prepared to defend your honor?"

"Maybe," Simon said, and sighed. "Less than charitable of me, I know. But there are dozens of appropriately sentimental young men in London. I can't imagine why she hasn't settled on one of them."

"Couldn't say. I wouldn't choose you if I were a starry-eyed young idiot."

"So much flattery will spoil me," Simon said.

"Hey, I think it's a good thing that you're not running around babbling about fate and dreams and misty April whatever. But I don't do it myself." She shrugged and turned back to the fire, closing her eyes. "Maybe she wants what she can't have. That's human enough."

She said it very casually, but it was a reminder nonetheless. They both fell silent, each feeling the sudden, electric tension in the room. Perhaps, Simon thought, what was between them meant that they couldn't count on anything to be casual or to remain so. All that they could do was to try to get past these moments.

So he looked away from Joan, with the firelight playing over her face and throat, and back to the pile of invitations. "Three garden parties in the next fortnight. Someone's very confident of the weather."

"Don't you start," she said. Was there relief in her voice? Or disappointment? "What will I have to do at those?"

"Wander about and gossip, as far as I can recall.

Perhaps play croquet or go boating, if you feel active, or—do you play cards?"

"Three kinds of poker. Will that be okay?"

That was how Simon ended up teaching her piquet. He went to some pains to explain first that one didn't gamble for money, or at least ladies didn't, at least not at garden parties. "Quite probably not this one, anyway."

"Uh-huh," said Joan. She'd taken over shuffling the cards while Simon talked. In her hands, the cards hissed smoothly against one another, and she didn't even look down. "I guess I could always say we hadn't played much in America."

"Most people don't think you do anything else except perhaps shoot bears. And each other."

"Because everyone who lives in America is bugs-in-the-walls crazy, of course." Joan cut the deck and tapped it with quick, decisive movements. "I'm surprised they want to invite me to parties. I might get nervous and start stabbing people."

"Only if they offend you. Or cheat at cards."

"You're kidding me."

"Well, yes." Simon smiled at her. "Lady gunslingers are supposed to be much rarer. I don't think anyone's particularly nervous about you."

She stopped in the middle of dealing and gave him a disbelieving look. "But people do kill each other over card games?"

"Men can win or lose a great deal of money at cards," Simon said, "and sane men have been known to take extreme measures with a fortune at stake."

Joan shook her head. "There's only three or four things someone can knife you over. If you're a free human, that is—I bet anything goes with the Traitor Lords' people. None of them is a game. Or money."

"We do hang murderers," Simon pointed out. "We don't think it's all right."

"But you don't think it's crazy."

"Perhaps it's a sign that the world is crazy," he said, remembering late nights discussing just such things. "I confess I've felt that way myself from time to time."

Joan laughed shortly, with black humor in it. "If you're feeling it only from time to time, you're doing a hell of a lot better than most of us."

"But not you, surely," Simon said, half in jest. "You have proof otherwise, don't you?"

"Like hell I do." Joan leaned forward, spreading her hands in illustration. The deck of cards rested forgotten on the table between them. "Sure, something out there likes us. Is it more powerful than the things that hate us? I don't know. Is everything going to turn out okay? Nobody knows. Even the visionaries can't see all the future."

"Why not?"

"Powers and Entities, did you ever get the wrong girl!" She picked up the deck and started dealing again. "If I remember the priests right," she said after a moment, "and I never listened too closely, there are two theories. The first is that we're too human."

"Too human," Simon echoed, and thought of Gillespie. "Not entirely?"

"Me? Probably, or as near as makes no difference. I can't see the future or start fires. Maybe I'm carrying something—magic doesn't take hold as much on Dad's side..." She looked off at the fireplace for a second, cleared her throat, and went on. "Anyhow, it's probably nothing big, and it's sure nothing that shows up."

"But there are people in your time who aren't completely human?"

"Sure."

Simon stared frankly, like he couldn't have done with Gillespie. "Then what else are they?"

"I don't know that either. Things from Outside. Some of them are the Dark Ones probably, or close. Some of them aren't. We call the others the Watchers, and I couldn't tell you why."

"I could," said Simon, thinking of *The Book of Enoch* and a quotation from it: *There were giants in the earth in those days…*"It's having their blood that lets you see the future, then? And that blood's not strong enough in most people?"

"That's one way of thinking about it. Some people don't think even the Watchers, or the Powers—if they're different things—could see the future very well. They say there isn't a future after you get to a certain point or there are too many futures, or both. It'd be nice to think there was a great plan, but nothing's set in stone, is it? Or I couldn't be here."

"Unless you were meant to be." Simon found that a comforting thought. Amid a storm of revelations, he liked to think that some guiding force was behind everything.

"Maybe," Joan said, and she looked dubious. But there was something of gratitude in her face as she picked up the cards again and of understanding. "You never know."

Chapter 26

"LOVELY," ELEANOR SAID, TURNING FROM HER MIRROR to take a better look at Joan. Her eyes widened then, and her mouth fell open a little. "No, beautiful."

"That'd be more flattering if you weren't as surprised." When Eleanor blushed and started to murmur an apology, Joan laughed, waving it away with one white-gloved hand. "No, I understand. This really isn't anything like street clothes, is it?"

She'd been surprised herself. Long dresses and bright colors seemed almost normal now. She'd even—sort of—gotten used to the corset. But the skirts and blouses she wore every day, and even the high-necked, long-sleeved dresses she wore to parties, didn't begin to compare to this getup. Ball gowns and everything that went with them were a whole different world.

Even now, Joan wanted to take off her gloves and run her hands down the blue silk, or to spin the way she had after the maids had left. It was a stupidly undignified impulse but a compelling one all the same. "You're looking pretty gorgeous yourself," she said as distraction.

Eleanor wore a silvery-white gown, high necked compared to Joan's, with short puffed sleeves and pink ribbons trimming it. Her hair had delicate pink rosebuds wound through it and had been piled high on her head, a style even more impressive when Joan's own scalp was still on fire from a similar procedure.

A bit like ritual scars, in a way, all this stuff. "Hey, I can endure pain!" That's what you want in a wife—especially here.

"You really think so?" Spots of color burned high on Eleanor's cheeks, and her eyes were almost feverishly bright. "I wasn't quite sure about the color—perhaps I am still too pale to wear white—but it's the thing for young girls. And—well—I thought it was best."

She was too pale normally. Now, though, her pallor was hard to notice. Besides, Joan knew what *I thought it was best* meant. White was for purity. People in this demented place thought that was important, and Eleanor's had been called into question. She wanted to make a point.

"I do. You look great." Joan grinned at her. "And if anyone says otherwise, I'll break her nose."

Eleanor laughed. The sound was brittle and too high, but she did laugh. "Don't do that. Pugilism's not at all the thing this year."

"Bah," said Joan cheerfully. During the days before the dance, she'd worried. Now she felt the calm that came over her at the start of every mission, and she knew that she was ready. She looked decent, and she could dance well enough to get by. Her corset hid the flashgun really well, and the slit in her skirt, right above the long dagger strapped to her thigh, didn't show at all.

Everything was good.

———

Waiting downstairs, Simon wanted to drink, to pace, and quite possibly, to throw things.

There was simply too much that could go wrong.

Yes, Joan had danced before, but with him and in private. Yes, she'd been to a party or two, but always with him or Eleanor close at hand and with little one-on-one conversation. Yes, she'd met Alex and talked to him without any ill effect, but in a crowd when they'd met more or less by chance.

From what Joan had said, Alex had seemed interested. If he'd taken the bait, this evening would be his opening move. Gossip would have let him know that Joan was coming. He would have had ample time to prepare, and he would almost certainly be able to talk to her alone.

And do what? said the more reasonable part of his mind. *Guess who she really is? Insanity.*

True. But Alex could well guess that something was wrong, that Joan was trying to trap him, that her connection to Simon was deeper and less carnal than it appeared. All the arguments that had seemed so favorable to Simon at the beginning of this endeavor now looked utterly foolish.

And if Alex didn't guess? If he used his powers on Joan?

She can defend herself. And you want *him to make the attempt on her virtue. Or have you forgotten the reason you're helping her in the first place?*

It seemed different now.

Cold feet.

At first, Simon welcomed the sound of footsteps from the staircase. It was a distraction from his thoughts. It also promised that they would soon get the evening started and, thus, over with all the sooner.

Then he looked up, and everything in his chest seemed to tighten unbearably.

Joan was beautiful.

The dress was pale blue silk with indigo trim that complemented the violets tucked into Joan's hair. The dress flowed down her body like water, showing all the slim strength of her figure. Above the bodice, her breasts were creamy and inviting, pushed high by the corset, and her neck was long and slender, bare of cloth and hair alike. Looking at her, Simon was conscious of instant, aching desire.

That wasn't new. The regret was.

She looked like she belonged.

In that moment, Joan could have been any lady Simon had ever met, flirted with, or kissed. They could have met in some ordinary, unremarkable way and now be looking forward to nothing more than dancing and no worse threat than gossip.

He might not have been sending her into the arms of his worst enemy.

Simon swallowed. "You're exquisite."

"Thank you," she said lightly and smiled. "I'd like to think so. I can't do anything else in these clothes, so I might as well look good."

A certain light in her eyes and a rush of color in her face belied the casual way she spoke. Joan wasn't one to lose her head over compliments or dresses, Simon knew, but when she thought he was looking elsewhere, she smoothed one hand down her skirt as if to make sure it was real.

He wondered if any of the old fairy tales had survived to her time. Had she, in her hard and bloody journey from girl to woman, ever heard about disguised princesses and fairy godmothers? Would she have listened if she had?

Joan made an odd princess, and he was no fairy. And if she was transformed so that she could go to a ball and meet a man, then that meeting was still for an older and a grimmer purpose than had been in any of the romances.

Love and death, one of his teachers had said, *are the two great forces for change. In some respects, they are virtually identical.*

There was the regret again, as sudden and sharp as a knife to the throat. Not that he'd know anything about that, Simon thought. Joan would. That had been her world.

He shook his head quickly, trying to throw off his thoughts, as Eleanor came down the stairs. She looked flushed and nervous, but not actually unwell. She would come with them, though he and Joan had both said she could pretend to be ill. There was some cause for joy yet. He just had to hold on to it.

"I'm sure," Simon said, falling back on the old familiar phrases, "that I'm the most fortunate man in town tonight."

------*w*------

The first thing Joan did as they entered the Coles' ballroom was check for exits. There was the hallway she, Simon, and Eleanor had come through, two small rooms on the left side, and a large set of double doors on the right. People moved quickly through all of them. There were maybe forty or fifty guests, plus servants and the band, but in motion they looked like more. Like ants in a hill.

"Quite a crush, isn't it?" Simon murmured from behind her. "Don't worry. We don't trample more than six or seven people an evening."

Joan laughed. "That's reassuring. I'll only have to be the eighth slowest person here."

"You'll manage that easily enough."

That was true, considering that a number of older women and men were seated in the corners, talking and watching the dancers rather than dancing themselves. Joan saw a few of their heads turn as she, Simon, and Eleanor made their way across the floor, and she drew herself up. The knife at her thigh and the gun in her cleavage were comforting. They reminded her of who she really was: Joan, daughter of Arthur and Leia, who'd faced a million worse things than a ballroom full of overdressed, overfed primitives.

She looked through the crowd for Reynell but didn't see him. At least she'd have some time to adjust.

The room shone. Candles on the walls and in a chandelier overhead reflected in the long mirrors, doubling their light. Light sparkled off gems too, at the women's necks and hands, sometimes even in their hair or on their clothes. It was almost blinding. It was also gorgeous.

She ended up in a small clear space on the side of the floor, next to Simon and Eleanor, looking out at the whirling dancers themselves: white lace, emerald silk, gray-silver skirts that moved like the ocean before a storm; young men with flushed faces dancing stiffly with demure girls; older men with bushy whiskers chuckling at their partners; flowers, jewels, and motion.

Through the music, a voice. "Simon!"

It wasn't Reynell. The voice was too cheerful for that. Slightly loud too, but anyone would have to be a little loud here to be heard. Joan turned and saw a tall, skinny redhead making his way toward them. "And Miss Grenville," he went on. "It's such a pleasure to see you here again! Your guest too, of course."

The first thing that made Joan think she liked him was his wide and sincere smile. It was a little doglike in its sincerity, but dogs were pretty damn trustworthy. Also, Simon was laughing even as he bowed, and even Eleanor was relaxing.

"Henry," said Simon, "it seems like an aeon. This is Mrs. MacArthur. She's the daughter of my mother's friend. Lived in America until very recently. Mrs. MacArthur, this is Henry Meyers, an old friend of mine."

"Charming country, America," said Henry, and then added with a laugh, "or so I hear. I haven't had time to visit myself, so my opinion is based on every kind of wild tale. I'm sure you've heard most of them."

Joan grinned back at him. "Not nearly enough. I like hearing what other people think about it."

"In that case, I must press my advantage now, when you've just arrived, and ask you and Miss Grenville for a waltz each. If Simon will permit it, of course. Fearsome guardian that he is." Henry widened his eyes in mock fear and shrank back, pressing one hand to his throat.

"You should've gone on the stage, Henry. You're wasted on this crowd," Simon said.

"But this crowd is so very charming. Miss Grenville, may I?"

Eleanor blushed but smiled and didn't look away. "I'm very much out of practice."

"All the more reason to dance with me then. I'm sure you'll do excellently. You'll look even better in comparison to me, and everyone will think you're the soul of charity."

However goofy he acted, there was something warm and genuine in his eyes when he looked at Eleanor. Joan didn't know if it was love, but it looked at least like honest liking.

Maybe that was what Eleanor responded to, because she smiled again and placed her fingers in Henry's outstretched hand without either hesitating or freezing up. "If you're willing to be patient," she said, "I'd be glad to."

"For you, my lady, I would wait until the end of time."

"Since that's settled..." Simon drawled. He turned toward Joan, holding out his hand. "Mrs. MacArthur?"

Touching him was like picking up a live wire. More pleasant, sure, and probably less lethal—at least in the short term—but it focused all her attention on a single moment of contact. The whole world narrowed to the hand holding hers, the one on her back, and Simon's body in front of her, warm and lean and inviting. Joan looked up into his face and caught her breath at the desire there.

They couldn't act on it, but that didn't matter. Here and now, while the music played, they could at least come as close as would ever be wise.

No, Joan thought as they started to move. They'd already come closer than that.

———

Other women were better dancers. Oh, Joan did well enough, but she had to catch herself a few times during the fastest part of the song. Other women were better flirts too. They'd have chattered gaily, pouted, beamed, looked up at Simon from under their eyelashes, and generally done their best to be alluring.

Yet in ten years of dancing, Simon had never enjoyed himself as much as he did during that one waltz with Joan.

There were good reasons for it, reasons that had nothing to do with desire or sentiment. It was important to remember that. Dancing with a woman of a decent height, for instance, was a relief. A man got neck cramps looking down at a tiny partner. Having a dance partner who wasn't marriage minded was also a refreshing change, as one felt less like a stag at bay.

Simon reminded himself of these things. Both of them were true, but neither was an adequate explanation. Not since he was sixteen had his nerves been at such a fever pitch. He was painfully aware of the few inches between them and of the firm warmth of Joan's body, even through the silk of her gown. It was a wonder, he thought once, that he could dance—or walk.

But the dance itself was a pleasure, not the horror of frustrated desire that he'd been expecting. It was good to move with Joan, to have her echo his steps with perfect confidence. The fact that following didn't come naturally to her made it better, as if she was trusting him specifically when she responded to his lead.

Of course, that was nonsense. He and Eleanor had trained Joan well, and she was so utterly professional that she wasn't likely to balk at following anyone in a dance.

Yet he couldn't help but feel pleased. After all, he was the only man in the ballroom to whom Joan would've complained if she hated the whole affair. She hadn't. She was smiling up at him instead, and the desire in her face blended with friendly challenge: *Do your worst. I can keep up*.

Surely he was the only man in the room who knew she was having a good time.

When the waltz was over—too damn soon—and Simon had walked Joan back to the edge of the floor, he found Archie from the lecture already standing with Henry and Eleanor, and another young man was drifting through the crowd in their direction. "Mrs. MacArthur, how very good to see you," Archie said. "And you too, Simon."

"Yes," he said, "how fortunate."

"Your sister," Henry said, "dances divinely, by the way. You should take a turn with her, Simon. Keep her from being plagued by fools like me. It's the sort of thing that must be tiring for a young lady."

Eleanor didn't look particularly tired, but she had fallen silent again, probably because Archie had arrived. Though Archie and Eleanor had been introduced, they weren't on comfortable terms with each other, and Simon heard and appreciated the hint in Henry's suggestion.

Besides, he would have to leave Joan alone for their plan to work, and dancing with Ellie might keep his mind off that plan. Simon found that he also didn't want to watch the way Joan was smiling at Archie now, lifting an eyebrow and shaking her head at some compliment or other. She'd turned a little, and Simon could see her face only in profile, but her expression wasn't unlike the way she'd looked before while dancing with him.

She was a very good actress. She had badly needed his help. A façade could have many levels, he knew. Where did he stand with hers?

Joan didn't have to worry about working with Archie or Henry. She would be discreet, Simon knew; she would do nothing to endanger her mission. He almost wished she wouldn't be. It would have given him more reason to object.

He'd never been a jealous man. He knew very well that he'd had his chance already.

"Yes," he said abruptly, turning to Eleanor. "Ellie, would you do me the honor before all your dances are taken?"

"Of course," she said, and placed her hand in his.

She was still nervous, Simon knew, but she was here and she was relaxing by the minute. That was something, and he inwardly thanked Henry for it. He tried to think of that.

Mostly, he tried not to see Joan.

Chapter 27

"...AND SO WE ENDED UP GOING BEFORE THE HEAD-master," Henry said, leading Joan back to the side of the room, "both of us soaking wet. Simon claimed that it had all been my idea, of course."

"Of course," Joan said, laughing. The first four dances had gone damn well. She'd been lucky in partners too. Henry had talked easily the whole time, and Archie almost didn't speak at all. The middle-aged man who'd claimed her for the third set had been glad to discuss mythology, and Simon...had been Simon. "He was the ringleader a lot?"

"Off and on. We all took turns, though. To be honest, it was me as often as it was Simon or—Alex." Henry stopped short.

Reynell stepped out in front of them and bowed smoothly. "Mrs. MacArthur. Mr. Meyers. Good evening to you both."

"Evening," said Joan, and quickly scanned the crowd for Eleanor. She wasn't nearby, thank the Powers, but either dancing with someone or getting refreshments. Simon, of course, was nowhere in sight.

Henry was making his own greetings, as stiffly polite about it as someone with his personality ever could be. He probably didn't know about Reynell's weirder activities, but he sure knew something. That was all over his face.

Reynell, who couldn't have missed the look, just

smiled. "If I'm not interrupting," he said, "I was hoping to claim a dance with Mrs. MacArthur. Unless, of course, she's otherwise engaged."

"No," Joan said, "I don't believe I am." She smiled at Reynell and then back at Henry. "It's been a pleasure, Mr. Meyers. I hope I'll get the chance to talk to you soon."

"Yes, of course," Henry said, clearly worried but just as clearly unable to say anything.

Poor guy. Joan wished she could've said something: *I know what he is. I have this under control. It's all right.*

Though she really didn't know about either of the last two.

This was the next step, though. And, hell, it was just a dance. How bad could it be?

Dancing with Reynell was like rolling in carrion.

That was stupid, and Joan knew it. Reynell was handsome and well dressed. He danced well. He didn't try to grope her or breathe in her ear. Outwardly, he was a great partner.

And Joan had never been sensitive. The only auras she'd ever seen were the aftermath of concussive fire. She'd sensed the Dark Ones by having sharp eyes and keen hearing, and by knowing what to look for. There'd never been anything more about her. She'd never seen more than the flesh.

So there was no reason why she should want to throw up right now.

Reynell's aura *was* probably black and as rotted as a bad tooth. In the underworld, his hands were probably dripping with blood. Joan had no way to know that, though. She couldn't actually feel the corruption oozing out of his palms and over her body because it didn't work like that, and she wouldn't sense it if it did. Everything she felt was psychosomatic.

She kept repeating that to herself. It let her smile up at Reynell without gritting her teeth.

At least he didn't speak for the first few seconds of the dance. That gave her time enough to get herself under control and to note that he'd clearly been trying to impress her by coming out of the crowd like that. That was a good sign. It helped to analyze him, and it broke the whole thing down into information gathering and mission objectives. Colder things. More sterile things.

"You dance very well, Mrs. MacArthur," he said.

Bullshit. Between her lack of experience and her urge to pull away, she'd missed two steps already. He clearly wanted to get her attention back, though, so she smiled up at him. "Do I? You're too kind."

"I've rarely been accused of that."

"Then let me be the first. I'm rather out of practice, and I know it. This sort of dancing's new to me."

"Ah, yes, you're new this Season, aren't you?" Reynell tilted his head and smiled, a slow, insinuating thing. "Here to guard Miss Grenville's virtue, I hear."

That was the opening shot you didn't talk about—virtue, or the lack thereof—that in ballrooms. A proper woman of this time would've said something shocked and cutting to Reynell, or maybe even slapped him. For once, Joan wished she were proper.

"That implies, sir," she said, meeting his eyes squarely, "that her virtue is in any danger."

"She's a lovely young woman."

"Respectable and intelligent as well." With a little shrug, Joan added, "Besides, any serious danger to her honor would hardly find me much of an obstacle."

"Oh, I'm sure you can be quite intimidating if you try."

"I've heard that before." Joan gave him a playful look. "Do I scare you?"

"No. But then, I don't frighten easily."

"Good to know."

The tempo changed and they sped up to follow it. Joan looked over Reynell's shoulder to avoid getting dizzy and watched the dancers beyond them. A very few were visibly bored or nervous; most were smiling and some laughing. But then, so was she.

Was anyone in that crowd faking it as much as she was? You could hide all sorts of things if you knew how.

"Have you been acquainted with Miss Grenville long?" Reynell asked very lightly.

Want to know how much she's said about you, you son of a bitch?

Joan shook her head. "A year, maybe, through writing to her and her brother. Only a month or so in person. And, of course, it's hard to be really acquainted with someone that intellectual."

"Oh?"

"Well, she doesn't talk very much about herself. It's all mythology, philosophy, poetry. Interesting, but it doesn't give me the feeling I know her very well." Forcing a laugh, Joan added, "And it makes me feel pretty vain."

"A little vanity suits beautiful women."

"You seem to think so, the way you're encouraging it. Why do you want to know about Miss Grenville?"

The question was innocent enough, but she thought

something flickered in Reynell's eyes before he answered. "Merely curious. You said she introduced you to spiritualism."

Gushing like Thompson was not the way to his heart. Joan shrugged again and said diffidently, "She gave me books, at least. And got me to go to that lecture."

"And now that we're no longer surrounded by ardent devotees, what did you really think?" He gave her a conspiratorial smile. "I promise I'll never tell."

"I think it would be amazing." Joan let that lie for three seconds and then added, "If I were convinced that it was real."

"But you're not?"

"People see what they want to. I haven't seen anything myself. Until I do, I'm not going to make up my mind."

"Honest indecision? In this society?" Reynell widened his eyes, laughing. "You'll have to learn better, you know. You'll stand out like a sore thumb without some sort of ignorant devotion or other."

Her own laughter caught Joan by surprise. Yes, there was a reason Simon had liked this man once. Seeing it made everything worse.

"I'll do my best to be a fanatic then," she said, forcing cheer into her voice. "Just give me some time to catch up."

"I'd like to do more than that, if you'd be willing," he said not quite suggestively. "As I'm sure you've heard, I have something of an interest in the subject myself."

"I hope you're not offended then."

"Not at all. Your honesty's quite refreshing. And if I may, I look forward to showing you a great deal you haven't known before." His voice deepened just a little, enough to make his meaning clear.

As the waltz ended, Joan looked back at him. The heat in his eyes was unmistakable.

"I'm always interested in…new experiences," she said, leaving her hand in his as he walked her back toward the side of the room. "I hope you can provide a few."

"Be certain of it," he said. Then he bowed and drifted off, moving through the crowd with a grace neither she nor Simon had managed.

Joan watched him walk away. The doors to the terrace were across the ballroom. The doors to the hallway and the dressing room were a little nearer. But people were coming toward her already—Henry and Eleanor, she saw as they drew closer—and she had to stay behind.

So she lifted her chin, smiled, and let them take her off for a glass of lemonade. She danced with more men, talked a little and listened much, and managed to hold on to her dinner until she was back in her room.

See, she thought to herself then, as she raised her head from the basin, *you're doing just fine*.

Chapter 28

Two weeks later, Alex thought that the whole thing was coming together rather well. If Simon and Eleanor had mentioned anything to Mrs. MacArthur, they clearly had not included any particular slurs on his own good name. They couldn't, after all. The actual circumstances had been far too odd to tell a stranger, and anything they could make up would implicate dear Eleanor as much as it would Alex.

Society certainly spread its rumors, but Society, by and large, thought that Alex was largely innocent and Simon far too quick-tempered. Of course, doing such things with a young girl hadn't been quite proper, but in the end, it was only a foolish party game gone wrong. Especially now that Eleanor was clearly not suffering any of the more visible consequences of impropriety.

Nonetheless, he broached the subject—he hoped—before Mrs. MacArthur could. It was at a garden party at one of the few houses near the city that could manage that sort of thing, and they were walking under a line of stately oaks. "I suppose you've wondered," he began, after a suitable period of looking distressed and brooding, "why Mr. Grenville and his sister avoid me."

"A little," she admitted, and her face went grave and attentive. Rather gratifying, really. "I'd thought maybe you just didn't know each other, but—"

"No, I'm afraid not. We used to know each other very

well." He sighed. "And I'm afraid it's rather my fault that we're no longer on speaking terms."

"What happened?"

Alex sighed again and ran a hand through his hair. "A spiritualist experiment gone badly. Very badly. I know you're skeptical about such things."

"Just unconvinced so far," Mrs. MacArthur said. "I don't claim to know everything. And I've never done any of these experiments. I'd like to know what you think."

Better and better. Alex looked off into the distance, down the lane of trees toward the wrought-iron fence beyond. "I wish I knew myself," he said, with just the right touch of self-recrimination. "Miss Grenville had volunteered to serve as medium. She truly seemed glad of the experience. I tried to call forth a spirit. I succeeded."

Mrs. MacArthur's eyes widened, and her mouth opened a little. She didn't gasp or draw away, though, and neither did she laugh. She gave him a long, thoughtful look instead, weighing his claims against some internal standard. It would be great fun to see how she'd respond to a summoning. Breaking that much self-control would be worth it, even without Simon's pain as relish.

Alex cleared his throat. "I'm still not sure who— or what—I summoned. I was far less prepared than I should've been. Whatever the spirit was, it took control quickly. It was very hostile. Dark."

As all real power is in the end. What would you have me do, Simon? Alex could see the other man now, walking with his sister at the end of the lane. *Work one-handed? This isn't some schoolboy game. We're not bound by old men's rules, and there's no pride in second place. You'll learn that. A new experience for you, I should think.*

Bitterness cramped his gut and closed his throat. Alex looked away from the figures on the grass.

Mrs. MacArthur put a hand on his arm. It was an impulsive gesture, and she drew her hand back after a moment, but the sensation of her touch remained. She looked unsettled too, either by the story or by the contact. "It must've been awful," she said. "For both of you."

"It was. I was trying to think of what to do when Simon came in. I don't know quite what he'd heard, but he obviously assumed the worst. And I was in no mood to argue well." Reynell rubbed his face, wincing in memory. "I can't blame him for his actions then. When I came to, he was gone. With Miss Grenville."

"And the...spirit?" A trace of skepticism remained in her voice. For the moment, though, she listened as she might have done to a ghost story on a winter night, not quite believing but willing to be convinced for the time being.

"Simon must have found a way to banish it. He has a little knowledge of that sort of thing himself, if he's not given it up entirely since the incident. We went to a great many lectures together as boys."

They'd even bought admission to some of them. Others, like most of those they'd managed to attend at school, they'd sneaked into. A sudden memory rose up, clear and warm, of twelve-year-old Simon keeping lookout while Alex squirmed through a gap in one of the hedges.

If a master comes, I've dropped a ball somewhere and I'm trying to get it back.

Alex, you know I'm no good at lying.

Everyone's got to have some fault, I suppose.

Just try to be quick.

As the nun said to the bishop.

Stop making me laugh. It looks bad.

Those days had been warmer and full of more sun, and the world had stretched out wide before the two of them, ready to be explored or conquered. Alex supposed he was man enough to admit that the memory hurt now in the face of Simon's betrayal.

More than man enough to be revenged for it.

Judas was hanged, wasn't he? Seems too quick, somehow.

"Sounds like a bad misunderstanding all around," said Mrs. MacArthur. "I'm sorry to hear it."

"You're very kind," said Alex.

She really was a handsome woman, he thought. Her slim figure suited the frothy white dress she wore very well. Her hair, tossed in the light breeze, shone golden, and best of all, her hazel eyes were bright with sympathy for him.

Alex felt a sudden rush of kindness toward her. It would be best, perhaps, not to harm her in the end. There were plenty of other women in the world. Perhaps setting Mrs. MacArthur up as his mistress and making her happy in that station would be the way to hurt Simon.

After all, they said that the best revenge was living well. A man of Alex's abilities had many ways to ensure that.

"She has a great deal of range," Eleanor was saying, "but she needs more precision to be really skilled. But then, she's young…and I'm dreadfully afraid I'm babbling at you, Simon. I'm sorry."

"No," he said, and tore his gaze away from the figures walking by the line of trees. Eleanor was talking to him now. She'd gone to the opera the other night with two of her friends from school, and today she had been sitting in the sun and smiling. The last thing Simon wanted to do was discourage any of that.

And yet her words fell on his ears like rain, pleasant but meaningless. "I'm sorry," he said. "You're not babbling. I'm tired, that's all."

"Yes," she said carefully. "It must be very taxing escorting two young women all over town. I can't imagine it's how you usually spend your time."

"Hardly," said Simon. "But I'm finding that I quite enjoy it so far."

That was devilishly true. Perhaps he'd needed to get away from his habitual clubs and his studies. Perhaps his enjoyment of the last few weeks had merely been a matter of fresh perspective or a heightened appreciation of everything that was at risk.

He feared, however, that it was really due to the company. To Joan, to be precise: smiling a challenge up at him while they danced, muttering under her breath when he beat her at cards, looking askance and skeptical during lectures and unguardedly amazed at the Royal Zoo. Talking seriously with Eleanor about sensational novels and Greek myths. Telling him about magic in her world, her hands moving in quick, descriptive gestures.

She'd moved into his memories with as much ease as she'd moved into Society. Simon wasn't sure he was comfortable with either.

"Simon." Eleanor's voice was gentle. "Pretending doesn't really help either of us, does it?"

"Pretending?" he asked, drawing his attention back to her, now with guilt added to his uneasiness. If he was neglecting Ellie in addition to everything else…

But she wasn't looking hurt. Her gaze went to the end of the lane, and she pressed her lips together quickly. There was nothing out of the ordinary where she was looking. Joan was laughing up at Alex, and he was shrugging gracefully and shaking his head. Nothing too scandalous there. He was a grown man, she a grown woman, and her husband had been dead three years.

Eleanor swallowed.

Simon realized that his nails were digging into his palms. He made himself unclench his fists and put a hand on his sister's shoulder. "We can go elsewhere," he said, "if it would be easier for you."

Eleanor shook her head. "He…he's going to be in Society for quite a while," she said. "I'd best get used to it, hadn't I?"

"You shouldn't have to."

"But I do. Besides, it—it must be worse for you, in a way, and you don't avoid him."

"That's different," Simon said lamely.

In the silence that followed, he had to look back again. Joan had drawn closer to Alex now, and they were talking more seriously. Sunlight danced on both of them, drawing gold from their hair. They looked quite the matched set.

"I worry about her too," Eleanor said.

"Worry. Yes."

Seeing Joan with Alex was very like watching a

snake charmer and the swaying cobra in front of him, knowing that death waited with one wrong note.

There had been moments over the past two weeks when Simon hadn't known who was the charmer and who the serpent. Of course, it was beyond unlikely that Alex would use any magic on Joan in such a public setting, particularly with Simon around. Simon told himself this and then told himself again.

Simple charm could have a great influence. So could deceit. Alex had always been able to get any woman he wanted. There were plenty of tactics that he was willing to use unscrupulously, even without bringing magic into the picture.

Was ever woman in this humour wooed? Was ever woman in this humour won? The lines from Shakespeare came back to Simon, mocking and sure.

No. Joan knew Alex's true nature. She was no innocent. She'd come here to kill the man, for Heaven's sake.

You wouldn't let her. You said there was a chance he'd repent.

Eleanor was watching him closely now, her eyes mild but concerned. "I think," she said slowly, "that the sooner this is over—whatever it is—the better we'll all be. It's hard on Joan as well."

"Is it?" Simon turned away from Joan and Alex. "Has she talked to you?"

"No, of course not," Eleanor said, blinking. "You told her not to. But she's been restless ever since the ball, especially on nights when they've met. I hear her walking the floor next to me sometimes when she thinks everyone's asleep."

His first thought was of the night in his library, of the

pain on Joan's face and the way she'd looked at the desk, alone and surrounded by darkness. She'd seemed less shadowed, under less strain, when they'd come to London.

But perhaps she'd just become better at concealing it from Simon, or he'd made himself blind to it, as he'd been blind to so many things in the past. If he went to her one night, offered comfort...

It was quite possible that she'd turn away. At best. After all, he'd had his chance once. If she chose to seek distraction with someone she didn't work with, someone who hadn't rejected her once, he couldn't quite blame her.

On the heels of that thought, Simon realized that Joan might be losing sleep for many reasons now. God knew his own nights hadn't been entirely restful, with her in his mind.

He wished he could be certain that he was in hers.

Eleanor looked up at Simon, biting her lip. "You... won't tell her I said anything, will you? I wouldn't want her to feel I was gossiping. I'm just...well, worried."

"I'll keep it a secret," Simon said, and tried to smile. He would, after all, because he doubted anything good would come of confronting Joan with the information.

No matter how much he wished otherwise.

Chapter 29

"MEETING REYNELL AGAIN?"

Joan was in the hall, putting on her hat and gloves, when Simon came around the corner. The way he looked her over, though she wore the same pink-and-gray dress he'd seen many times before, stirred her blood. The way he asked the question irritated her. It was too knowing somehow and too resigned.

This was your idea, buddy.

So she shrugged and glanced in the mirror before she replied. "I do sometimes see other people, you know."

Simon nodded. "But this time—"

"Yes. We're meeting some of his friends." She added, "Spiritualist friends," trying to remind Simon of the reason for all this.

He'd been acting more than a little weird lately: hiding out in his study most of the time, not talking a whole lot when she did see him, and almost flinching every time Reynell's name came up. Second thoughts, maybe, now that push had come to shove. Maybe deceiving his old buddy seemed worse now, or maybe the possibility of having to kill Reynell was scaring him.

Maybe he was just scared now that they were coming closer to their goal. Joan could sympathize.

She'd had no chance to talk to him about it, though. Either he "wasn't to be disturbed" or they were in public or with Eleanor. One of these days, Joan thought, she'd have it out with him, and to hell with "not to be disturbed." Not right now, though. "I'll be back before dinner," she said, and headed out the door.

———※———

Simon knelt in darkness. After he'd traced the necessary designs on the floor of his "private study," he'd blown out the candle, leaving the room in darkness. Then he'd closed his eyes. No special clothing this time. It would only remind him of what he was trying to leave behind.

The floor in this room was harder than its twin back at Englefield and colder too, made of stone rather than wood. Simon acknowledged the cold, recognized the hardness, and then sent the thought away, letting it become part of the black formlessness that was slowly filling his mind.

He breathed in slowly, smelling sandalwood, cinnamon, and a touch of opium. The last was an unfortunately necessary part of leaving his body and the reason he'd done it only a few times before. There were houses in France that he still remembered in his nightmares. He'd seen them only briefly, but that had been enough.

That thought too became part of the blackness. Simon held still with the backs of his hands resting on his thighs, filled his lungs again, and tried to think of nothing.

It was hard, harder than it had been since his first time, when he'd had to overcome both his own disbelief and the impatience that was part of being fifteen. Now there was neither, but dread had taken their place. Simply knowing how much he needed to succeed at this would keep him from doing so, and yet that knowledge clung to him long after he'd lost awareness of his knees and stopped consciously smelling the incense.

But he was stubborn, and he was trained.

In time, fear vanished. Anticipation vanished. Simon no longer thought of Joan and Eleanor or of how much he risked on this journey. He simply floated in blackness that wasn't true blackness because it really had no color; he existed no longer as a body or even quite as a mind. There was an eternal void that was also the form of everything, and Simon was almost a part of it.

Not quite. He was separate enough to feel the power as it began to wash over him like a warm breeze and to clutch it as he'd grabbed for Aladdin's reins on that cloudy day back in early June.

The power filled him, and Simon was suddenly aware of himself again. He had a presence but not a human one. There were wings, instead, beating without any command of his, and the feeling that he was hovering in the air. When he looked down, he saw a hunting bird's talons, faint and blue.

Owl, he thought, embracing the familiar, and his form seemed more solid with the word.

The room was back too. Now it was overlaid with green and blue and gold, gold particularly in the circles inscribed around Simon's body, which still knelt on the floor. The circles looked brighter and more real than anything else in the room, as if stone, wood, and even flesh were no more than the sheets laid over the furniture in a closed house, with only what lay beneath them to give them shape.

God willing, he thought, the book would stand out the same way.

Flapping his wings, he wheeled away from the body and out through the wall.

—⁓—

Outside one's body, travel was much simpler: only a matter of thinking hard enough about the place where one wished to go and being familiar with it. Simon had known Reynell's house a long time. As he flew through the streets, he only had to keep a part of his mind trained on the house. It pulled at him like a magnet, and he knew exactly which way to go.

That was fortunate. Simon could easily have been distracted for a very long time by the things he saw on the way.

There were spirits in the air, dancing, ephemeral things. Simon spoke to a few of them briefly, but they mostly kept their own counsel, if they had any to keep. The people below him were more interesting. He could see auras in this form, after all.

Some of the people in the streets had a swirl of bright colors surrounding them, like a child's toy or a music-hall advertisement. Others were dimmer. Or darker. Some of the latter were blotched in places with what seemed like rot. Simon saw one man who walked inside a black cloud, and he didn't stop to look twice.

Houses had auras too, as golden as a hearth fire or dull wool-jumper gray or, in one case, a very oceanic blue-green. The last time he'd seen Alex's from this vantage point, it had been an almost ethereal shade of silver. When Simon drew closer, he realized how much that had changed.

In the physical world, it was a handsome, well-made house in the fashionable part of town. Alex's father kept mostly to the country these days, so Alex had the place all to himself. Looking at it from the astral, that much—and more—was plain.

The silver had become gray but not merely dull, as the other house's aura had been. This gray was dead and leprous, with a slight reddish cast that suggested rust or worse. The whole aura seemed to crawl, and the windows yawned like mouths.

Beyond them—what?

Simon flew up to the study window but didn't approach. Not yet. Alex might not suspect anything specific, but he had wards up all the same. Simon could see them as he grew closer, rising concentric circles around the house that glowed faintly green. If he wasn't very careful, Reynell would know about the intrusion.

Then again, wards had always been one of the areas where Simon had bested his friend. Alex had teased him about it when they were boys—*You'd make a good parson, Grenville, with a mind like that. Thank God you have me to keep you out of danger, eh?*

When Simon got close enough to make out the patterns, he saw what he'd been expecting and nearly laughed. Whatever skill he'd gained elsewhere, Alex was as clumsy at ward-craft as he'd ever been. There was a point, just at hand, where a bit of unraveling would let Simon slip in like a cat through a stable door.

He stopped himself midair, reached out with one claw, and just...nudged one of the symbols. Very gently.

It floated out of the way, and he slipped past, through the window and into the study.

He almost screamed.

There was something here. Simon didn't know if

it was Joan's book or not. If it was, even incomplete, it was more powerful than he could've imagined. The whole room was covered in blackness. It writhed and rippled. It hissed—or something did, just loudly enough to insinuate itself into the senses.

Somewhere beneath it, Simon saw blood oozing from the walls.

This isn't the book. Or it isn't just the book. Something horrible happened here.

Alex, what are you doing?

Simon tried to peer closer, to see if there was a spot where the book itself—or whatever—lay. Slowly, beyond the spasmodic movements, a deeper darkness started to appear—

Something moved behind him.

Simon bolted forward toward the window, thanking God that shock had kept him from coming too far into the room. He made it as far as the sill before a tentacle wrapped around his leg.

The…creature…surged forward. Its tentacle pulled back at the same time, tugging at Simon. His leg burned at the touch. Simon pulled back, raking at the creature with his other claw, and the thing shuddered in what might have been pain.

Its grip was strong, though. It yanked again, and this time Simon went with it.

As he did, the world started to blur. The walls of the study melted like spun sugar in the rain, and the air crackled black and white. Simon felt that he was moving—spinning—very fast, not just toward the tentacled creature but toward something much larger. Some*where* much larger.

It was taking him home.

Simon cried out, seven short words of Power. Strength poured out of him, leaving him as weak as an invalid, but coursing into the burning gold runes that appeared in the thing's strange not-flesh. It lurched backward.

Then it threw him, casting him away from itself without any aim, only with its own version of desperation. Simon flew, and the world became a whirlwind around him.

He could not perceive most of the places he passed through. God was that merciful, at least, or perhaps his own mind intervened to save itself. All he saw was a jumble of shapes and colors, most unrecognizable but some sickeningly familiar. They rushed by at great speed, as if he were looking out the window of some absurdly fast-moving train.

Simon clung to humanity by teeth and nails. He thought of a world where things fell down and triangles had three sides, where people walked upright with two arms and one head each. For a minute, he held those thoughts—but they were too abstract, and the shapes he saw blasted them out of his mind quickly.

Then he pictured Joan's face. Not as it had been recently, laughing above silk dresses or under broad hats. He thought of her at her most savage, when she'd sprung up from the library table with the letter opener; he remembered her in the circle of stones. He clung to that memory of strength and prayed for the whirlwind to stop.

Then it did. And he was somewhere else.

The sky was greenish gray, lit sullenly by flickering lightning. Dark shapes moved there too, huge and purposeful. Their outlines hurt the eye.

Simon hung in the air below them, still a spirit and hopefully beneath their notice.

Below him was a city. Or what had been one once.

In places, the buildings still stood, high steel squares with many small windows, most of them broken by now. Other buildings raised jagged, shattered edges to the sky or had disintegrated into a welter of rust and beams. Between them, the narrow streets were full of rusting metal boxes.

Automobiles? Simon had seen illustrations in the papers. These were sleeker, though, and smaller. The shape might be similar—in the future.

He'd been thinking of Joan.

Logically, he had no way to be certain he was in her time. She'd given no real descriptions, named no identifying features save squalor, and a hundred worlds might be as bleak or worse. In his gut, though, Simon knew where he was.

This is her world.

Another flash of lightning allowed him to see more clearly.

The automobiles were packed together, with maybe an inch or two between some of them, in a jam worse than any London traffic he'd ever seen. Thousands of them, Simon thought, maybe hundreds of thousands. Even with one person in each, there'd been a vast river of people in those streets once.

The knowledge crept into his mind, sickening and inescapable. *They were trying to get away.*

He was suddenly very glad that he couldn't see into the automobiles. Perhaps, he told himself, they were all empty. Perhaps everyone had gotten out, when it became clear that driving wouldn't help, and had escaped on foot. He doubted it.

We were losing, Joan had said.

White mounds were piled against the buildings. Not snow. As he watched, an...object...fell from the top of one, rolling down it and finally coming to rest against the rusted side of an automobile.

Figures moved in the darkness: human figures, or near enough, running from the shelter of one building to huddle against the side of another. No—not running. Scurrying.

They were prey. And they knew it.

One of them looked upward, responding to who knew what. Simon glimpsed a face, very small from that distance, that was one-eyed, gaunt, and desperate. Then a formless darkness whipped down and blotted it out.

The others ran instantly and as one. Their very organization was horrible in its meaning. This death, horrible as it was, was no shock. Perhaps no death was in this place.

Darkness followed very quickly.

Simon would have screamed. But he knew nobody could hear him.

Chapter 30

WELL, THAT WAS…ILLUMINATING. AND I NEED A BATH.

Spending time with Reynell was better in a crowd. He still smirked and posed and preened at her, he still had his disturbing moments of actual charm, and Joan still wanted to get everything over with and shoot him in the head right there. But there were people to distract him, whether by chance or intention.

This crowd hadn't been great, though, even if some of the magical theory had been interesting. It was really disturbing to see how enthusiastic some of them were about Reynell and how even the ones like Cole and Cunningham stayed quiet. Either Reynell had messed with people's minds or there was something wrong with them. Or both. Probably both.

Thomson had been there, of course, and had looked ready to cry when Reynell had spent most of his time flirting with Joan. *Sorry, kid. It's for your own good anyhow*. The others seemed to have given up attracting his attention as a lost cause. A few of them, to their credit, didn't seem to give a damn.

A few of them had actually seemed to know what they were doing. Joan had said as much to Reynell, though implying less than she knew, and he'd looked pleased. "Your judgment seems quite sound. I'm very impressed."

"You should see me buying hats," she'd said.

So it had been a success. She still needed a bath.

Joan opened her eyes as the carriage drew up to Simon's town house, sighed, and let the footman help her out. "Are the Grenvilles both home?"

"Yes, ma'am," he said, opening the door. "Miss Grenville's in the library, ma'am, and Mr. Grenville's in his personal study."

"Of course he is," she muttered dryly. She handed the footman her hat and cloak, stepped into the house, and almost swore aloud.

The sensor behind her ear had suddenly flashed red-hot. Magic, active magic, and powerful stuff. Joan looked toward the stairs. "How long has Mr. Grenville been in his study?"

"These three hours, ma'am."

"Thank you."

Ignoring the worry on his face, she picked up her stupid skirt and almost ran for the stairs.

Of course, everything could be fine. Some spells took a couple hours. Most of them required more than one person, but in theory you could probably do them on your own. There were spells that might have set off her sensor, even from the hall.

But those were huge spells, with huge effects, and you'd tell someone before you were going to cast one.

Probably.

Unless you were used to a world where nobody believed in that sort of thing.

Joan reached the top of the landing and hurried down the hall.

He would have told her, though. Oh, he'd been weird and distant lately, but they were allies, weren't they? Even friends, she'd thought.

The door was the way it had always been, light wood with brass fixtures. Nothing had changed. No flashes of strange light came from underneath it. Joan looked around quickly, making sure that no servants were watching, and then pressed her eye to the keyhole.

Darkness.

It was silent inside too, but the room would've been designed for that. Simon wouldn't want anyone to hear him chanting, even when things were going well.

The sense of magic was even stronger here. If Joan hadn't known better, she'd have thought the sensor was burning through her skin.

Simon would've told her if he'd been planning something big. Wouldn't he?

If you interrupted magic at the wrong time, things could get really bad. If you didn't interrupt it when you needed to, they could be even worse.

You don't have a lot of time. Shit or get off the pot.
Fine.

The knob wouldn't turn, of course. It was locked. Joan took one more look up and down the hall and then grabbed a pin out of her hair and knelt in front of the door.

She wished she'd had time to get her lock picks, but a kid could pick an indoor lock in this age. Even with a hairpin, it took Joan only about five minutes before she felt the tumblers turn and the bolt release.

The knife slid easily from her sleeve as she rose, and she clasped her hand around the hilt, welcoming its solid presence in her palm. Joan opened the door a crack and stepped back instantly. Flattening herself against the wall, she held her breath for a second.

Nothing came out. She let her breath go, edged forward a little, and peered inside.

In the light from the hallway, she saw a bare room with circles traced on the floor. Simon knelt on the floor within them, motionless.

She smelled incense: cinnamon, sandalwood, and opium. *Oh, Powers.*

In seconds, she was in the room, lighting one of the candles on the floor and reflexively pushing the door shut behind her. Even before she saw the runes in the circles, Joan knew what he'd done or tried to do. She'd seen it before.

You never, never tried astral travel without getting someone to watch you. It had become a chore for kids in her time: sit by the priest while he goes off exploring, and then go and fetch someone else if he doesn't come back after however long it's supposed to be. A common task, if a scary one. Joan had done it a million times.

Now she wished she'd paid attention to what happened once the watching child actually fetched another priest.

"Simon," she said in a sharp but not loud voice.

Nothing.

"*Simon.*" She raised her voice this time. "Wake the hell up."

Still nothing.

She grabbed Simon under his arms—he was still breathing, she noticed with a rush of relief, but he didn't react at all—and dragged him outside the circle. His head hung slack, wobbling with every movement. Joan pretended she didn't see that.

Fear was a cold lump in her chest. She couldn't think about it, or it would grow and paralyze her.

Laying Simon on his back, she tilted his chin upward. His eyes were open, but they'd rolled back into his head. "Hey!" Her voice was as loud as it could be without shouting. "Come on!"

Still he lay silent and motionless.

Joan slapped him. The first time was light. When *that* didn't get anything, she drew back her arm and really let him have it, sending her palm into the side of his face with a meaty *thwack*.

He didn't move. In the silence that followed, she heard Eleanor's indrawn breath.

"I—" Joan started, prepared for anger or tears or just *what the hell are you doing?*

But Eleanor ignored her, rushed past her, and knelt by Simon. "Oh, God. What's happened?"

"Astral travel," Joan said, and went on with no thought for tact or current phrasing, just following the cold sense of urgency that had taken her over. "You've got to stay calm, okay? If you freak out now, everything's going to go right to hell."

"The servants said—" Eleanor began, and then shook her head. "No. Wait. Astral travel? Projection, you mean?"

"Yes." Joan abruptly remembered the little leather book she'd seen Eleanor reading. "Do you know anything about it?"

All the color was gone from Eleanor's face. She closed her eyes for a moment and then nodded. "Yes. I need…a pitcher of salt water. And a knife. And…and a bandage."

It took five minutes to collect everything. Joan was worried that the servants would object, but one look at her face and they had gotten out of her way. She ran back up the stairs, pitcher and bandage in one hand and skirts in the other, and into the room, where Eleanor now stood, hands open at her sides.

"Is there a knife?" Eleanor asked faintly, as Joan set the water down in front of her.

"Yeah." Joan slid hers back out of her sleeve, turned it around, and offered Eleanor the hilt.

Eleanor gulped. "I was thinking it might be better if you did it. I've never…I might faint or flinch or something."

"All right. Where?"

Eleanor bit her lip, closed her eyes, and held out one hand, palm upward, over the water.

It was a quick cut. Joan was at least good at that. Eleanor didn't scream or draw back. She just held herself very still for a second. Then she turned her hand over, so that the blood fell into the water and began to spread, drops of red becoming crimson flowers. She started chanting in a language Joan didn't recognize. Whatever the invocation was, it took only about a minute.

"That's all," she said then, her voice high and wavering. "Salt to break the spell and blood to be an anchor. We just throw it over him—but please—can you—"

Maybe it was her hand. Maybe it was just the idea of drenching her brother. It didn't matter. Joan grabbed the pitcher in both hands, turned in one smooth movement, and threw its contents over Simon.

If he needs an anchor, she thought, *better give him more than one.*

She dropped the pitcher, hearing the crash as it broke and not giving a damn, and knelt by Simon again, her hands on his shoulders. "Rise and shine, Grenville," she said. The words came out thick. Her throat hurt for some reason. "*Now.*"

Simon's shoulders jerked under her hands. His head snapped back, and Joan put her hands out instinctively, stopping him just before he cracked his skull on the stone floor. "Joan," he said hazily.

"Yeah, me, you idiot!" she snarled at him. "You—"

"My God," he said, oblivious to her anger. "Joan, how did you live there?"

Chapter 31

ELLIE STARED AT HIM, THOUGH SHE WAS OBVIOUSLY trying not to. Every time Simon met her eyes, she went red and looked away for a moment, but then her gaze would jump back to him, and her hands would twist in her skirt. Simon couldn't blame her. If he looked half as bad as he felt, he would draw anyone's attention.

And Simon rejoiced in every bit of it: his boneless limbs, his aching head, and the tight dryness in his throat. He hurt, but he *felt*, and he felt with his own body. For a few moments after he woke up, he'd simply flexed his hands, staring at them, and then looked down his body at his legs and arms. Everything was whole. Everything was there.

Eleanor could stare as much as she liked. She could, if the impulse took her, have stood on her head or shrieked at the top of her lungs, and Simon still would have been glad because she would have been present to do it. This was his world. He could have wept with joy.

But she was looking upset, and so he smiled. It wasn't hard, despite his weariness. "I'll be all right, Ellie. I'm just a little worn out at the moment."

"That's very good to know. I'd hoped—" She broke off quickly.

One of her hands was bandaged, Simon saw now. There were shards of blue china scattered around the floor. "You did it," he said, staring back at her now. "Didn't you?"

Eleanor looked down at her hand. "I cast the spell. Joan threw the water."

"Thank you." He tried to put everything he felt into the words: relief, joy, gratitude. Love. "You saved my life, Ellie."

Her head came up, and for a moment, her eyes glowed with both happiness and pride. "I could hardly do anything else," she said softly. "After all, you did the same for me."

In that moment, he understood some of the constraint that had been between them, understood it even as it vanished. *There was never a debt*, he might have said, but she'd felt one even if he hadn't. Now they were on even ground. Eleanor would stand a little straighter from now on, he knew, and meet the world more squarely.

If this misadventure had done only that much, Simon would have been glad of it.

Getting up went all right. With a substantial effort of will, Simon even managed to do it without taking Joan's hand. "All right," he began, and took a step toward the door.

It was as if the entire world moved, and not the way he was going. He stumbled forward, clutching at the wall. "Simon!" Eleanor gasped behind him.

Then Joan was at his side with one of her arms around his back, holding him steady. Highly mortifying. She didn't laugh, though, and she didn't immediately start cosseting him. She just held Simon still while he gasped for breath and pushed wet hair out of his face.

"He's all right," she said matter-of-factly. "This happens. Wasn't just astral travel, though, was it?"

He shook his head, panting. "Guardian beast. Spirit. Something. Had to get away—blasted it. It threw me—"

Exhausted and giddy, he might have gone on, letting Eleanor know everything he'd tried to keep from her, if Joan hadn't interrupted. "Yeah, that'd do it. At least you can stand. I've seen men be carried out feet first after this kind of thing."

"So he'll be all right, then?" Eleanor asked.

"Should be," said Joan. "It might take a couple days. Can you go tell the servants that he's sick or something? I'll get him out of here."

"Oh. Yes, of course."

As Eleanor departed, Joan took a quick look around the room and then sighed. "You can tell me how to clean up later, I guess. Hold on to me."

"Don't you want to know—" Simon began, but Joan shook her head.

"I want to know later," she said. "And I will. For now, we're moving."

They'd closed the door and gotten a few steps past it when Mathers and one of the footmen hurried up to them. Whatever Ellie had told them, it had certainly sounded serious. "I'm all right," Simon said again through the swaying dizziness.

Mathers replaced Joan with cautious efficiency. "Very good, sir. James, send for the doctor."

Simon considered objecting, but there was really no reason to. It would only make him look strange. His doctor would examine him, find nothing, and conclude that it was some sort of chill or fever—or, if the opium showed up, would tactfully caution him against it. The man was discreet.

Besides, right now, he just wanted to lie down. The joy at being back in his own world was fading slowly, but it was fading, and he was becoming conscious of, among other things, the clammy wetness of his clothes. So he let James send for the doctor, he let Mathers dry him off and put him to bed, and he sank gratefully onto his pillows.

Home.

The doctor asked why his hair was damp. Simon told him something close to the truth, that Joan had woken him with a pitcher of cold water when other methods failed. "Hmm," the doctor said, and went on with his examination.

"Exhaustion," he pronounced at the end, "and strain. Keep to your rooms for the next few days. Eat bland food and avoid strong drink."

"I'll do my best," said Simon.

The world was now fading. He didn't want to let it. It was too dear to him just now, even when he couldn't move his head much: the familiar furnishings of his room, the noises from the street outside, the smell of wood smoke from the fireplace. The sheets were crisp and cool against his skin.

Joan slipped in, closed the door quietly behind her, and walked over to Simon's bed. There she stopped and stared down at him, arms folded over her chest.

"Projection? On your own?" Her voice was low, but it had the parade ground and the barracks in it. "Great idea. Fucking terrific idea. You people have a real highly developed survival instinct, you know that? Forget what happens a hundred years from now—how the hell did we survive this long?"

"Well," said Simon, smiling up at her. It was good to see her face, even when it was angry. "We don't usually encounter legions of the damned here."

Joan glared at him for a few moments, but then she sighed, unfolded her arms, and sat down on the edge of his bed. "That's the problem with living in this world, I guess. You're not prepared for the worst. I wish you'd told me, though. I would've stuck around."

"Believe me, I wish I had told you," he said. "But you were doing your part. If you'd stayed, I wouldn't have thought it was safe."

"Scrying on Reynell, huh?"

"On his house." The memories came flooding back, and Simon swallowed. "The book's there, I think. And...I don't know what else. It's a dark place. Whatever he's done—whatever he's doing"—he could only pray it was the latter, knowing that neither of them would be in a position to stop it for a while yet—"it leaves traces behind."

"I'd have expected that," Joan said evenly. "And then there was a guardian that could see the astral, and it threw you to my time?"

"I think so." He described it in as much detail as he could so that Joan could recognize it, yes, but also just to get it all out. As he talked, he saw recognition on her face.

"Sounds like it," she said, and turned her head away from him, looking out the window.

The sky outside was a hazy blue. It couldn't compare to the brilliant hues in the country, away from the smoke of London, but it was bright and peaceful. Somewhere, it wasn't. Somewhere, there were piles of bones and patches of moving darkness.

"Those automobiles," Simon said. "People were trying to escape. They knew something was coming, didn't they?"

"They did," said Joan.

For a minute, she was silent. Then, without turning from the window, she sang in a low voice:

"And in the streets, the children screamed.
The mothers cried, and the prophets dreamed."

She sat in the afternoon sunlight, utterly respectable in blue serge, her hair still mostly neat after everything. There was no hint of anything wild or untamed about her, let alone otherworldly, but her voice made Simon shiver.

"Have you been there?"

"Maybe. There are a couple places that fit the description."

"Then every city is like that?"

Joan turned. Her smile was a knife slash. "No. Some of them are black glass and poisoned air. The bombs fell there at the end, and they don't even leave bones. Nobody goes there."

"God," he said. Even with his eyes open, nightmarish images flashed in front of him.

"You really didn't get it, huh?"

"I thought I did," he said quietly.

"Yeah." Joan sighed and her face softened a little. "Bad enough when you're used to it. It must be hell to see if you're not. I'm sorry, Simon."

Simon shook his head, though the motion made him wince. "Hardly your fault, was it? Projection on my own—fucking terrific idea."

For once, he seemed to shock her. Joan drew back for a second and then laughed, bright and golden. "I deserve that. Shouldn't underestimate you. But damn, I thought you'd burst into flames or something if you swore like that."

"Me? Not at all." It was a pity that they hadn't met in

his own world—at the theatre or one of the salons or any of the other places he'd gone back when a bit of scandal or an aching head had been the worst consequence the world held for him. "One tries to speak nicely in polite society, though. And around ladies, in general."

"That kind of lets me out, doesn't it?"

"Hardly," Simon said, with more strength than he'd planned to.

Joan laughed again, startled for a second time. For all that there'd been no self-pity in her question, it had been sincere. "You're really sweet sometimes," she said and added quickly, "It'll probably get you in trouble."

"As opposed to the placid and uneventful life I've been leading?"

"Well, you don't need more excitement, do you?" Absently, Joan reached out and brushed a lock of hair away from his forehead. It was a gentler motion than Simon would have expected from her, calming and very pleasant. She didn't move her hand away afterward, and he was glad.

"How did you get in, anyhow?" he asked. "I swear I've got the only key to that room. Did you—ah. You picked the lock, didn't you?"

"If you can call it that."

He had to laugh at the disgust in her voice. "I'm just as glad it's not up to your standards, considering everything. Not all of us have your talents."

Joan smiled, conceding the point. "It's just training," she said. "Well, a lot of training."

There might have been wistfulness in her voice. Simon couldn't tell, not really, but he remembered how she'd taken to dancing and riding. Now she couldn't do either without playing a part.

"If you want to," he said, "you can use the room I was in. To practice, I mean. I'll have a key made for you."

She stopped for a second and blinked. Not a woman to squeal or gush, Joan, but he could see surprise on her face and then delight. "Really?" she asked, and hastily cleared her throat. "I mean, I won't be disturbing anything?"

"Not a thing," Simon said. "In fact, once I get my strength back, you'll have a sparring partner if you'd like one. I could use a few lessons, I think."

"Hey—" she said, totally abandoning the patterns of speech she'd mastered. "Hey—thanks. Really."

Simon let his eyes drift closed and thanked God when there was only unmoving darkness in front of him. Joan's body was a vague warmth by his side. He wanted to move toward it, but even dazed and weak, he remembered some of the proprieties. "You shouldn't be here," he said, hearing himself slur the words a little as weariness advanced on him. "Dreadfully scandalous, you know. People will talk."

"What people?" she asked. Simon knew that she was smiling and that her eyebrows were raised just a little. "And what exactly do they think you're going to do to me like this?"

"God only knows," said Simon. Though he could imagine. Not that he could manage any of it right now. Still he welcomed his arousal at the thought, faint as it was. It was more proof that he was alive.

"Or maybe," Joan said, speculative and amused, "they're worried about what I could do."

The idea was simultaneously laughable and stirring. Simon had seen certain little-discussed publications showing bound men, haughty women, bonds and whips.

The dim heat he'd felt earlier grew stronger. "I doubt anyone worries about my virtue," he said thickly.

"How sad for you." Joan started to get up. "But if—"

Despite his exhaustion, he wanted her badly in ways it was best that he couldn't carry out right now. But when Simon caught her wrist, it had nothing to do with sex. She was warm and human; she was the one person in his household who'd lived through what he'd seen. "Please," he said. "Stay. Until I sleep."

If Joan had looked at all askance in that moment, Simon would have summoned up the remains of his dignity and sent her away.

But she didn't even look surprised. Quite the contrary. In fact, she had a look of recognition on her face when she sat back down. "Sure," she said. Her hand found his hair again. "Sure. I'll stay."

Chapter 32

SOMETHING WAS WRONG.

The first thing Alex noticed was his creature's absence. The thing wasn't much for greeting him—or, rather, he'd bound it not to greet him the way it would have liked—but he could sense its presence from two rooms away. He knew, from the moment he put his foot on the second-floor landing, that it was gone.

Simon.

Alex yanked open the study door, stepped in, and slammed it behind him. He'd long since stopped worrying about what the servants would think. They knew better than to talk; he'd made sure of it when he hired them. And there were more important things to do right now.

He stalked over to the bookcase and pressed a spot on the underside of one shelf. A narrow drawer slid out, and Alex allowed himself to breathe again when he saw his manuscript looking just as it had when he'd put it away the night before.

Sitting down at his desk, he took a yellow candle out of the top drawer and lit it. The smoke rose almost immediately, smelling strong and sweet, a bit like roasting pork. Alex stared into it for a second, let his eyes unfocus, and pronounced a long harsh name.

The strands of curling smoke grew and solidified, turning pink. Unlike in the past, though, their outlines remained fuzzy, and Alex could still see the shapes of his study through them. *Wounded*, he thought, and indeed there were vivid gold shapes burnt into the writhing flesh of the creature.

It would be no good to him for weeks. Alex swore and then focused his will again. "Tell me what happened."

In a moment, he was looking through the creature's eyes—or whatever—as Simon's astral body opened a gap in the wards and slid in.

Didn't think it was a trap, did you?

There was at least some pleasure in that. Even if it wasn't unmixed. Simon had fallen for the trap because Simon still didn't think much of him. *If I'd bothered to study wards as intensely as you did,* Alex fumed, *I would have been much better than you by now. But I got better at other things. More important ones. As you found out.*

In the creature's memory, Simon went very still, as if stunned. It struck then, grabbing Simon by one leg. They struggled for a while.

Then everything went blindingly gold. Enraged and wounded, the creature flung Simon outward along the dimensional roads. He vanished into a maelstrom of shifting worlds, and the creature went elsewhere.

Alex couldn't follow either of them and keep his mind. Not yet, anyhow. He muttered another word, dismissing the thing. No point wasting the candle, after all. It had cost him no little effort to make. One couldn't get...materials...like that easily.

He wondered idly if Simon had made some provision to get himself back. Perhaps he was dead now, or as good, his mind blasted out of space and time. The prospect should have made Alex entirely happy or at least relieved. He could deal with Simon readily enough, but doing so was a dashed inconvenience.

But, as it had been when he set the hounds on Simon, Alex's pleasure was mixed with regret. He shouldn't have felt it, of course. Simon's treachery should have killed off any feelings save hatred, and yet he did. A mark of a sensitive nature, perhaps.

I never wanted *this*, Simon, he thought at the absent man. *You could've left me alone, you know. A friend would have.*

Alex found the bottle he kept in his desk and poured himself a glass of port. He couldn't make himself drink it immediately, though. Instead, he stared down at the ruby liquid, all his pleasure in the day gone.

And it had been such a good day. Oh, propriety had forced him to spend it with a gaggle of Society maidens and their beaux, but he'd been able to talk mostly to Mrs. MacArthur. She seemed more receptive by the day, both to the theories Alex advanced and to his own person.

He'd even thought that she might make more than a plaything in the end. It would be no bad thing to have an apprentice for some tasks, and a woman wouldn't be the threat a man would, particularly when Alex was confident that he could keep her loyal.

After Harrison's séance next week, he'd thought, she would be as good as his. The man was an amateur, of course, but one with a few visible gifts. More importantly, the party would be private, quiet, and dark.

Harrison was suggestible enough in Society matters. A word in his ear would secure Mrs. MacArthur an invitation. After the day's conversation, Alex was certain she'd attend.

Yes, it had been a good day. And now it was spoiled.

If Simon was still alive—and it was best to assume he was—he knew more than he had before. He probably didn't know about the manuscript, but Alex was well aware of how his study looked in the astral. Seeing that, Simon would naturally try to intervene, preaching choirboy that he was. Particularly since Alex was winning over his mistress day by day.

Well, the wards would hold very well against force. Simon couldn't direct any attack from a distance that Alex wouldn't be able to rebuff, just as Alex doubted he could take care of Simon remotely, now that he was prepared.

Simon would seek him out, probably in private. Eleanor's name was at stake, after all, and now her friend's.

Alex thought of the creature and of the other…allies… that he'd made since the Great Ones had started teaching him their secrets. He smiled into the dim room. Perhaps it would be for the best if Simon did decide to have it out with him.

Perhaps that would even give Alex the opportunity to make Simon see reason. And if not, a man could do only so much on his own. Even the Church said that.

He downed the rest of the port and got to his feet, fingering the ring on his left hand. It was plain gold with only a small emerald, not outstanding in any way. Alex had been very careful about that. Just as carefully, he now took it off and slipped it into the innermost pocket in his waistcoat. Where he was going, it didn't do to show jewelry openly. Even he could be overwhelmed by a gang of thieves.

The sun was setting when he left the house, carrying a large black bag and walking briskly.

Allies didn't come cheaply, after all. And if Alex was going to use them in the future, now was the time to start the diplomacy.

———∿∿∿———

It didn't take long for Simon to fall asleep once he let himself. Joan wasn't surprised. Projection took it out of you, especially when it went wrong. And Simon hadn't exactly been relaxing lately.

Now, watching him, she thought that she'd never *really* seen him relaxed. He'd come close sometimes when they'd gone riding together back at Englefield and during their first week in London when she'd sat in his study and they'd played cards. At those times, Joan had seen a little bit of the way he had used to be: as careless as the average wealthy man in this time, though more learned than most.

He had the beginnings of lines around his eyes now. Not many of them, but they were there. Compared to the other men she'd met at balls, he was thinner as well and wearier. Henry had mentioned it once. *He was never what you might call stout, but now—well, we'll make him go to a lot of dinner parties*.

Someone should. Poor bastard. Joan passed her hand over Simon's hair again, took a few strands of it in her fingers, and let them fall.

It was hard on him, this new duty. She wished it hadn't happened, but she couldn't wish that Simon hadn't gotten involved. He was a good man, too bound by this world's idea of honor, sure, but maybe that helped even while it exasperated her. She could trust him the way she would never have trusted anyone from her world after only two months. Not just to keep her secrets and not stab her in the back, but to know what needed doing and to go after it.

To be her partner.

In his sleep, Simon murmured something and turned toward her. As if of its own volition, Joan's hand slid through his hair again and then downward, leaving her palm cupped against his cheek. His skin was warm and still damp from the water, a little rough with five-o'clock shadow.

He looked very young and very old at the same time. Very mortal. Very tired.

Two hours before, he'd nearly died—or worse—trying to figure out where the book was. Trying to help her like he'd been doing for more than a month, like he'd offered the first time he spoke to her, though she'd been covered in blood and holding a gun.

Rage surged up inside her, blinding and white-hot. *He's going to come out of this*, she snarled silently—at Reynell, maybe, or the Dark Ones or the universe itself. *You do whatever you want with me. Maybe I deserve it. But he's going to be alive when this is over and whole and happy. Or I'll rip your goddamn face off and feed it to you.*

The anger left her shaking and shaken too when it passed through her. She wanted to spring up and go for someone's throat, to put her fist through a window, to fight something. Anything. She wanted to run away.

There hadn't been much use for emotion in her life, but she wasn't a moron and she wasn't a robot. She knew what it meant, this rage. Same thing as the fear she'd felt earlier when Simon lay without breathing.

I care about him. A lot.

She pulled her hand away from Simon, stood up, and leaned her head against the window. The glass was cool against her forehead. Joan closed her eyes.

You couldn't surrender. Not to the Dark Ones, not to their minions, and not to yourself. But the first part of a fight was knowing your enemy.

I love him, she thought slowly, and then spat it out. *I'm in love with him.*

Oh, God. I'm really fucked now.

Chapter 33

"LUNCH, SIR," SAID MATHERS, SETTING THE TRAY DOWN by Simon's bed. "And a letter for Mrs. MacArthur."

Being sick had some advantages, Simon had discovered. A healthy man couldn't have a woman sitting by his bed without causing comment—oh, Mathers was far too well-trained to say anything to Simon's face, but he would have looked very purposefully blank, and the others would have talked among themselves for days. But now, as long as Joan stayed safely in the chair, nobody would bat an eye. He was sick, after all. And Eleanor couldn't be expected to attend him all the time.

She and Joan had traded off shifts. Ellie read to him, mostly—they were halfway through *Kidnapped* by now—and Joan picked up the book occasionally too, reading in a low, rough voice and sometimes stumbling over Italian names and long words, but with a verve that kept Simon listening attentively. She talked more than Ellie, though. Over the past two days, she'd asked questions and given her opinion on subjects from horse racing to theology.

Now she picked up the letter, and her face went blank for a second. When Simon glimpsed the handwriting on the envelope, he understood why.

Of all the things they'd talked about, they'd never mentioned Alex. After that first day, Joan hadn't brought up the mission. She'd stuck to trivia and philosophy, or she'd read about pirates. Simon hadn't forgotten either Alex or the tasks that lay ahead—how could he?—but they'd slid into the back of his mind. Until now.

"I do a lot to save the damn world, you know," she said dryly when Mathers had gone.

"Oh?"

As she read, she pronounced each word with elaborate, ceremonial care. "The privilege of your company is requested at a Demonstration of Mediumistic Powers and an Exploration of the Realms Beyond."

Despite his worry, Simon had to laugh. "Standard wording, I fear."

"If anyone I've met here got a good look at the 'Realms Beyond,' they'd come back with their pants wet and their brains running out their ears, if they came back at all." She added as an afterthought, "Except you, and Reynell."

The name came out flat, and Joan picked up the letter again. It was a hasty motion, aimed at disguising something. Revulsion? And if so, at Alex or the situation? Or at herself?

Her behavior hadn't been what Simon would expect of a woman wrestling with her own desires, but then, it wouldn't have been. She was a better actress than most.

"Who's holding it, and when?" he asked, trying to disrupt his own thoughts.

"Thursday. Mr. Harrison. I *think* I met him."

"That means Alex is probably behind it. Harrison's tremendously attentive to Alex's concerns."

"Which means I should go to the damn thing." Joan looked down at her skirt, thoughtful. "What do you wear to a demonstration of whatever?"

"Good God, I have no idea."

In the course of the discussion, her face had become slightly flushed and her eyes brighter. Strategy? The thrill of the chase? Or something more?

Simon sipped his tea and didn't taste it. The toast could have been paper. "I could get the book," he said abruptly, "while you and Alex are at the séance, at least."

Joan stared at him. "You? Play ninja? After Reynell's watchdog got a taste of your blood?"

"I can handle the guardian," he said stiffly. "At least if I'm prepared."

"Yeah? And how are you going to get in? Got the Ninth Ring?" When he looked baffled, Joan waved a hand. "It makes you invisible. And it's only a story, anyhow. Nobody can turn himself invisible—can you?"

"If I could do that, I would've told you at once."

"You told me," she said, "that breaking in was a bad idea. And I had a lot more advantages than you do now."

It was horrible logic. But it was sound. "He might be killing people," Simon said. "Or worse."

Joan nodded. "He might be. And he might not. You don't have any proof that he's still doing whatever he was doing, just that he's done something bad enough for it to show up. That's not any change from when I got here, is it?"

He couldn't read her face.

She'd had plenty of opportunity to press harder, to become more acquainted with Alex and his household. She hadn't taken it. There might even have been a few moments where she could've struck. Poison, at least, would be subtle enough, and the Joan who'd come through the portal would've counted her life well spent if she could've killed Reynell with her last breath.

She wants the book first.

Simon could destroy it. Would destroy it. And Joan knew that.

She promised me.

That was laughable. He'd seen the world as it would be, and now even he found it hard to hold on to his principles. If he'd been raised in the world he'd seen—if he'd traveled two hundred years and left all he'd known to see it put right—he wouldn't have stopped for the honor of one man, or even for whatever mystical consequences came of being forsworn.

Joan wouldn't have. At least, not the Joan he'd met.

It's just tactics, Simon told himself sternly. *She's waiting for the right opening.*

Of course it was. Of course her feelings hadn't changed. He knew she was a good actress. It was only natural that she'd be able to pretend to like Alex.

Simon wanted badly to believe that.

<hr />

It seemed like a bad idea to ask your maid what to wear to a séance, and the small book of etiquette Joan had bought was no help at all. So she found Eleanor in the drawing room and asked her.

Eleanor closed the leather-bound book she'd been reading—a different one now, Joan thought—and frowned. "Is it after six?"

"Eight."

"I'd wear evening dress, then. It's more likely to be a party in disguise than anything serious." Eleanor sounded like she was trying to reassure herself, and she didn't quite succeed. "I don't want to intrude, and I –

certainly mean no offense, but are you certain you want
to go to this?"

Joan laughed. "God, I'm certain I don't. I don't like
the crowd, and I don't see why everyone thinks the dead
want to come back and chat. You'd think they'd either
be resting or have more important things to do. But I
have to."

"Oh." Eleanor gave her a slow, searching look,
opened her mouth, and then shook her head. "Be careful, then. I mean, I'm sure you are anyhow. And I certainly don't mean to imply that you need the warning.
But these gatherings can be more dangerous than most
people think."

Stupidly, Joan half hoped this one was. There'd been
a restlessness riding her for the last couple days due to
the séance itself, as well as Simon making suggestions
that were incredibly dumb, especially for him, and generally being trapped in a small house in a crowded city.
The walls pressed in on her, and she wanted to hit them.
To hit something, anyway.

None of that was Eleanor's fault, though, so Joan just
nodded. "I know."

"It might not be. Most of them are just party tricks
and imagination. But if Mr. Reynell's there..." She
broke off, dropping her gaze to her lap.

"Then he's going to try to pull out all the stops. Don't
worry. I can stay a couple steps ahead of him."

"I'll pray that you do," said Eleanor. Her voice was
even quieter than usual, the whisper of a child who
didn't quite dare to name the thing she hoped for or the
thing she feared.

Chapter 34

IT WAS STRANGE TO BE TRAVELING BY HERSELF AT NIGHT.

For one thing, she wasn't really by herself. Betty, the maid who waited on Joan in London, was sitting silently across from her, and the driver was at the front of the carriage. Joan had led ambush teams with fewer people. She'd also done a fair number of solo missions, many of them at night. And now, just because she'd left Simon and Eleanor behind and the sun had set, it seemed new and a little scary.

Not without reason. Joan watched the twilight streets go by, a maze of winding alleys and wide roads turning unpredictably and crowded, even this late. If she had the wrong house—if something went wrong—how would she ever get back?

Betty would know, Joan told herself. So would the driver. And if neither of them was available, she at least knew Simon's address, and she could hire a carriage herself. She had several pounds in her purse and a few more in the bag she'd strapped to her leg, next to her knife. Everything would be all right. If it wasn't, she would deal with that. Even so, she was relieved to arrive at a well-lit house and be shown into a crowded drawing room.

Harrison himself was tall, balding, and gaunt. He'd have been intimidating if he'd worn dark clothes rather than the bright, elaborate outfits he favored. He'd also have needed to keep silent and stand still. "My *dear* Mrs. MacArthur!" he cried, fluttering his way across the room as Joan entered. "*So* glad you could attend—hope you had an easy journey—"

"Thank you," she said after Harrison had gone on in that style for a bit and then stopped to take a breath. "Very easy, yes."

She greeted his wife as well, though she didn't have to come up with nearly as many responses there. The woman was much quieter and almost seemed lost in her own world half the time. Anyone probably would have to be, married to someone like Harrison.

Thomson was there, looking simultaneously vague and intense as usual, and chattering to a couple of other young women. One or two of them chattered back; Cole, nearby, kept quiet. Joan saw Cunningham lounging near the sofa, talking with another man and a striking dark-eyed woman. Archie was already coming over, beaming.

And Reynell turned from his conversation and met her eyes.

He held her gaze for a second and then smiled. His look of slow appreciation suggested he saw every inch of her and liked it a lot. At first, that look had made Joan shiver. Now she hardly noticed except to make sure he was still interested enough to work at it.

Not that he came over to meet her at first. That would've been too common and too available. Instead, he watched while Archie made his way past the furniture and then turned back to his partner, content to wait. Archie, Reynell's body language said, was no threat.

Joan wished Reynell wasn't right about that, both because he was a smug bastard and because Archie seemed like a nice enough guy. Young, but nice. The sort Joan might have tried to get into bed—if he wouldn't have taken it exactly the wrong way and if she didn't have a mission. He would, and she did.

So she treated him like a brother, like a member of her squad back home, and was pleased when he fell into conversation with a little red-haired girl from Thomson's set who seemed smarter than her friends. That left Joan alone for a minute, and Reynell found his way to her side.

"I thought I'd never get the chance to talk to you," he said. "Your companions are so…devoted."

His eyes mocked and invited her to mock with him. Joan let herself smile for a second, shaking her head. "He's very amiable."

"I know. It's rather sad, really."

Joan lifted an eyebrow. "For whom?"

"Me, of course," Reynell said, as if astonished that anyone could think he'd meant anyone else.

This is a hell of a game.

"Well, I'd hate to make you sad," she said, sipping her punch. "Not when you've been so…educational. When do we start, anyway? And how?"

Reynell laughed. "Soon. Very soon. Impatient?"

"Curious."

"I hear it's a painful thing, unsatisfied curiosity."

Joan lowered her eyelashes. "I do my best to endure," she said. "What happens?"

"I presume our host will give us some instruction." Reynell glanced toward the middle of the room at the woman talking to Cunningham. "Mrs. Stewart has volunteered to be our medium tonight, I understand.

NO PROPER LADY   251

It's very generous of her to put herself in Harrison's…
hands…like that."

It was very clear what he meant. Joan blinked.
Harrison—and Mrs. Stewart?

Maybe he's really good in the sack.

The image made her bite the inside of her cheek.
Reynell saw it and grinned, only a little smugly. "Can I
get you something more to drink before we start?"

"Yes, thank you," said Joan, without thinking about
it. That was standard practice around here, and at least
it gave her a minute or two alone. She wanted to take a
look around, partly out of curiosity and partly to be sure
she knew all the exits.

There were candles around the couch and a bowl of
water at one end. No sigils or wards, but a set of silk
ropes lay on the couch itself. None of the ropes back
home had been silk, but the memories came up anyhow.

It wouldn't be like home. The gorgeous, if misguided
Mrs. Stewart wouldn't have volunteered if people
regularly lost their minds, and Harrison didn't have the
air of a man who drove his subjects insane. Still, Joan
shuddered.

"Worried?" Reynell said from behind her. Joan
flinched and then cursed herself, both for the reaction
and for not hearing him come up in the first place. Too
many damn people in the room talking too damn loudly.
"You needn't be. We've never lost a guest yet."

"So you're due?" Joan asked, turning toward him.

As he handed her the glass of punch, he let his hand
brush hers for just a moment longer than he should have.
"Never fear. I'll make sure it's not you."

Harrison clapped his hands. The room fell silent,

or as silent as a roomful of people ever could, and the guests turned toward the couch. Harrison stood at its head now, Mrs. Stewart beside him. "My dear friends and fellow explorers," he began, "I want to thank you all for your attendance here. It's faith such as yours that will take us from the darkness of prior days into a new dawn of spiritual enlightenment."

He turned to look at Joan. "And I am gratified, most gratified, that we have a new arrival in our midst, a new initiate into the mysteries that were old in the days of Atlantis and that we are only now rediscovering. It is my fondest hope, Mrs. MacArthur, that what you see tonight will give us another ally and you a source of guidance on your own path."

Applause blew through the room like dry leaves. Joan made a slightly awkward curtsy and smiled.

"I am gratified, also, by Mrs. Stewart's gracious offer to be our means of communication with the world beyond. For the purposes of this exercise, her hands will be bound, for when we cannot reach out with our hands, we must perforce do so with our minds and souls."

Perforce. He said perforce. Joan kept her gaze fixed straight ahead. She couldn't look at Reynell.

Mrs. Stewart lay down on the couch. The redhead who'd been talking to Archie—a slight girl in pale yellow silk—moved in a circle around her, lighting the candles. As they sprang to life and the faint smell of burning wick and melting wax filled the room, Joan no longer wanted to laugh, and her disgust faded into a faint background presence.

Harrison was pretentious as hell. Stewart was doing the whole medium thing to get into his pants. But that didn't matter. This was ritual. Joan had grown up with it, and it was deadly serious.

One of the young men, who'd clearly done this before, turned out the lights, and the room dwindled to the circle of candle flames. Above them, Harrison's long, gaunt face was like something out of a nightmare.

He reached into the bowl of water, wet his fingers, and very carefully began to draw shapes on Mrs. Stewart's forehead. As he finished each one, he intoned a name. Greek, Joan thought, remembering some of the texts Eleanor had showed her, or maybe Latin. Hard to tell.

Behind Joan's ear, her sensor began to heat up. Whatever Harrison thought he was doing, it was working.

Then Mrs. Stewart began to float: one inch up, then two, until she was hovering half a foot above the sofa. The train of her dress hung beneath her. It rippled in an unfelt wind. Joan gasped, since people would expect that.

Reynell put a hand on her shoulder in response and then left it there. His touch sank down through Joan's clothes, warm and viscous. *You're not feeling that*, she told herself, and took a hasty swallow of punch.

"O spirit," Harrison began, "we welcome you to our company tonight. You honor us with your presence and your knowledge. If it is in our power to make your rest easier, you have only to ask."

"I?" said something, using Mrs. Stewart's voice. "I need nothing of you. I am the Wanderer. I am the restless. All things are mine to see. All are mine to tell, or not to tell, as I will. What is it you wish?"

Stewart's eyes opened. They were bright blue from

side to side, without pupil or iris. One of the girls screamed a little.

Joan relaxed. The Wanderer was one of the neutral spirits, not really a power of light or dark, and sort of liked humans. Opportunistic little bastard, they said, under the pretentious talk. Liked its booze. Still nothing to mess with.

Any of the spirits could cause trouble, if only by deciding that it liked a body enough to stay there. Joan wondered what was worth the risk to these people, if they even thought about it that way.

She expected Thomson to ask something first, some idiot girlish romantic thing. Cole stepped forward instead, her face as grim and set as any warrior's before a battle.

"I want to know about a baby," Cole began. "A little girl. Nine weeks old. Her name was Anne Elizabeth. Is she there? Is she happy?"

The voice of the Wanderer was subtly different from Stewart's, deeper and wavery, like someone talking under water. "Of course she's not here. She's gone onward." Then a pause, and Stewart's head turned jerkily toward Cole. "You'll meet again."

"Thank you," said Cole. Now her voice broke, and she stepped hastily backward. "Thank you," she said again.

More came forward after her, and some of them did ask the stupid questions Joan had anticipated: *Where's the will? Which horse should I bet on tomorrow?* Nobody, surprisingly, asked about romance explicitly, though Thomson asked where she'd be next year and got sulky when the Wanderer said it didn't know. It had said the same thing to the man asking about the horse race, but he took it with a sigh and a shrug.

Joan watched with what she hoped was the appearance of calm. She tried not to think that the Wanderer might refuse to leave if someone like Harrison told it to and tried not to think about what she would do then. She held her breath as he went through the whole ritual with the water again, commanding the spirit to depart "without harm or malice to any here." Mrs. Stewart sank down until she was lying on the sofa again, but Joan didn't relax until the woman stirred and opened normal dark eyes.

"Well," said Reynell, as the other guests began to chatter in excitement. "What did you think?"

"I admit I'm impressed." It came out as a croak. Joan looked down at the glass of punch in her hand and took several rapid sips. Now it was warm, but it did the job. "More than I thought I'd be."

"It happens that way to some people. You held up well, though. No screaming, no fainting."

"I do my best," said Joan. "Do people generally faint?"

"Young ladies, sometimes. Generally if there's a likely young man about."

Joan laughed and let Reynell escort her to a seat, watching the room on her way. Harrison was talking to Mrs. Stewart, of course, smiling and leaning in close. His wife was smiling too. Joan wondered if triads sprang up even here under the thirty-seven layers of clothing and manners.

She'd never been one for women, and she sure hadn't been attracted to Harrison, but a slow warmth spread through Joan at the thought. Adrenaline, probably. It usually wasn't this strong, but she was used to running around when she risked her life. She clamped down on it.

At least, she tried. But then she had to look at Reynell,

and that was worse. He was at least physically attractive, and her body had no conscience. Joan shifted in her seat. "What happens now?"

"Now?" Reynell smiled at her. "Now, or at least soon, we go to bed like good little boys and girls." He emphasized "bed" just a little, and Joan, horrified, felt her nipples harden immediately.

Adrenaline, my ass! What's wrong with me? "I see," she said. "That's too bad. We've hardly gotten to talk at all this evening."

"It's a pleasure I'd like to prolong as well. Perhaps we could meet another time without quite so many people around." Reynell leaned forward, lowering his voice. "It would be very nice to talk privately."

There it was. The opening she wanted. Only part of her could look at it tactically, though. The rest responded blindly to the promise in his eyes and his voice. She was fully aroused now, and it took every atom of willpower to keep her thoughts coherent.

Trying to distract herself, Joan tightened her hand around the punch glass and then stopped. She didn't look down. That would have given the whole thing away.

He drugged me. It was like a brief splash of cold water. The lust was still there, but the shock gave her space to think, at least for a while. *A love potion?*

Not by the feel of it. Besides, he wouldn't waste mind control on some random woman, not when he thought she was already attracted, and people in this time had sex and love all twisted up here. An aphrodisiac, then.

Son of a bitch.

"If you'd be amenable," Reynell went on, picking up her gloved hand, "I'm sure I could arrange something."

NO PROPER LADY   257

"I'd like that," Joan said, and took a deep breath. She could feel Reynell's eyes on her breasts as they swelled beneath the green silk. "I'd like that an awful lot."

"And I'd hardly deny a lady any pleasure. I would offer you my escort home, Mrs. MacArthur, but that might cause problems." He bent over her hand, touching his lips to her knuckles. "So we'll have to be content with the future. The very near future."

Chapter 35

BY THE TIME SHE GOT INTO THE CARRIAGE, JOAN WAS almost unbearably turned on. Whatever Reynell had put into her drink had kicked in all the way. She felt every inch of her clothing as it rubbed against her skin, every motion of the carriage on the way back to Simon's. If Betty hadn't been there, she might have at least started to take care of it herself.

She wondered if Reynell had thought of that. Was the drug designed so you could be satisfied only with a partner? With a man? Or did he assume that she, like the fainting morons of this time, wouldn't think to handle the problem on her own?

Hard to say. Joan wished desperately that she could at least experiment.

Instead, she clenched her fists and looked out the window, watching the stars overhead and thinking about anything but sex. The drug would work its way through her system. She just had to wait it out.

It wasn't even worth using the antidote.

Joan slipped into the house, handing her cloak to the sleepy boy who came to meet her, and sent Betty away. She'd get herself out of the dress somehow. Having someone else undress her right now would be a really bad idea.

She hurried through the dark hallways, and she didn't see the light under the study door until it opened just in front of her. Joan jumped backward.

"I'm sorry," Simon said, retreating back a step. "I heard footsteps. I didn't mean to startle you."

"Not your fault," Joan said, cursing at herself silently. Lust was no excuse to get stupid.

He looked her over for a second. Shadows fell across his face, making it unreadable, and Joan swallowed hard. Even his gaze seemed to brush tangibly across her skin.

"Will you come in? I'd like to hear how the evening went."

If she were smart, she'd say she was tired. Oh, sure, debriefing came before her needs, even when those needs had been boosted by magic or alchemy or whatever, and it was important to share information as soon as possible. But it wasn't like Simon would disappear in the middle of the night.

"Sure," said Joan, and followed him back into the study.

I'm not sleeping with him, she reminded herself. *I shouldn't. He won't.*

Then I don't have anything to worry about, do I? And there's no harm in looking.

Simon waited for her to sit down and then dropped into the chair next to her. Now Joan could see his face and the lines of tension on his brow. "Are you all right?"

He'd waited up for her. He was worried. Joan felt a sudden warmth in her chest. It didn't match the sensations lower down, but it was more disturbing in its own way. She'd been trying to forget that she loved him. "Yeah. Things are coming along pretty well."

"Ah. Are they?"

Had his voice gone flat there, or was she imagining things? They were both tired. Joan shrugged. "He suggested meeting in private sometime soon."

"If he went that far, he must be fairly certain of your interest," Simon said, and this time Joan definitely heard the flatness in his voice. "Unless he's playing some deeper game."

"Possible. But I doubt it. I'm pretty sure he thinks I'm really drawn to him." Joan shifted in her seat. Embarrassment and lust made a great combination.

"Ah." Toneless. Whatever bee he had in his bonnet was buzzing louder. "You're going to take him up on the offer?"

"When he makes it," said Joan. Annoyance was starting to shoulder its way in among her other feelings. Honestly, it was a relief. She raised a hand. "Don't worry. I'll give you your chance to talk to him. Though the logistics could be a problem."

"Could they? How so?"

Joan shrugged. "I don't think he'll come by here. He'll invite me over to his house instead. If he wants to do more than talk, I'm going to have a hard time finding the book. We'll have to think up some distraction."

"Before or after?"

"Whatever it takes."

"Of course. Stupid of me to ask, I suppose." His mouth twisted with distaste.

That was it.

"Are you fucking kidding me?" Joan snapped her head up and glared at Simon. "You were there, weren't you? You saw what the world becomes. Do you think for a goddamn second I'm going to turn down a chance to stop it just so I can act like one of your innocent little ladies?"

That got through, and he winced. "No. I—"

"Let me be perfectly clear," she said, imitating for a

second the snottiest of the well-bred women she'd met. "First of all, this was your idea. If you didn't think it through, if you have a problem with it now because it's not proper or modest or whatever, too bad. If there's a chance to save this stupid world, I'm taking it. If that means I have to sleep with Reynell or the whole damn city or a herd of goats, then I'm going to do it. And I'm going to smile about it if I have to."

Thanks for that mental image, by the way. Ass.

"Well, you certainly haven't had a problem…smiling… so far."

"Is that what this is about?" She felt like a giant ball of spikes now: weariness and revulsion, anger and thwarted desire combined. "This is my duty. Do you really think I'm going to bitch about it every chance I get?"

"No." Simon looked down at his hands and then back up. "I'm worried that you might be getting too fond of your…duty."

It took a moment to sink in.

"You son of a bitch."

Joan almost hit him. She was on her feet, her fists clenched, before she was even conscious of moving, and stopping herself was an effort that was almost physical pain. "I could kill you for that back home. There are maybe four things I could kill someone for, and that—"

She broke off and spun toward the fire, pulling the knife from her sleeve.

Simon made some kind of incoherent sound and stood up fast, knocking over his chair. Ignoring him, Joan held her arm out over the stone hearth and put the blade against her open palm.

"I give you my oath by blood and iron," she said, and

the words came back to her as clearly as when she'd made the vow to the priest, with her mother crying in pride and fear. "I give it by the fixed stars and the wandering, by our dead and our lost, by all we have left behind and all we still hold. I am a warrior of the free people, and I will fight to my death against the enemies of humanity. Let me be broken, nameless, and voiceless if I ever forsake my duty. Let men and Powers both abandon me if I turn against the light or show favor to the darkness."

"Joan—"

She didn't even feel the cut. "This is my word. This is my will."

In front of her, the fire went on crackling away as if nothing had happened. Joan stared at it.

"You didn't have to do that for me," Simon said behind her.

"I didn't." The clarifying anger had ebbed, leaving Joan dog tired and still, stupidly, horny. *As my honored ancestors would say: oh, what a world, what a world.* But the oath had left her feeling less polluted, both by Reynell's touch and by her own reaction, like she stood on solid ground again. "Though I guess I thought I did at the time."

He sighed. "For what it's worth, I never really thought you wouldn't stop him, regardless of your feelings. I just didn't know what they were."

Joan laughed, harsh enough to hurt her throat. "Ask Betty. She knows how many baths I've taken in the last couple weeks and how hot they've been. Among other things." There was really no need to mention throwing up. "For five years, he's been in every nightmare I've had. The ground turned to ash where he walked. He's not like he was in my dreams—but do you really think I could look at him and see anything but a monster?"

"But you'd been so eager to kill him, and then you started hesitating…"

"I'm scared, you moron." It came out half choked. She didn't turn. "Not of dying. I'm going to die here no matter what, and maybe it's better if I go down fighting. But I only have one chance. If I make a move too soon, if I don't do everything just right…then there was never any point to my coming here at all."

The words hung in the air; the fire itself seemed to shape them.

"I'm sorry," Simon said. "I was a cad and stupid, and I'm sorry. Will you let me see your hand?"

"Sure." The cut was shallow, just beginning to sting now. Joan turned away from the fire and sat back down. Simon dug a handkerchief out of his pocket. There was a little pocket of silence between them and a sense of healing there. "At least I'll be wearing gloves tomorrow, I guess."

"There's that. And this doesn't look bad at all." His touch was warm on her wrist.

Joan nodded, trying not to feel. "It should be okay. I heal fast."

"You're fortunate."

"Partly. There are spells we get once we take the oath."

"Oh?" He wrapped the handkerchief around her hand and tied it deftly.

Joan nodded. "It's a dangerous business, but we do what we can." She watched him: the long lines of his body, the way his hair fell as he bent over her hand, the sudden glint of his eyes in the firelight. "I'm an assassin, Simon," she said abruptly. "I'm pretty good at pretending to feel things. Or not to feel things. You should remember that."

"I do," he said. "That's part of the problem."

"What do you mean?" She knew what he meant. It sang through her, sending the arousal she'd almost managed to bank into bright flame again.

Simon looked up at her, his eyes very dark. "I wanted to know how you felt about me," he said. His voice was low, ashamed but excited. "Not a very worthy impulse, I understand, but—"

Joan held up her hand, its improvised bandage white in the dim room. "Let me clear that up for you," she said, and leaned forward.

—⁓—

Kissing Joan was like drinking neat rum—almost uncomfortably hot and thoroughly, almost instantly intoxicating. It wasn't like kissing any other girl in Simon's experience. There was nothing naive or submissive about her, as there had been with Society girls. There was nothing practiced or seductive either, though he didn't doubt she had experience. She was all wild demand and hunger, bordering on greed.

It was agony to push her away, even a little. He struggled to find the breath to speak. "Do you really think this is wise?"

"I don't think it matters." Her lips were a little bruised now, and her smile was bright and hot.

"Joan—" he began, feeling the obligation.

Her eyes met his. Behind the lust, they were

essentially clear. "Do you really think it'll help anything if we stop now?"

God help him, he didn't.

Chapter 36

SIMON ROSE FROM HIS CHAIR, HALF PULLING JOAN AND half lifting her into his arms. He tried to be gentle for a moment. Then Joan wound her hands in his hair and pressed her body against his, her breath hot against his neck, and his control snapped.

He claimed her mouth with almost painful violence, startling himself—but not pulling away. Not when Joan didn't. Not when she groaned instead and writhed, rubbing her breasts against his chest and her hips against his aching erection. He couldn't have stopped himself then for anything.

All he could do was step away a little, not enough to stop kissing Joan but enough to bring his hands upward and stroke her breasts. The corset was a damnable barrier, too stiff and too thick to permit much contact, but above it, where there was only thin silk between Simon's hands and Joan's skin—ah, there was warmth and firmness, and he couldn't bear even the silk any longer.

It ripped easily. Joan did tense for a moment when she heard the noise, and Simon started to pull back, to reassure and inquire. Her hands were on his shoulders, though, drawing him to her and pulling downward at the same time so that they were both settling to the floor. He went willingly, kissing her neck and the smooth skin of her breasts, clearly visible now above the shredded neckline of her gown. Joan tilted her head back and caught her breath.

God, she was gorgeous, and, God, she was enthusiastic, and Simon didn't have anywhere near enough control to do her justice. Another few minutes of this, and he was going to spend in his trousers like some clumsy sixteen-year-old with his first woman.

When one of Joan's hands dropped to the buttons of his flies, Simon almost did. His hips thrust forward toward her palm, almost of their own volition, and his cock bucked against her fingers. The world began to go white around him. He pulled himself back from the brink, barely, and somehow caught her hand.

"No. Not like that." It was amazing that he got the words out. He was yanking his trousers open as he spoke, heedless of snapped buttons. They opened, after what felt like an eternity, and he shoved them down. When his swollen cock sprang out, Joan made a low, appreciative sound in her throat.

Hunger.

Simon shoved her skirt up and out of the way with one hand, a clumsy motion that Joan, thank God, either didn't notice or didn't mind. He slid his other hand up her leg, feeling the firm muscle through the thin cloth of her drawers, and then farther up. Joan parted her thighs for him almost at once. She was soft and hot and astoundingly wet.

Oh, God, yes.

At his touch, Joan thrust her hips upward, circling them. Her breath was coming fast now, her face flushed. Simon moved over her and forward, just nudging at her sex with the head of his cock.

Somewhere, he found the presence of mind to speak once more. "Tell me yes. *Please.*"

She opened her eyes. The rim of hazel around the

black pupil was very thin now. "Yes," she said, husky and impatient and feverish. "Hell, yes."

The first thrust forward was ecstasy in itself. Tight, wet—and Joan rising to meet him, her mouth on his neck and her hands low on his back now, urging him on. He went again, and the world began to diminish, to center itself in his plunging cock and the woman beneath him. *Good*, he thought, and *good* again, and then there were no more words.

Joan cried out into his neck, a shout of pure primitive triumph. Simon felt her climax beneath him. Her nails scored his back, creating a dim pain that only increased his pleasure. He might have shouted at the end himself. He neither knew nor cared.

Smell was the first part of consciousness to return: sweat and arousal, strangely pleasant with a touch of lemons and roses. Simon realized that he had his face buried in Joan's neck and that her hair was spread out beneath them. Her skin was silky against his lips, and her body felt wonderful beneath his, all firm and warm with just a touch of softness. Already, renewed lust began to make itself known.

But they were still on the floor, he thought, and still mostly dressed. Simon remembered his urgency then and his violence. When he opened his eyes, he saw the beginnings of a bruise on Joan's neck and didn't remember how it had gotten there.

Simon flushed and winced a little inside, even as his body started to respond again. If he hadn't remembered how wet Joan had been, or how quickly she'd come once he'd thrust into her, he would have damned himself for the worst kind of brute.

As it was, he found himself absurdly embarrassed
when Joan turned her head to look at him and absurdly
relieved to see her languid smile. "I didn't think about
the floor," he said, apologizing nonetheless. "I hope it
wasn't too uncomfortable."

She laughed, rippling and easy. "There's a floor?"

It was all right. Any remnants of tension fled, leaving
Simon relaxed as he hadn't been in months. "There's
supposed to be."

"Oh, well." She shrugged. It was quite a diverting
movement. "I don't think I could've made it to a bed."
Firelight spilled down over her face, making it glow, turning her hazel eyes luminous and her hair to molten gold.

"Would you like to try now?" Simon asked.

Joan shifted under him and then lifted her eyebrows
and laughed again. Her laughter fell around Simon like
the fire's warmth. "*You've* been eating your Wheaties,
haven't you?" Incomprehensible statement. It didn't
matter, though, because she leaned up and kissed him,
long and hard. "Absolutely."

———※———

It had been years since Joan had felt so comfortable
in anyone's presence. She didn't think she'd ever felt
so much like laughing as she did sneaking through the
house behind Simon, neither of them quite daring to turn
on a light and both of them wincing at every squeaky
board. Not since she was a kid, anyhow, and maybe not
even then. Her childhood hadn't ever been safe enough
to be silly.

She did start laughing when she got to Simon's room.
"You've seen it before, you know," he said. He was

standing beside her now and sliding his hands slowly up her back. Heat followed them: a more comfortable sort of heat this time, though, now that the first clawing desperation had been sated.

"Yeah, but I didn't notice."

"Notice what? I never thought you'd care so much about interior design."

Joan shook her head and turned, grinning at him. She gestured to the bed with one hand. "How many people do you usually fit in this thing?"

Now Simon laughed. His hands ran up her neck and then back down, light touches that made her squirm against him. "No more than five or six a night. I'm a moderate man, you know."

"Uh-huh," she teased back. "I hope I can live up to your standards then."

Simon bent and kissed her neck. "Oh," he said. His voice was low and husky. Against her back, she could feel that he was doing very well on the recovery front. "You've already done that and more."

There was only one way to answer a comment like that.

This time, it was slower and gentler, as far as either of them could manage, without the bruising force there'd been earlier. This time, Joan slid her hands through Simon's hair as he kissed her, rather than tangling and pulling. This time, when his mouth moved back to her neck, it was with no hint of teeth. She felt her lust building quickly, but it was building, not already at the point of no return.

They had time. Time to get undressed, for example, though that took longer than either of them would have liked. There were too many hooks on the back of Joan's

dress and far too many knots on her corset. By the time
Simon had gotten both of those off, Joan was fairly well
used to hearing him swear.

But at last it was off. The flashgun came with the
corset—Simon must have noticed but didn't ask. Nor
did he ask when Joan slipped off the garter and the knife
it held. He had his priorities straight, after all. And besides, when the weapons came off, so did the rest of the
goddamn complicated underwear, and Joan stood naked
before him in the dancing firelight.

For a moment, she was conscious of her scars, here in
this time where women were supposed to be white and
unblemished. For a moment she was glad of the shadows.
Then pride rose up. Joan straightened, tossed her hair
back over her shoulders, and met Simon's eyes squarely.
There might, she thought, have been a moment of tender-
ness in his gaze. More importantly, there was plenty of
desire. She heard him catch his breath, and smiled.

The view from her end was pretty spectacular too.
Simon's clothes had come off with relative ease—men
had it good here—but he'd been too busy trying to re-
move Joan's for her to take a good look. He deserved
one. Naked, his body lived up to every promise it had
made under his clothes and more. Not a warrior, no—he
had more than a hint of softness about him, and now
that made the men back home seem too thin, too sharp
and desperate—but an active man. His chest was broad,
his stomach was flat, and his cock jutted upward from
between lean, strong thighs.

She might have taken a step forward, or Simon might
have. Joan wasn't really sure and she didn't really care.
His skin felt amazingly good against hers. The sparse

hair on his chest rubbed against her hard nipples, and she made a quick involuntary sound of pleasure. Going slowly began once again to seem hard.

But she wanted to, so she stepped back, took Simon's hand, and led him to the bed. He followed, briefly surprised but not at all shocked, watching her with a combination of desire and curiosity. "Lie down," Joan said.

She began with his neck, trailing her mouth downward from the sensitive spot behind his ear—there was a pressure point there that would make men curse and stumble back if you jabbed it, but the light touch of her tongue just made Simon moan—and pressing her body against his, her hands light on his shoulders again. His hands were nowhere so innocent. They grasped her buttocks and pressed her against him so that she could feel him hard and hot against her stomach. By the time Joan reached his chest, she was slick again, not quite aching for him but getting damn close.

Slowly, she told herself, and tried. She even sat up to touch him, running her fingers through the dark hair on his chest, flicking them over his nipples, and grinning when he drew a breath that was more of a hiss. Then Simon sat upward and captured one of *her* nipples in his mouth, and Joan did more than hiss. She groaned and wriggled her hips against him, lust racing through her now. When he moved to the other breast, she threw her head back and closed her eyes, blind for a second to anything but that pleasure.

It took a hell of a lot of willpower to swing off Simon, but she did. He started to reach for her and then stopped, as if frozen, when Joan slid a hand between his legs. Slowly she moved upward, stroking his thighs and then cupping his balls gently, her fingers moving in small circles over the soft hair and softer skin. It had been a long time since she'd touched a man. She had never, she thought, touched one with so much pleasure.

"God," Simon said hoarsely. His eyes had closed somewhere in the process. Joan wrapped her fingers around his shaft, and he said, "God," again. This time it was considerably more emphatic. His cock pulsed in her hand, thick and rigid. When she slid her fingers upward, she found wetness at the head.

When she ran her tongue around it, Simon cried out, and his fists clenched on the sheets. "You—ahh—don't have to—"

Joan laughed and slid downward, taking him into her mouth. He tasted musky, far from unpleasant, and she wanted to make him come that way sometime soon. Not now, though. Whether it was the aphrodisiac or Simon himself, she was hot again, wanting again, and she couldn't wait much longer. She gave the head of his cock one final flick of her tongue, making him moan again, and then sat up.

Straddling him again was wonderful. Taking him inside her was damn near mind-blowing. She cried out this time—once in pleasure and then startled when Simon caught her hips before she could begin to move.

When she looked down, she saw that he was smiling up at her. "My turn now," he said, and his hand, big and warm, moved down. He ran his fingers through the curls between her thighs, found the place that was stiff and eager for his touch, and slowly began to rub it. "Don't move."

His voice was low, almost a whisper, a caress itself.

And his touch was patient. Light. Skilled. Joan might have been surprised if she'd been able to think. Instead, she held very still, biting her lip, fighting the urge to arch forward and rub against Simon's hand. All her attention focused on his touch and on making sure it didn't stop—more so as he rubbed faster, a little harder, and suddenly the conclusion wasn't just likely but fucking inevitable.

Joan didn't notice him leaning up, but suddenly his lips had closed over one of her nipples again. Then his hand was moving even faster, and she threw her head back, biting her lip. That time she managed to come without screaming, though she'd never in her life know how.

As the surges inside her died away, she and Simon started moving. Now there was urgency. Simon seemed at the end of his patience, and that was fun too. His hands gripped her hips again, but this time they urged her on, faster and faster, with his eyes on her face or watching the way her breasts moved with each thrust. At the end, his eyes closed again, and he thrust upward one final time, letting go and taking Joan over the edge again as he went.

"You don't have any scars," Joan said, sometime later. She was lying on one side, trailing the tips of her fingers over his chest. Even after two rounds of sex—and those quite the wildest Simon could remember—it felt wonderful. He thought he might start purring. "None. It's pretty impressive. Didn't you ever fall off anything?"

"I did. And I do. Have a scar, I mean." He wiggled

his right foot and then caught Joan's arm. "No, don't get up. It's not worth looking at."

She grinned. "What happened?"

"Nothing terribly romantic. I slammed it in a window trying to sneak out of school one night."

"Why?"

"I was twelve."

This time, her smile was rueful. "Okay, fair enough."

He ran a hand down her arm, brushing the long scar there. "I shouldn't ask where you got yours, should I?"

"Not this late at night," she joked, but her eyes were serious, watching his face. Looking for any hint of disgust, Simon thought, and he met her gaze seriously. "There's the flashgun, of course, where it fastens on. You know that one."

He glanced down at the scar in the crook of her elbow. "Is it always there?"

"Not always. It has more of a kick with the major vessels and closer to the heart." She rubbed the little circle absently with one hand. "I've attached to the femoral sometimes if I had time to prepare in advance and someone to supervise. And if I could eat a steak afterward."

"Does it hurt?" he asked.

She shook her head. "Not during. The gun's got anesthetic. Aches a bit after, though. The tattoos hurt worse."

There was one of them on her back, high enough that he could see why her ball gowns were relatively modest: a spiraling blue shape near her spine. Another, also blue but more angular and runic, adorned the inside of each thigh. "They look like they took a while too."

"Oh, yeah." She winced but with pride. "The priests

tie you down when they do it. Only way to make anyone
keep still. And you have to. They're magic."

"What do they do?" he asked, stroking his finger over
the blue spiral.

"These? Speed. Strength. Protection. Other people
get other things."

"But everyone has them."

Joan nodded. "It's a sign that you're grown up."

"Enduring pain," he said dryly. "I suppose that's a
reasonable enough mark of adulthood. Particularly in
your time—no offense intended."

"None taken," she said, amiable and relaxed. "There's
a reason I came back."

Abruptly, Simon pulled her into his arms, rejoicing
not in sensuality now but in the sheer feel of her, warm
and alive and whole against him. He held her tightly,
perhaps too tightly—in recompense, perhaps, for the
time in the library before when he couldn't.

Joan sighed, contented, and rested her head on his
shoulder. "I'm glad I got to meet you too," she said.

Then she sighed and pushed herself upward. Her body
was shadow and silver, now that moonlight had replaced
the dying fire, and her hair fell around her like Danae's
cloud. "I'd better head out. Before anyone wakes up."

"You could stay here," Simon said. He told himself it
was a sudden impulse, but he knew he was lying.

And he knew what the answer would be, even before
Joan shook her head. "If I could stay, I would."

Chapter 37

THERE WAS ALWAYS A MORNING AFTER.

Not that Joan had any regrets—even the faint damn-it's-been-a-while soreness was good, since it brought back hot memories and gave her the satisfied feeling of hard work well done—but logistics had gotten a lot more complicated all of a sudden.

The ripped dress, for one. Much as she'd enjoyed Simon's company the night before, Joan looked at the shredded bodice and cursed him quietly. The tear was a simple one, but it was in a very revealing place. So, wincing inwardly, she stuffed the dress into the cupboard where she kept the rest of her more damning supplies. At least today was Betty's day off. That gave Joan something of a reprieve.

She found a blouse that would hide the bruise on her neck and a skirt, and then went downstairs.

Eleanor was in the library. Her usual book was on the desk, but for once she was paying no attention to it, looking out the window instead. She jumped a little when Joan came in.

Was Eleanor going back to her old nervousness? She hadn't dressed in black or anything, and she smiled, but she did drop her eyes. Joan sighed inwardly even as she smiled. "Hey."

"Good morning." At least that came without stuttering or hesitation. "Are you all right? Did the party go well?"

"Pretty well," said Joan.

Eleanor looked her over, trying to be surreptitious. Her eyes lingered on the high collar of Joan's blouse. "I'm sorry I wasn't awake when you came back."

She was worried, Joan realized, and she was a lot less innocent than most people here thought girls were. It did look bad: a late night in the company of a bastard, followed by plainer clothing than usual with a high neckline.

"Don't worry about it," she said. It came out sounding rougher than she'd meant it to, more like rejection. "I mean—"

She reached over and put a hand on Eleanor's. "Nothing happened. I swear. There was a crowd. Reynell tried flirting with me, like usual. That's all."

Not exactly the truth, though, not about Simon and, more importantly, not about Reynell. Joan thought she'd done a fairly good job of hiding that, but Eleanor gave her a long, measuring look before she nodded. "I'm very glad to hear it. Did you have a good time?"

"Not really." Joan sat down on the edge of the desk. "I don't really like messing with spirits. Especially not when I'm with people who don't know what they're doing."

"You don't think *anyone* there does?"

Joan shook her head. "I think there were people there who can call things up. Reynell might be able to put them back down again. But eventually he's gonna run across one that he can't make go away or one that puts its mark on him before he does, and then—" She brought her hands together with a sharp clap.

"Oh." Eleanor frowned a little. "You seem to know a great deal about them."

"Yes," said Joan.

"It's odd, really, that they should be so much the same between your world and ours. When yours is so different, I mean."

"Maybe," said Joan. "But maybe they come from outside all worlds, so that wouldn't be so strange."

Eleanor walked back to the desk and closed her book, smoothing her hand down the leather cover. "You're here to do something very serious," she said. "Aren't you?"

"Yes," said Joan.

"It's to do with Mr. Reynell."

"Yes." She waited.

Eleanor looked down at the book. "Oh," she said, and left it on the desk. "Simon says we might go to the theatre tonight. Would you like that?"

—∿∿—

Theatre dresses were low necked, but a broad velvet ribbon hid the bruise all right, and Joan pinned on a brooch to make it look like jewelry instead of camouflage. She let Betty fuss over her hair a little more than usual too, and peered into the mirror for just a moment longer, looking at the masses of rose satin and the piled curls.

Dumbass. You need infatuation right now like you need a hole in the head. Still, there it was. When she thought of Simon, her pulse sped up. Stupid, but undeniable.

And when she met him in the hall and saw the way he looked at her, Joan found herself smiling like a complete moron. She couldn't even be properly embarrassed about it. Not when he was smiling back the same way. On him, it looked gorgeous.

"You'll have a good time tonight," Simon said, as he

walked into the theatre with her and Eleanor. "It's an excellent play—and has a very well-known actress in the lead part."

"That," Eleanor said, quiet and wry, "will guarantee a packed house no matter what the play is."

She was talking more tonight, her small jokes more frequent. That might have been a good sign. There was energy there, nervous energy, though, Joan thought. She hoped that Eleanor hadn't found out about her and Simon or that she wasn't upset if she had.

They tried not to be too obvious. Joan didn't know how successful they were. Simon pointed people out to her and Eleanor alike, but when Eleanor was distracted, he sometimes bent close to Joan and told her something he'd never think of mentioning to his sister, or he ran his fingers up her neck for a moment. Joan thought it was fairly subtle, but she had no real way to be sure.

Not that she was objecting.

"It is a tragedy," Simon said, leaning over to her when the curtain fell for intermission.

"Hmm?"

"You're smiling."

"So are you."

"It's a very thoughtful smile. I'm contemplating the meaning of life." He straightened up as Eleanor got to her feet, turning to her with a slightly less joking look. "And how did you like it?"

"Oh, very well, thank you." They were heading out of their box now into a hall filled with richly dressed people. Joan strained to hear Eleanor as she went on. "I've seen it done before, but the staging here was—"

She stopped short. A gaunt woman in ostrich feathers bumped into her, sniffed loudly, and stalked on. Eleanor didn't seem to notice.

Joan followed Eleanor's gaze across the room and saw, as she'd expected, Reynell. He was standing in a small group of young people, holding a drink in one hand and leaning against a wall. When he saw Joan, he bowed—the drink didn't even wobble—but he looked from her to Simon and Eleanor and didn't step forward.

Oh, Powers.

All right. I'm supposed to be crazy about this guy. What do I do now?

She turned to Simon. His hands were clenched at his sides now, and if she put a hand on his arm, Joan knew, she'd feel the muscles as tense as wire. Much as she wanted to touch him, though, to give him some kind of reassurance, she couldn't. Too many people were watching, and one person in particular.

It was time for the mission now.

"I'm going to go and get some fresh air," she said, just a little too loudly. "It's a bit hot in here."

Simon frowned. "Would you like me to come with you?"

"No, don't trouble yourself. I'll only be a minute. Besides, I'm sure Eleanor could use some refreshment."

That much, at least, was true. Ellie was staring back and forth between them and then at Reynell, looking more troubled than she had in a long time. *Hell*, thought Joan, but she couldn't worry about it now. *I'll just find the book and stab him, and this will all get better.*

First she had to make herself an opening. She patted Eleanor on the arm, then slipped through the crowd.

Of course, she couldn't actually go outside. Ladies didn't do that. There was a small open window on the other side of the room and enough people to provide plenty of cover between it and Simon. Joan squeezed between people to get there, smelling rich food and heavy perfume, and tried not to think about what would happen in an attack.

At the window, she stared outside, letting her hair blow back and taking deep breaths. It really was a relief—at least until she felt a gloved hand on her shoulder. "I've missed you horribly, you know."

"It's only been a day," she said, laughing nervously. The nerves supplied themselves, at least. She only had to fake the laughter.

Reynell met her eyes as she turned and let his tongue slip out, passing over his lower lip for just a second. "A day can seem like an eternity," he said, "especially without the company one desires. I can only count myself lucky that chance brought you here."

Does this really work on people? Maybe just on girls he's drugged.

"Why do you say that?" She dropped her eyes. "I do have to get back soon. The play will be starting."

"But before it does," Reynell said, sliding his hand down along her arm, "perhaps we can make more private arrangements." His hand reached hers, clutched it, and pressed a slip of paper into the palm. "Bring a maid, if that will satisfy your hosts. Only take care to bring a discreet maid."

He smiled at her, utterly sure of himself.

"Nothing could keep me away," said Joan.

Reynell raised her hand to his mouth and slowly

kissed the knuckles. "I'll be counting the hours," he said, and then he was gone.

Turning back to the window, Joan opened the paper.

Tomorrow night, it said, in perfect handwriting. *Ten o'clock.* And an address.

Ten o'clock. Not horribly late for town life. Still too late and too private to be anything but sex. At least he was honest. Joan folded the note and slid it into her reticule. Her hands shook only a little.

Calm down. You're ready for this. You've been getting ready for years.

That was the problem. Five years of training back home and more than a month here. Suddenly, time had weight, and Joan felt all of it at her back. Everything she did from now on would be important, either because it would affect the mission or because…well, because it would probably be one of the last times she did it.

Here we go.

She crossed the room again and found Simon standing by himself. "Where's Eleanor?"

"Over that way," he said, gesturing roughly toward the area where Joan had been. "Talking with a friend from school, she said. I thought with so many people around, and since you were talking to Alex—"

"'Just a distraction.' Goes great on a tombstone," Joan said, and laughed a little too sharply.

Then Simon's hand was on the small of her back, firm and warm, and she felt her racing heartbeat slow. Arousal ran second now to relief. She looked up, met his eyes, and saw confirmation.

"There are two of us, you know," he said mildly. Then, frowning, "Are you all right? Did he—"

"He didn't do anything that wasn't in the plan. And I'm fine." She took a deep breath, hardly even feeling it. "But we'll need to talk when we get home."

Chapter 38

THE NOTE WASN'T SURPRISING, REALLY. STILL, SIMON read it slowly and then read it over again. If there was ever a time to have all the details of a situation down, it was now.

Joan paced while he read. She picked up one book after another and set them down again, took a diffident sip of tea and then abandoned the cup, and finally took the poker and began, entirely without need, to stir up the fire. Color flamed in her cheeks, and her eyes were so bright that she looked almost feverish.

She hadn't bothered to take off her evening dress, but she had pulled the pins out of her hair, one by one, shortly after they'd entered the library. Now her hair hung loose and golden over the rose silk, completing the picture of a woman in an advanced state of distraction.

Not that Simon could blame her. Not that he didn't have his own inner maelstrom of relief that things were finally coming to an end, regret that it was this end, a now almost nonexistent glimmer of hope that Alex could be redeemed or at least could meet an honorable death, and what he could now freely admit was bitter jealousy where Joan was concerned.

He spoke from the last. Everything else was too momentous, too intense. "If it's possible," Simon said, putting the note down, "I would rather not give him the chance to get very far."

Joan spun around and stared at him. For a second, her eyes were blank, and Simon waited for anger. She laughed, though. There wasn't much humor in it, but it was laughter. "Powers help me, neither would I. If he weren't a wizard, it might be a good idea, tactically speaking. But—you know what I mean?"

"I do." There were spells that used sex as a conduit. There were some that needed only close physical contact.

"Yeah. I'd rather not sleep with him. Besides, he probably wouldn't trust me enough to roll over and fall asleep after."

"No," said Simon. "I doubt he falls asleep with anyone else in the room these days."

"So," said Joan, flopping down at the desk and drumming her fingers on the surface, "I need a distraction once I get in there. Something that'll keep him busy for a little while so I can look for the book. Something that goes off before too long. I don't want to eat or drink anything he gives me, and I can make only so many excuses."

"The book's probably in his study," Simon said. "If you're in his bedroom, it might take you ten minutes to get there. Five if you're in the drawing room. That's assuming you're not interrupted."

"I'll deal with interruptions," said Joan, and then shook her head when Simon's alarm clearly showed. "Nonlethally. I've got enough knockout darts to take down a horse."

"And the guardian?"

"Flashgun. A couple shots should take care of it, from the way it sounded. Maybe not kill it, but at least send it off for a while. Long enough."

The image of that thing with its tentacles around Joan

made Simon's throat close. But he knew better than to try to protect her against her will. "I hope so," he said. "I'm afraid he's probably hidden the book fairly well. You can lock the door behind you, probably, which will buy you at least a little time."

"The longer I have, the better. I want to make sure the book's gone before I have to deal with Reynell at all." Joan frowned. "So a fire wouldn't work. He'd go to grab the manuscript himself. A break-in, maybe?"

"Possibly." Simon leaned back in his chair, closing his eyes, and rubbed at his temples. "It'd have to be something magical, though. Otherwise he'd just send a footman to deal with it. And that—"

"—means you'll have to do it," Joan said. She didn't sound happy about it, which Simon supposed made them even. "Unless you can make something and send that in with me."

He shook his head. "The wards would pick up anything like that instantly. I suppose I'll have to turn out-and-out housebreaker. He'll never believe you'd bring a manservant to something like this, and his servants would never let me in otherwise."

"I don't like it," Joan said. "We don't have anyone on the inside. You break in, and we're opening this thing up to police, servants, you name it. It's not just us and him anymore, and that makes it a whole less predictable. But—"

The door opened.

Both of them looked up. Joan stood, one hand going to her side—and then saw Eleanor. She was standing just inside the doorway, her face pale but set.

Before either Joan or Simon could speak, Eleanor

pushed the door closed and then clasped her hands behind herself. "I could do it," she said. "I could be the person on the inside."

—∿∿—

Simon looked like he'd seen the dead walk. Joan wasn't so surprised. This made sense when she thought about it: Eleanor's nervousness, her questions about Reynell, the way she'd been studying magic. "You were listening," she said.

"Yes," said Eleanor, and swallowed. "And I-I spied on you earlier, I'm afraid, when you met with Mr. Reynell. I saw him give you a note. I'm sorry. I know it was deceitful, but I had to find out."

"Why, in Heaven's name?" Simon asked, sounding like someone had throttled him.

"Because I kept finding out other things," Eleanor said, looking like she might faint. "They were little things, but they came together, and I started to see that something very large was going on. And that I can help."

Simon stared at her. "You don't know any more about housebreaking than I do."

"I don't have to. Nobody looks twice at a maid. You know that. Most people don't look twice at me, anyway. I don't think even Mr. Reynell has, since I've come back, except to try to scare me. He doesn't see me as a threat. I don't think he sees me at all." She smiled wanly. "Certainly his butler won't know me or care. And I know a little magic. I could do enough to set off the wards, and then I could scream and run away."

"You think they'd let you get far enough into the house to cast a spell?" Joan asked.

"I think so. At the very least, I could let Simon in one of the back doors. If I said I'd forgotten to give you something and then pretended to get lost…I think I could manage."

"Absolutely not," said Simon, coming back to himself. The hope vanished from Eleanor's face, and she looked down. "There's no way I'm letting you—"

"Think about it for a second," Joan interrupted, holding up a hand. "She could be useful."

Simon turned to her, eyes narrowing a little. "This isn't about your mission," he said, "and I told you when we started that I wouldn't have her recruited."

"Exactly when do you think I recruited her, huh? When she listened at the door, or when she spotted me with Reynell? Besides, everything's about this mission. It has to be."

"I'm well aware that you think so," he said icily. "But this is my sister. She doesn't have to be, and, by God, she isn't going to be."

"Not even by her own choice?"

"She's a child."

Joan snorted. "She's eighteen. Old enough here to marry and breed. And I was in the field three years younger—"

"—because your world is like something out of Dante. That doesn't mean anything. It certainly doesn't mean I shouldn't protect her."

"Yeah?" said Joan. "Well, did you ever think maybe so much protection's why she—"

Simon knew what she was going to say. It was obvious from the way his eyes flashed. He opened his mouth to interrupt as Joan was about to go on—and then Eleanor cleared her throat.

It was a very quiet sound, but it made them both turn. Heat spread across Joan's face, and she saw Simon flush as well. *Right. We're both assholes.*

"Um," said Eleanor, "I wanted to say that I wouldn't be in nearly as much danger as either of you would. Not even if I went."

Simon blinked. "Well, *no*," he said. "You shouldn't be."

"Why shouldn't I?" Eleanor swallowed again. "I mean, it isn't as though I don't worry about you or as though what happens in there won't affect my life. And if I didn't go and it went wrong, don't you think I'd hate myself for that?"

Her voice cracked on the last word, and she looked hastily down at her feet.

It took about two seconds for Simon to get out of his chair and put his arms around her. "Ellie," he began, and then stopped. Joan looked away. She'd have left the room, but that would have been more disruptive.

Eleanor sniffled. "You can't tell me nothing will go wrong, Simon. I couldn't believe you. I'd want to, but I couldn't."

"It wouldn't be your fault," he said, "if it did."

"Wouldn't it?" Eleanor looked solemnly up at her brother. "Why not? If you'd left me in danger when you could have done something about it at very little risk to yourself, wouldn't you feel as though you were to blame?"

"That's different," said Simon, but halfheartedly. He looked down at Eleanor for a long moment. "Is that the only reason you want to do this?"

"No," she said very quietly.

"Is it to try to be like Joan? Because—"

"No." Eleanor blushed and looked over to where Joan sat. "I like you a great deal, but I can't be like you, any more than I could be like Rosemary. I...hope you understand."

"Of course I do," said Joan, and left it at that. "Why, then?"

"I had no part in saving myself," Eleanor said, and her voice was almost too quiet to hear. "I don't even remember it. And now when I see Mr. Reynell, he's... larger than he should be. Scarier. Like an ogre in a fairy story. I thought that maybe if I could do something to him, just a little thing, it wouldn't be so bad. He'd be more human."

Her nerve failed her at the last, and she didn't look at Simon when she talked. Joan did, though, and saw him look like he'd been punched in the gut.

"I see," he said, and then stood quietly for a long time, not looking at anyone or anything in the room. "Give me your word, then, that you won't take any unnecessary risks. You'll let me in, set off whatever distraction we need, and then hide. You won't confront Alex."

Eleanor's face lit with surprise and pride, fear and love. Joan looked away.

"I swear it," Eleanor said, lifting her head and speaking clearly. "I swear by the stars and the children of the stars, by the greater Powers and the lesser."

It was like an oath from Joan's world but different. From one of Simon's books, she thought, particularly given the way Simon almost flinched at it. He managed a smile, at least. "Then God go with us all," he said. "And we'll talk about this tomorrow."

He didn't look at Joan when he left the room.

—*ᴧᴧᴧ*—

Sleep was long in coming that night. Past midnight, Simon was still awake and well acquainted with every crack in his ceiling. He was turning over for what might have been the fiftieth fruitless time when he heard the door open. He spun around almost instantly, less from any sense of real danger than from a general irritation of the nerves.

Joan closed the door behind her and stood silently looking at him. She was wearing a dressing gown again, with a nightgown underneath it this time. With her hair loose and flowing over her shoulders, she looked surprisingly young, and yet there was something in her face that could never be so.

"I'm sorry," she said.

"You were right."

It hurt to say it, hurt both because of his pride and because of what it meant. He watched Joan's face carefully, looking for triumph, and found none. Instead, she shrugged. "Maybe. But I said it wrong." She smiled in a way that was half a grimace. "They should've sent a better diplomat."

"I'd rather not work with a diplomat," said Simon. He sat up a little and held out a hand to her. "And I'd certainly rather not do anything else with one."

Joan flashed a grin. "Probably not. Our best diplomat was Winston. He's a friend of my father's—about the same age too—and has a giant beard."

She joked, but the weariness was still in her voice. It was in her body too, despite her straight shoulders and high chin. Not just the fight, he thought, or maybe the fight hadn't just come from Eleanor's offer. Did everyone's nerves go *twang* before something like this? "I'm sorry too," he said.

"Good to know." She sat down on the bed beside him and ran her fingers through his hair. Through the window, the moon picked both of them out in silver light. Neither of them spoke for a long time.

There was too much that they might say if they did. All of it seemed ill-omened, the sort of thing you told someone that you would never see again. Simon was magician enough to know the power of belief. If you acted as if something were true, maybe it would be. So he said nothing.

He wondered if Joan had the same reasons. *Everyone I love is there*, he remembered her saying. He wondered if that was still true, and if she'd prefer, at the end of whatever happened the next night, to leave this world to try to find whatever was left of those she'd known.

When she met his eyes, hers were sad and filled with the same awful knowledge. It didn't matter what she felt or what he did. It couldn't. Nothing was certain, and they would be risking everything. That was all either of them needed to know.

Simon rose, then, and kissed her. It was like coming home. They had all the time in the world and not nearly enough.

Slowly, Joan slid her arms around him and pressed her body close, her mouth sweet and warm beneath his. She moved to his neck after a little while when she felt him harden against her, grazing the skin lightly with her lips, tracing every inch until Simon moaned. More than lust was rising in his blood now; there was a warmth that felt almost magical.

Pulling away a little, Simon ran his hands down Joan's body, grazing her breasts, until he found the knot holding her dressing gown closed. He undid it with care, and he knew Joan watched him. The gown fell away easily. She half sat, half lay before him, almost exposed, and then she reached for the hem of her nightgown and drew it upward.

There was none of the impatience or the frank sexual hunger that he'd come to expect. Not that Joan blushed or tried to hide herself. That sort of reaction would be as alien to her as this time was. But she took as much care removing her nightgown as he had untying the knot of her belt, drawing it slowly upward to expose slim, strong thighs and the sleek golden triangle where they met. Simon caught his breath.

The fabric moved farther upward, traveling the lean, scarred length of her body. Joan drew it higher, over her head and then off. Her bare breasts rose high and firm, dark pink nipples hard and thrusting toward Simon, as if begging for his hands. He made himself wait, though, until Joan reached for him again.

Then he drew her toward him so that her naked skin pressed against his. Her gasp was both satisfying and tempting. He wanted to hear it again, so he cupped her breast in one hand, flicking his thumb over the nipple. Joan writhed. Her hand, on the small of his back, pressed harder, pushing him against her so that the hair between her legs rubbed deliciously against his stiff cock.

Simon groaned, but he didn't enter her, not yet. He wanted to feel her first, to feel all the firm muscle and smooth skin, to read her scars like he might a book. He ran his hand up her arm and then down her back, gliding over the tattoo there. *Protection*, he thought, and left his hand there for a while, as if, by its warmth, it might activate the mark or lend some new power to it.

He could indulge that fancy for only so long, though, before Joan's urges and his own body's had their way. When she trailed her fingers down his spine, they left heat behind them. When she gripped his buttocks, Simon groaned again and slid his hands down to hers, cupping them and squeezing gently. She squirmed again, eager, even if not impatient, and the friction made Simon gasp.

"You're lovely," he said, his voice thick. He still couldn't speak of love. It felt too much like doom. "You're so bloody lovely."

Another day, she might have laughed and denied it. Now she looked up at him and smiled. "So are you."

One of her hands slid between them, found his cock, and stroked once. Slowly. Simon thrust forward into her hand and cried out. *Now*, he thought, with a tidal certainty that he'd never before felt with a woman. *Now*.

She was wet against his hand, and she opened easily, eagerly. Nonetheless, his first thrust forward was slow and gentle. Joan's body closed around him, arms and legs as well as her sex, and Simon began to move very slightly inside her. He looked down at her while he rocked forward and back, watching her eyes and the almost serene pleasure on her face.

Even the moonlight couldn't make her silver, not entirely. She was too dark for that. Too vivid. The most living person he'd ever met.

They fell easily into a rhythm. No struggle upward to a peak this time, nor overwhelming fall. Instead, Simon seemed to float there, aware of his own urgency and yet willing to wait, wanting to wait. Not wanting this to be one more thing that was done, that was in the past, as he went forward into—what?

He didn't want to think about it. Right now, he didn't have to. He moved slowly, Joan warm and strong below him, and lost himself in *now*.

It was almost a disappointment to feel his pleasure rising, his own climax approaching, and he tried to hold it off. Then Joan was there with him, coming around him, her eyes open and wide with surprise. He'd never seen such joy on her face before.

Simon kept his own eyes open when he came, trying to burn Joan's face into his mind. Trying to keep it always—however long *always* lasted.

Afterward, Joan lay with her head on Simon's chest, one arm thrown across him. She felt deceptively boneless. Simon suspected that she could snap alert at one wrong sound, though he was far from inclined to test that theory.

Joan didn't speak. Her eyes went from the window to Simon's face and then back to the window for a long moment. Then she sighed.

She was going to leave now, Simon knew. She'd say something about having to go, push herself out of bed, and leave. It was very practical of her.

"Could we get under the blankets or something?" Joan asked. "I'm not feeling the cold yet, but it's only a matter of time."

"You're staying?" Simon asked, blinking down at her.

Joan opened one eye. "If you don't mind."

He put one hand on her arm in case she got any ideas about getting up. "Of course I don't. I—" Simon

tried to process his thoughts, tried to get past the feeling that he'd been given a gift he'd never expected.
"But—the servants?"

"Hell with 'em," Joan said, wriggling closer to his
side. "Gossip doesn't spread that fast. It's one night."

Either he truly believed her or he wanted to believe
her, and Simon didn't care much either way. He pulled
the blanket around them both, rested his chin on Joan's
head, and closed his eyes.

One night, he thought, and tightened his arms around her.

Chapter 39

ALEX WAS REASONABLY CERTAIN THAT JOAN WOULD show up.

The potion, after all, had been very potent. The woman must have been nearly frantic by the time they'd met at the theatre. The strained note to her laughter had certainly borne that out, as had the tension that had gone through her body at his touch. Whatever Simon might have been doing to her, Alex thought, he certainly wasn't leaving her particularly satisfied.

Still, some doubting part of Alex half expected, when ten o'clock arrived, to find Joan's maid with some excuse. It was possible that Simon would prevent her from coming. It was possible that her own nerves would have gotten the best of her. And there were always unexpected complications when dealing with women. One simply never knew.

Alex had prepared himself for some disappointment, a temporary setback, at least. He could always try again. Delay did increase desire, or so they said.

Still, after so much time, he was impatient to see the culmination of his plans—his own carnal pleasure, Simon's pain, and perhaps an aid to his magical practice or an agent in the Grenville home. There were a number of possibilities at hand, and Alex badly wanted to grasp them.

He'd given most of the servants the night off, saying that he'd have a quiet supper in his rooms—which he had—and retaining only two maids and the butler. Casborough had been serving him long enough to be unshockable and knew enough not to ask inconvenient questions. At Alex's request, he'd prepared the drawing room by lighting a fire, turning the lamps down low, and placing glasses and decanters on a low table.

Wine did great things for an evening, after all. If it didn't, Alex could always slip a little more of the potion into Joan's glass. When Casborough opened the door, a few minutes past ten, Alex felt a thrill that he hadn't quite been expecting. Physical desire and more emotional satisfaction mixed deliciously. In a very short time, he would have everything he wanted.

Perhaps he wouldn't even have to kill Simon afterward, or his sister. Alex smiled and rose from his seat to greet his visitor.

Joan was wearing an evening dress: blue and white, frothing with ribbons, and long sleeved but temptingly low cut. Her hair was loose, almost unbound, and there was a wide velvet ribbon around her neck. Alex wondered idly where she'd told Simon that she was going. He'd know the truth soon enough, anyhow.

"Joan," he said, taking one of her hands in both of his. Her eyes widened most gratifyingly. "It's so very good to see you."

"And you," she said, her face already flushed. Through her glove, her hand was a little cold.

Nerves, Alex thought. Best not to rush things. If he blundered here, Joan could run straight back to Simon. Not that she'd ever be able to do anything to his good name, not after having come here more or less unescorted, but there was no sense in ruining the game. He waved Casborough away and led Joan over to the wide sofa. "I thought you might care for something to drink," he said.

"Oh—" she began, looking over at the decanters. "I—a very little, please."

Alex poured slowly, letting her hear every sound he made in the otherwise silent room. "Don't worry," he said. "I'd like to have you well aware of everything."

"That's practically a given," she said, laughing a little as she took the glass.

It wasn't taking her long to relax, Alex thought. In a way, that was good; in another, it was less than flattering. "I do hope," he said, watching her toy with the wine, "that you've been doing all right. Particularly after that little display we witnessed."

"Very well, thank you," she said.

Alex lifted an eyebrow. "No nightmares, then."

She caught her breath. Rich color spread up her neck and over her face. There was a little pulse in the hollow of her neck, beating fast now, like a rabbit's heart as the animal cowered before a predator. Alex was hard almost instantly.

"No," Joan said. "No nightmares." She added, "You have a very nice house here," her eyes darting around the room.

"Yes," Alex said. "It's very spacious. The view from my bedroom window is particularly excellent."

"Oh?" She tilted her head and looked up at him. Unconsciously, it seemed, she wet her lips.

"Mmm." Alex sat down beside her, almost close enough to touch but not quite. She was breathing quickly now, he noticed, with desire or fear, or both. He hoped for both. Forcing women was no fun, but a little fear always made seduction more interesting. "Are you the sort of woman who enjoys a good view?"

Joan caught her bottom lip between her teeth. "Maybe," she said. "Though I must admit I haven't seen very many."

"Then tonight should be quite enlightening," Alex said, and reached for her.

Her shoulders were tense beneath his hands, but she didn't pull away, and her mouth opened at the first touch of his tongue on her lips. Alex slid one hand up to the back of her head, tangling his fingers in her hair so that pins scattered across the couch, and the other down to the base of her spine, crushing her to him.

Joan made some muffled noise and wriggled against him, perhaps struggling from surprise or perhaps trying for closer stimulation. Either way, the friction felt wonderful. Alex took her mouth again, taking her lip between his teeth—gently, but not too gently—as he pressed her down into the sofa. He hadn't meant to take her here, but if circumstances got the better of him— well, there'd be the rest of the night to move upstairs.

He found the buttons of her dress with one hand, cursing the need for secrecy that kept him from ripping the damn thing off. Still kissing Joan, he began to undo them.

Then a woman screamed.

Alex didn't raise his head at first. He could calm Joan easily enough, and Casborough would handle whichever stupid girl had lost her wits at the sight of a mouse or something. Nothing he had to worry about. But then the world flashed green before his eyes, and he smelled something sharp and bitter.

The wards.

Simon.

He pushed himself off Joan and onto his feet, frustrated desire only adding to his anger. "I have to see to this," he said. "I'll be back. Call one of the servants if you need anything."

"But what is it?" she asked, eyes wide. "Are we in danger? Is it a burglar? Should I—"

"Wait. Here."

He stalked out of the drawing room. Casborough met him on the way. "Sir," he began. "I beg your pardon, sir—"

"You had better," Alex said darkly.

"—but one of the maids saw a shape, sir. A dark one. Toward your bedroom. And I'm afraid there's all sorts of damage in the dining room, sir. It hardly seems— shall I call the law?"

Human was what he'd been about to say. The shape hardly seemed human because it wasn't. Perhaps Simon had set aside some of his more inane prejudices after all. It would have been a good sign—except that Simon had done it to him. "No," Alex said. "Stay out of the way. I'll handle this myself."

—◆◆◆—

Joan watched the door close behind Reynell. In her mind, she saw the house as Simon had drawn it for her: the dining room down a long hallway from the drawing room, with the staircase in between. She tore open the loose stitches closing the slit in her skirt: there were the knockout darts on one side of the band around her thigh.

Reynell would be out of sight by now. Joan palmed the darts and headed for the door.

The hallway lights were dim, and there was nobody around. No cover either, though. Joan could see the staircase up ahead, but there wasn't a door or even a niche between her and it. She walked quickly. Running would look too suspicious. She had the darts, but if a servant got a scream out first, she was screwed.

I got nervous, she said silently, rehearsing, *and then I got lost.*

Down the hall, something crashed. Something heavy. Joan's sensor had gone off pretty strongly just as Reynell had started feeling things. Maybe Eleanor or Simon had set up something large. She hoped it was that. She couldn't afford to check.

As she reached the staircase, a shape appeared ahead of her. Large. Male. Joan slipped a dart into her hand and raised her chin. The man was in rough clothing, she saw now, with a cap that hid his face, the kind a stable hand might wear. She should be able to scare the hell out of him with rank alone.

"You—" she began, quiet and imperious.

Then she saw that it was Simon.

They couldn't talk. There wasn't time, and it wasn't safe. Joan met his eyes, though, and the glance was like a shot of good whiskey. Whatever happened now, she had somebody at her back.

Joan took the staircase as fast as she could, her skirt looped over one arm, and it still took forever. The carpet was thick enough to almost trip her up once or twice, the flashgun between her breasts jolted her at every step, and the knife and flask under her skirt chafed her thigh. Before she was little more than halfway up, her corset started stabbing her in the ribs. If she'd had time, she'd have asked Simon to cut the whole damn outfit off her.

One turn, midway between the floors, hid them from anyone watching below. They bolted around it and farther up. Not a second too soon.

"What the hell do you mean you don't know?" Reynell was at the bottom of the stairs, shouting at someone. "Find her. Bring her back to the drawing room. You have someone watching the front door, don't you?"

The answer was inaudible. Joan climbed faster. She didn't look at Simon.

"Then there's only one place she can be."

As they reached the second-floor landing, they heard him start to climb. Joan started toward the hallway and then turned back when Simon's footsteps stopped.

He spoke quietly. She still heard every word. "You know where to go."

"I do. And—"

"I'll delay him. Then lead him on. You'll never get the book otherwise."

Joan grabbed his shoulders and yanked him down to her. The kiss was hard. Her nails dug into his shoulders, and his hands pressed her to him with bruising force.

"Don't die," Joan whispered, and then ran off down the hall.

—◆—

Fourth door on the right. Locked, as Joan suspected. Didn't matter: what a hairpin had done in five minutes, her picks did in one. She grabbed the flashgun out of her corset and bolted into the study, slammed the door behind her, and locked it.

The guardian wasn't there. Maybe Simon had hurt it too badly. Maybe Reynell didn't want to waste his strength when he was in the house. That didn't matter either. Joan thanked the Powers for small favors and took a hasty look around.

Outwardly it was a normal enough room with a fireplace, a low sofa against one wall, a large desk facing the door, and a bookshelf behind the desk. No blood. No dead virgins. But Joan's sensor was almost flaming. This was the place. Reynell kept the book here, and he'd done more than that in the past.

She crossed the room to the desk and began yanking out drawers and dumping their contents on the floor. Papers and booze in the top drawer. More papers in the next drawer. None of them were magical. The third drawer had more papers, and a false bottom. Joan smashed it open with the hilt of her knife.

A shower of tiny bones fell out, hit the carpet, and scattered. They looked like fingers.

Shouting in the hall outside. Not at the door, but close enough.

When she stepped toward the bookshelves, the sensor flared again. It actually hurt this time. Joan tipped out each book, rifled through it, and dropped it—but nothing. Badly written pornography, pretentious occult bullshit, even poetry. But nothing handwritten.

Damn.

She grabbed control of herself before she could panic. *Think. It's not in the desk, and it's not on the shelves. There's nothing else here that can hold it, unless he put*

*it in the sofa cushions, but it is here somewhere. Just
keep going. One step at a time. It's something hidden.*

The bookshelves were pretty thick.

Joan reached out a hand. It was torture to go slowly,
to slide her fingertips over the bottom of each shelf, but
she made herself do it anyhow. The yelling outside was
closer now. There was a sound like thunder.

She told herself she didn't hear it.

On the third shelf, she felt a small bump, no bigger
than a fingertip. It could have been a knot in the wood—
but it wasn't. Too regular.

Joan drew her hand back quickly. There was no point
in taking risks now. She drew her knife, cut a thick wad of
satin off her skirt, and wound it around her fingertips until
it was almost an inch thick. Then she reached out again.

Nothing stung her when she pressed the button.
Nothing exploded. Instead, a thin drawer slid out. Inside
was a manuscript, rolled and tied with a black ribbon.
Joan grabbed it.

The writing was the same as in Reynell's note. That,
and a few sentences, was all she needed to know. *This
is it*.

She flung it into the fireplace, grabbed the flask from
under her skirt, and dumped the liquid inside over the
paper. There were matches on the mantel, and the cut
on her palm was fresh. As Joan opened it again with her
knife, she remembered her fight with Simon and what
had come after. It was a good memory for a time like
this, both the oath and the love.

"By blood and fire," she began, as her blood mingled
with the red-gold liquid from the flask. "I cast you out. By
sun and starlight, I destroy you. By my will, and the will

of all mankind and its allies, I send you back to the void where you belong. Your power is broken, and your place is not here. You have no part of this world. *Begone*."

A faint breeze blew around the room. It lifted the hair on the back of Joan's neck and toyed with the remains of her dress. She smelled jasmine.

The match seemed to drop very slowly, but when it hit, the book exploded. A burst of blue-white flame made Joan leap backward, grabbing her skirt out of the way. When she could look into the fire again, she saw that the manuscript was black already and crumbling around the edges.

Out in the hall, Reynell screamed.

He'd come in soon. Simon might be there first, or behind him, and Joan could probably get a decent shot off either way. But—this was something he had to do. They all had that need. Even Eleanor had, in the end, and Simon had seen her right to it. So maybe he had the same right.

Joan turned the latch again, unlocking the door. She thought about praying, but there were better ways to spend the next few minutes.

Chapter 40

JUST THE EDGE OF THE BACKLASH HIT SIMON, A GLANCING blow but quite enough to send him staggering forward, the world blurring in front of him. If he lived, he thought, he was going to have a devil of a headache in an hour or two.

The burst of force had sent Alex to his knees, screaming and clutching his head. Not likely fatal, or even really damaging, but it had at least bought Simon some time. With luck, Alex had seen no more of him than his shape as it vanished down the hall—lure enough to follow but no clear target.

The door opened easily, and Simon dashed into the study.

The feeling of evil wasn't as overwhelming, partly because he wasn't on the astral and partly, Simon suspected, because of the fire in the hearth. It was small but surprisingly warm. It was also the same blue-white flame that Simon had seen in the stone circle and in the scrying ring.

Simon couldn't see Joan anywhere in the room, and he didn't have time to look for her. Already he could hear Alex running down the hall. A hasty invocation to various protective deities threw shields of power up around himself. To deal with anything more physical, he grabbed the poker from beside the fireplace. Then Simon flattened himself against the wall beside the door and waited.

When Alex rushed in, Simon grabbed his arm and yanked, pulling him into the room. He kicked the door shut behind Alex and braced himself for the next attack.

It didn't come right away. Instead, Alex stared at the fire and the remains of the manuscript there. It seemed not to be a surprise but a confirmation he'd been dreading. His face twisted in wrath and thwarted malice, and he swung back toward Simon with madness in his eyes.

"You pious, interfering *bastard*."

What hit Simon looked like black fire, but it felt like living rot. It crawled over his shields like a mass of insects, seeking an entrance with revolting single-mindedness. The shields held, though, and then it was gone.

Simon closed his mind to it. Instead he looked at Alex, trying to see behind the rage. He thought of years past and of the future that might have been, of old men trading books and praising each other's grandchildren. That would never happen now, and he let himself sorrow for it, but there was still some hope that something might still be saved from this ruin. "Alex," he said quietly, letting the other man's arm go, "this doesn't have to happen."

At least Alex didn't laugh. Not at first. The blind rage vanished from his face, replaced by surprise. Then he cocked his head, looking horrifyingly like Eleanor when she was curious about something. "It didn't," he said, his voice hoarse from screaming. "Now it does."

"No," Simon said. "It's never too late."

A smile writhed across Alex's face. "Oh? Can I turn myself in? To whom, pray, and on what charge?"

"There are other ways. You know that." When Alex snorted and shook his head, Simon stepped forward.

"Don't do this. Don't waste your life more than you already have."

"I didn't know I was wasting anything. Time here, perhaps. But I've got plenty of that. And I'll have more soon."

"At what cost?"

"Who says there has to be one? Honestly, Simon." Alex waved a hand, indicating himself. "Does it look to you like I'm lacking anything? Or are you really going to try to convince me that I've given up love? Friendship? The spirit of Christmas, perhaps?"

"Well," said Simon, "at the moment, you rather appear to be short a book."

He'd been expecting a magical blow for that. Instead the inkstand flew at his head. Simon ducked just in time, and it smashed into the doorway behind him as Alex threw back his head and laughed. "At least there's some of you in there still, Grenville."

"I believe that's my line," said Simon. He spread his hands, though he still held on to the poker. "Or I hope it is. That's why I'm here."

"To reform me before it's too late."

"To tell you to get out of this while you can. I liked you once, Alex. I think you're still that man, at least a little bit, but many more deals with the Dark Ones and you won't be."

"Been studying for the clergy?"

"This isn't about sin, and you know it," Simon said impatiently. "That's simple. It's mortal. They're not. They'll suck you in, and you'll be lucky if they spit out the bones when they're done."

"I've the head for it."

"No man does."

"You don't give me nearly enough credit," Alex said, and then laughed again. The sound had barbed edges. "Besides, what would you do if I did repent? If I fell to my knees now and said that I'd been a bad boy? Would you forget dear Ellie or the valiant lieutenant? You'd make me pay in blood eventually, even if you claim otherwise now."

"No. I—"

"You give me your word, I suppose. The word of a gentleman. Just as you'd take mine, if I promised that I'd never do such things again?"

"No." It came out cold, and there was a raw place inside Simon that was all too glad to see Alex flinch. "You stopped being a gentleman a long time ago. I'm sorry. But there is a way—a *geas*—you could be better than this."

Alex flicked his eyebrows upward, unconvinced but intrigued. "You'd take it on too, I suppose? Let the past be past, the dead bury their dead, and all that?"

"No," Simon said a third time. "I couldn't forgive you, and I couldn't forget. But I'd rather have you live and hope you change. If I'd wanted to kill you, you'd have known that. A long time ago."

"You're very convinced—"

"You have this chance," Simon said, interrupting Alex's glib voice. He looked across the room and met the other man's eyes squarely, remembering the friend of his youth and seeing his enemy now. "I don't imagine you'll get another."

Alex fell silent. For a moment, he looked back at Simon, silent and thoughtful. Then he dropped his gaze, looking first to the fire and then down. He raised one hand to his face, rubbed his jaw, and the firelight flashed for a second on an emerald ring. "You're right," he said quietly.

"I—" It was Simon's turn to be surprised. His hopes began to rise.

Then Alex looked up, and they shattered. Alex's eyes were narrow, his mouth predatory, and his ring was starting to glow with a sick, greenish light. "You're right," he repeated, cool and amused. "This is my chance. *Carpe diem*, Grenville."

Oh, hell.

The light grew brighter very quickly. Simon began muttering phrases for an invocation that would almost certainly be too late.

Alex stepped forward, raising his hand. The emerald flashed—and then Alex staggered backward, gurgling, with one hand clutching the knife hilt sticking out of his throat. He turned blindly toward the far wall, where the knife had come from, and Simon turned with him.

"You kiss," said Joan, "like a goddamn squid." She stood behind the sofa, one hand resting lightly on the wooden back.

"You," said Alex. Blood poured out of his mouth as he spoke, and his voice was half choked.

The green light hadn't faded, though. It was getting stronger.

"You stupid bitch," said Alex.

Then he fell. But not for long.

―――∿∿∿―――

The green glow spread into Alex's hand and up his arm. Where it went, his flesh changed. The skin rippled and flexed, and the muscles beneath it bulged like tumors.

Spurs of bone tore their way out past skin and muscle, sprouting like rose thorns up his legs and down his arms. A slit ripped its way down his chest and grew teeth. His neck stretched out like a snake, and his face distended, becoming a rippling thing with three eyes and a gaping shark's maw.

The transformation took a few seconds. Then the thing that had been Alex was on its feet, looking around the room with red eyes.

"You *stupid* bitch," it hissed. A yellow tongue like a nest of worms flicked out over its lips, and it took a step toward Joan.

Simon drew a deep breath and shouted seven words, with all his voice and all his will behind them. Power poured into him and then through him in a wide gold beam that hit the Thing in the chest, driving it backward. The smell of burnt honey rose in the small room, wafting with the smoke from its chest.

The Thing howled, but its voice was too strong to give Simon hope. It shook itself. Blood ran down its chest and dripped onto the floor; it squirmed where it hit, the blood itself alive for a few seconds. The creature turned toward Simon.

This time, he'd prepared. This time, the words of power hadn't left him completely weakened. He had a little left. But not enough. Not nearly enough.

He started another invocation. It would hardly do anything to the monster, he knew, but maybe hardly anything would be enough. Maybe it would let someone else stop it; maybe Ellie and Joan could escape and find a way. If he was really very lucky, he'd at least get the spell done before the Thing ripped his head off.

There was the sound of ripping fabric.

"*Hey!*" Joan yelled. "Bastard. Over here!"

It didn't look. It was too smart for that.

A blast of silvery light hit it in the shoulder. It howled again and spun around.

Joan was still behind the sofa, but the bodice of her dress was gaping open, and the flashgun was in her hands. The tubes were out, their ends buried in the bare white skin of her arm. It was as grisly a sight as it had ever been, but it was a children's lullaby next to what she and Simon faced.

Simon kept chanting. He couldn't do anything else.

Now the Thing did turn. Its one flaming eye focused on Joan, and it stepped forward—hurt, yes, but not badly. It moved with the same unearthly speed it had before, and if it favored one side or the other, Simon couldn't see it. If they'd had more guns, he thought, or more people to feed energy to them—but they didn't.

Joan caught the flashgun tubes with one hand and pulled. The ends came out easily. As Simon stared at her, baffled, she met his eyes. There was resignation in her gaze and a strange sort of exultation. Suddenly he knew what she was going to do.

There was no time to say anything. Besides, Simon's breath caught halfway up his throat and he couldn't make a sound.

It didn't take long. She was very good. There was one swift motion, and then the tubes were stuck into her chest, just above her left breast. Right over her heart.

Simon took one jerky, useless step forward, his hands out and everything inside him screaming denial.

The gun began to glow.

The Thing screamed in a low clotted voice that shook the house, and it leapt forward. The remains of its lips peeled back as it went, giving it a red, wet grin. It lunged for Joan with everything, claws and teeth and snaky grasping tongue.

"Fuck you," she said, and the gun exploded.

Silver fire blossomed in the Thing's staring red eyes and spread like ripples in a pond, like the green light that had transformed Alex in the first place. Before the flame, strange flesh crumbled away to nothingness. The Thing's body jerked, twitched, and then fell.

So did Joan.

———— ᴡᴡ ————

Simon knew he must have run. He must have leapt over the couch at some point or run around it very quickly, because his hands were on Joan's shoulders before she hit the ground. He remembered none of it. He saw Joan fall. Then she was in his arms. There was nothing in between.

She wasn't a large woman. She'd been very light when they'd danced and made love. Now, bleeding in his arms, she felt very heavy. It was all Simon could do to lower her to the floor. He tried not to think the words *dead weight*.

There were things on the floor beside them. Some were shining silver, others corpse white, and Simon didn't really see more than a glimpse of any of them. But the tubes were clearly visible, lying like dead snakes, their ends covered in blood. There wasn't much blood on Joan herself, though, only a cluster of neat red circles over her heart. The wounds were almost bloodless, but they were very deep.

She was still breathing but not well. Shallow, spasmodic gulps of air shook her body. But she was breathing.

Simon had never needed spells for healing. He'd learned only a few, and those as an academic exercise. If he'd had time or energy for hatred, he would have hated himself for that ignorance. Instead, he made an arrow of his mind, focusing all his will on one purpose. He put his right hand on Joan's chest, above the awful holes, and started to chant.

She opened her eyes at the touch. They were clouded and her gaze was unsteady, but Simon could see awareness there and recognition. "Hey," she breathed.

There was a little fleck of blood at the corner of her mouth. Simon tried not to see it or to feel how cool her flesh was under his hand. He couldn't stop speaking, or the spell would fail. "Asclepius, Raphael, hear me. Blood and bone, do my will—"

Joan laid one of her hands on top of his and slowly smiled. "Don't worry," she said, moving her head very slightly from side to side. "It's okay. Best way it could've gone. I thought about this…a lot."

"Be now as you were before. Be whole."

She reached up and laid one hand against his cheek. "Never thought of you, though. Never thought I'd fall in love here."

Power flowed into him again, but it was sluggish this time. And where he wanted to shout, he could only manage a hoarse, desperate whisper. "I command it by all things made and unmade—"

"So I did okay," Joan said. "We did."

She closed her eyes again. Slowly, her hand fell from Simon's face, back to her side. "Okay," she breathed again.

"—by the secret names of the universe do I command—"

When the first dark spots appeared on Joan's dress, Simon realized he was weeping.

Chapter 41

SHE FLOATED, THOUGH SHE DIDN'T KNOW THROUGH what, or even with what. Her body was elsewhere. And it was ruined. She'd drawn too much from it at the end, and too quickly. She'd shattered herself with that final act.

Once, that would've bothered her. Now she felt no panic, no fear, not even any disappointment.

There was only contentment. She was tired. It had been a long day. Now there was time to drift, to let go, to remember a calloused, gentle hand stroking her hair and to hear her mother's voice singing: *Will you carry the word of love?*

It wasn't like it had been before, when she'd come back across the gulf between years. There was nothing to fear in this place, if it was a place: no screaming, no shouts or explosions. No darkness either, she realized as her mind relaxed.

Light, instead. So much light: blue and green, red and gold. Vivid, ever changing, formless.

Alive.

The light spoke to her in something that wasn't sound, in words that were only words because Joan was so recently human that she needed them.

The light said: Good job.

It said: You have served well. Faithfully. And the road has been hard for you.

"Yes," Joan said, because it wouldn't have been possible to lie to the light or whatever was beyond it. Not even out of kindness. She knew that, even as she felt its sorrow. She asked a child's question: "Did we win?"

Look.

She looked, or whatever you did without eyes, into unending green light, which became blue and white and gold in front of her eyes. It became shapes: tall silver-and-white buildings, spiraling into a sky so blue it almost hurt. Green fields around them, shining wide rivers, and roads that wound around the buildings, rich and brown, or hard and black.

Some of the buildings were familiar or almost familiar, give or take a caved-in wall or three. Joan had seen the shapes before, but they'd never looked anything like this.

Without moving, she was closer, close enough to see as a person on the street would. There were many men on the street, and women too. Their bodies were whole, their faces soft and shining like those of the people she'd met in Simon's time: people who could go their whole lives without worrying about mortal danger, who knew that, whatever might happen to them, the world would turn safely and beautifully in its orbit.

They *weren't* from Simon's time. Some of the men wore skirts, some of the women wore pants, and the vehicles that traveled the roads were like neither horse-drawn carriages nor the rusted hulks of cars from Joan's time. Instead, they were small dragonfly-bright things that hovered above the pavement.

Some of the people hurried. Some of them looked angry or sad or concerned. But all of them walked along the streets easily without flinching. They didn't look up at the sky every few moments, and they didn't jump at sudden noises. There were children among them. Some pulled their parents along by the hands, while others lounged in clumps or dashed through the crowd seeking some new amusement.

Alive. Free.

Joan heard a girl's laughter, high and careless.

Then she was somewhere else again, watching a man who stood in a lecture hall. He was laughing too, and she knew that laugh: quiet, self-conscious, like she'd heard it a thousand times growing up. She saw a woman getting out of some kind of plane and pulling off her goggles to show flashing hazel eyes. A young man walking into a building, talking earnestly with his friends.

All familiar, like the buildings had been. But like the buildings, they were made new again. Made whole.

It was stupid to be crying when she didn't have eyes.

"They're all right, then," she said to the voice. "They're all okay."

Yes. Their lives are their own. It is for mortals to make themselves happy or not so, but their world is a fair one. Such threats as exist are not great. They are not the terror you knew. The people who live there have a chance at happiness.

Do you wish to join them?

"I'm dead," Joan replied. "Or dying."

Not so. The young magician has some knowledge of healing, even if it is imperfect, and what power he has may yet be augmented. The beings he calls on are more real, in some sense, than he knows, and it is not their way to leave such deeds as yours unrewarded. Nor is it mine.

So—

You may disappear there and reappear in the time you see—weak, yes, but alive and in no danger of being otherwise. You will heal well there, I think. And no, he will not think you dead. You will *vanish*, and he will know nothing more. But he will hope.

Joan looked back at the shining city, at the way the sun glinted off the buildings and at the people who walked along the street enjoying the light and the warmth. "Will they know me?" she asked. "The ones I knew—back then?"

No. Some part of them—the part that hasn't changed—might recognize you, and they might feel more deeply toward you than one might expect between one stranger and another. But they are not really who they were. They have their own lives there, and you will still be very much yourself.

"It looks like a very gentle world," she said.

It is. They are not used to war or to warriors. You will be as alien there, in some ways, as you have been to those around you for the past few months.

"Does that mean I won't be happy?"

Happiness is always possible. And never guaranteed.

Joan withdrew a little, though she didn't know how she did it, and thought. She might have done so for a minute; she might have spent a few days. The light didn't seem impatient.

"This world—is it going to stay like that?" she asked, finally.

Perhaps. It's likely, at least, that it will reach that state, without much chance of interference from the past. Afterward? Even I cannot say. It's a peaceful world, but peace has two sides, and much of the old knowledge has been lost. For good or ill.

It was like crying without eyes. You couldn't draw a deep breath if you didn't have lungs, and you couldn't square shoulders you didn't have. Joan made the effort anyway.

"Then I'll stay where I was, if I can," she said. "I'll train others. Someone should—someone who knows what's waiting out there for Their chance. Who knows what the world could have been and what it might still become if there aren't people who can defend it.

A horrible thought occurred to her then.

"Unless that would make it all go wrong again."

The light laughed at her, spreading warm waves of mirth. No. No. It's a good thought, and a noble one. But that's not the only reason you go back, is it?

"No. Not the only one. I've spent my whole life just knowing duty. It seems strange to be going somewhere for love too."

When Joan looked directly at the light, it was a bright, cheerful red, the color of ripe cherries high in trees on a summer's day.

Go back, then, it said. Go and be as happy as any determined young woman can make herself. The ones you saw will never know how much they owe to any three people so far in the past, but they will dream of you sometimes, and those dreams will be happy. Nobody is ever truly parted, not forever, and no deed is ever fully forgotten.

Joan didn't say anything. She thought she should and then knew she didn't need to.

The light turned gold and grew brighter, and then it

was the gently glowing flame of a candle behind glass and she saw Simon's head bent over her. He was chanting and crying at the same time. Eleanor was holding the candle, and it wasn't quite steady because her hand was shaking.

If Joan had ever doubted her choice, that doubt would have vanished then. "We're in a lot of trouble," she said, and watched both of them turn to stare at her. She found the strength to grin. "How are we going to get out of this house before the police get here?"

Simon's face was a study in a number of emotions, but Joan didn't get to spot them all because she didn't get to look at him long. Heedless of his sister, the police, or the fact that Joan was lying on the floor, he bent and kissed her.

Oh, what the hell, Joan thought, giddy with victory and blood loss. She pressed up into his arms, listening to the broken words he muttered whenever his mouth left hers—love you, couldn't bear it, can't lose you—and stopped worrying about the police. *I don't think there's any law about killing demons.*

Epilogue

EVEN IN THE COUNTRY, AUGUST WAS TOO HOT TO DO much during the day. Everyone said so.

The doctor who'd examined Joan had been pretty damn firm about it. He'd also said several things about the effect of heat on the "female constitution" that had made Joan roll her eyes.

"Anyone who has to tromp around in ten pounds of cloth," she'd told Simon later, "is damn well going to feel hot. What does he expect me to do, lounge around naked?"

"Mmm. Medical necessity," had said Simon, tracing one finger down her bare back. "Can't be avoided. He's a very intelligent man."

Joan had snorted. "Yeah. Good luck keeping your servants if I never put any clothes on." She hadn't tried to avoid his touch, though. Far from it. They'd ended up on her bed doing things that Dr. Phillips would probably have wildly disapproved of.

Really, though, the orders themselves weren't so dumb, even if the attitude was. Joan didn't think the flashgun had damaged her permanently, but she did feel it. For a week, she'd stayed in bed, unable to walk farther than the door, and slept for about ten hours a day.

That had helped a lot with the police. They had turned out to be a pain in the ass: Reynell hadn't left a body, but he'd disappeared after Joan had come to his house. There were plenty of witnesses to say that she'd been flirting with him lately and that Simon had never liked him.

But the standards of the day, idiotic as they were, worked in Joan's favor. She was a lady, at least nominally. She'd been wounded very badly, and, in the end... well, there wasn't a body. What people did find, when they searched the house, incriminated Reynell much more than it did Simon or Joan.

One of the papers had already dubbed him the "Blue-Blood Bluebeard." Very witty.

The official story had Reynell luring Joan ("an unworldly American widow") to his house presumably with what the papers called "vile intentions." She'd put up a valiant defense of her virtue, he'd stabbed her, and Simon had burst in at just the right moment. Thwarted in his plans, Reynell had leapt out the window. Maybe he was dead now, or maybe he was living under another name. Nobody knew.

Once they were cleared of official suspicion, Joan, Simon, and Eleanor had left London almost immediately. It was better for Joan to recover in the country. It was also better for Eleanor not to deal with the gossip. When Reynell's family came to town, as one of them would have to, it would be good for them not to see anyone who'd been involved in their son's death.

Simon was indoors now, finishing a letter to Reynell's father. He'd lost sleep over that, and his face, which had grown less tense as Joan recovered, had been drawn and worn all day. It wasn't fair, really, Joan thought, but she couldn't do anything about it.

The Reynells were good people, Simon had said. They'd drawn away from their son lately, maybe because they'd suspected something of what he really was. Joan hoped so. It might make the next few months easier on them.

She hoped for other people's sake more often now. Maybe the mission had changed her or her timeless interlude in the light. Maybe she just had time these days. The weight of the world was gone, and sometimes it felt like her shoulders had grown wings in its absence.

The late-afternoon sunlight spread golden across Englefield's lawn, and the old oak tree was firm against Joan's back and scratchy in just the right places. She leaned back, one hand playing with the marigolds that grew nearby, and listened to music wafting out of the open windows. Eleanor was at the piano playing something slow and peaceful.

Joan waited.

Eventually, Simon raced out of the house like an overgrown boy, letting the door slam behind him, and tore across the lawn. It was alarming at first—Joan didn't think she'd ever be enough a creature of this world to stay relaxed through moments like that—but then she saw his face, and the mixed pain and relief there.

"Hi," she said, as he grew nearer and slowed.

"Oof." Simon flopped down on the grass beside Joan and laid his head in her lap, his hair very dark against the blue and white of her skirt.

She stroked his hair. "Done?"

Simon closed his eyes and sighed. "For all the good it may do. I don't think Lord Sherbrook will hate us— but—" He broke off, shaking his head quickly. There was a wound there, Joan knew, that still hurt. It was healing clean, though, and if it scarred, well, everyone had a few of those. "It doesn't matter. Did you hear from Gillespie?"

"I did." Joan grinned at the memory. "I'm going to be answering questions for years. He thinks you're crazy, by the way—turning your house into a school. And I don't know what your parents will say."

He shrugged. "We're not likely to have more than three or four students at a time, you know, and we've plenty of room. As long as I don't tear up the carpets— or, more importantly, the elms—they'll be pleased I'm doing something useful with myself."

"If only they knew," Joan said dryly.

"Civilizing young women is a very respectable profession. And one I have considerable experience—ow!" He batted her finger away from his ribs. "You're not supposed to be well enough for that."

"I do a lot of things I'm not supposed to be well enough for. This is the first time you've complained," Joan said. "Besides, I meant saving the world."

Simon yawned and shook his head. "That doesn't count. Not at all the thing in Society these days, you know. And you did most of it, anyhow."

"Like hell I did," said Joan. "I'd have been caught in five minutes without you showing me around. And I'd have gone crazy about halfway through if you hadn't been there."

"What did I do?" he asked, opening his eyes now and looking at her more seriously.

She shrugged. "You were there. You had my back. And…you were *you*. I couldn't have asked for—"

"Oh, you damn well could have. Several platoons, for one."

Joan laughed, but then she looked down at Simon,

and the laughter faded. Something was happening here. There was power in the air, solemn and momentous. So she answered honestly. "Yeah. But I could do without them. I don't want to think about doing without you."

Simon swallowed. Then he sat up and caught Joan's hands in his. His eyes were very dark. "I'd meant to ask differently," he said, and laughed. "I'd meant to be prepared. But—this feels like the right moment."

"The right moment?"

Simon smiled at her. "Would you like to—well, to work with me for a while yet?"

It took a second for Joan to realize what he was asking. Then warmth rose up within her, an echo of what she'd felt when she was in the light, and not a faint or a faraway one either. She met his eyes and smiled back.

"Always," Joan said.

Acknowledgments

So many people contributed to this book in one way or another! I'd like to thank Leah Hultenschmidt, my amazing editor at Sourcebooks, for taking a chance on this crazy plot, and Aubrey Poole for helping pull all the details together: you've both been an absolute delight to work with, and I hope to do so a lot more in the future! Thanks also to all of my friends for support, insight, and critiques and to my boyfriend, who gracefully put up with me successively biting my nails over cover letters and shrieking like a deranged howler monkey when I got the call. If I named names, this page would be longer than the entire book, but all of you guys rock.

So hard.

About the Author

Isabel Cooper lives in Boston, Massachusetts, with her boyfriend and a houseplant she's managed to keep alive for over a year now—a personal best. By day, she's a mild-mannered editor at a legal publishing company. By night, she's really quite a geek with polyhedral dice, video games, and everything. She only travels through time in the normal direction and has never fought any kind of demon, unless you count younger sisters. She can waltz, though.

LOOK FOR THE NEXT BOOK BY ISABEL COOPER

No Honest Woman

COMING APRIL 2012

The Eternal Guardians series...

TEMPTED

by *Elisabeth Naughton*

Isadora is missing. The words pound through his head like a frantic drumbeat. For her own protection, Demetrius did all he could to avoid the fragile princess, his soul mate. And now she's gone—kidnapped. To get her back, he'll have to go to the black place in his soul he's always shunned.

As daemons ravage the human realm and his loyalty to the Guardians is put to the ultimate test, Demetrius realizes that Isadora is stronger than anyone thought. And finally letting her into his heart may be the only way to save them both.

"ELISABETH NAUGHTON COMBINES DYNAMIC DIALOGUE AND SIZZLING ROMANCE WITH A WICKED COOL WORLD. DO NOT MISS THIS SERIES."

—*New York Times* bestselling author Larissa Ione

978-1-4022-6046-9 • $7.99 U.S./£5.99 UK

The Eternal Guardians series...

ENRAPTURED

by *Elisabeth Naughton*

For over two hundred years Orpheus has had an uneasy alliance with the Eternal Guardians. They've never quite trusted whose side he's on. Now he's been called to serve in the Guardian ranks. But that calling comes at a price—one that may eventually cost them all.

An assassin has been sent by Zeus to seduce, entrap, and ultimately destroy him. A woman who will dredge up a past he doesn't remember, a love that once condemned him, and a dark and deadly secret as old as the Eternal Guardians themselves.

April 2012

978-1-4022-6212-8 • $7.99 U.S./£5.99 UK

THE GOBLIN KING

BY SHONA HUSK

ONCE UPON A TIME...
A man was cursed to the Shadowlands,
his heart replaced with a cold lump of gold.
In legends, he became known as

THE GOBLIN KING.
For a favored few he will grant a wish.
Yet, desperately clinging to his waning human
soul, his one own desire remains unfulfilled:

A WILLING QUEEN.
But who would consent to move from the
modern-day world into the realm of nightmares?
No matter how intoxicating his touch, no matter
how deep his valor, loving him is dangerous.
And the one woman who might dare to try
could also destroy forever his chance at a

HAPPILY EVER AFTER.

"A WONDERFULLY DARK AND SENSUAL FAIRY TALE."
—Jessa Slade, author of *Seduced by Shadows*

978-1-4022-5985-2 • $6.99 U.S./£4.99 UK

Awaken the

HIGHLAND
WARRIOR

by Anita Clenney

A MAN FROM ANOTHER TIME...

Faelan is from an ancient clan of Scottish Highland
warriors, charged with shielding humanity from
demonic forces. Betrayed and locked in a time vault,
he has been sleeping for nearly two centuries when
spunky historian Bree Kirkland inadvertently wakes
him. She's more fearsome than the demon trying to
kill him, and if he's not careful, she'll uncover the
secrets his clan has bled and died to protect...

978-1-4022-5123-8 • $6.99 U.S./£4.99 UK